Fiona McCallum spent her childhoc
and wool farm outside the small tow
lia's Eyre Peninsula. While she now li
a country girl at heart. Fiona writes heart-warming journey of self-
discovery stories that draw on her experiences, love of animals,
and fascination with life in small communities. She is the author
of six Australian bestsellers: *Paycheque, Nowhere Else, Wattle Creek,
Saving Grace, Time Will Tell* and *Meant To Be. Leap of Faith* is her
seventh novel.

More information about Fiona and her books can be found on
her website at www.fionamccallum.com and she can be followed
on Facebook at www.facebook.com/fionamccallum.author

Also by Fiona McCallum

Paycheque
Nowhere Else
Wattle Creek

The Button Jar Series
Saving Grace
Time Will Tell
Meant To Be

Leap of Faith

Fiona McCallum

First Published 2015
First Australian Paperback Edition 2015
ISBN 978 174369240 0

LEAP OF FAITH
© 2015 by Fiona McCallum
Australian Copyright 2015
New Zealand Copyright 2015

Published by
Harlequin Mira
An imprint of Harlequin Enterprises (Australia) Pty Ltd.
Level 4, 132 Arthur Street
NORTH SYDNEY NSW 2060
AUSTRALIA

Printed and bound in Australia by Griffin Press

Acknowledgements

Many thanks to Sue, Annabel, Cristina, Michelle, and everyone at Harlequin Australia for turning my manuscripts into beautiful books, for all the wonderful support, and for continuing to make my dreams come true.

Huge thanks to Kylie Mason, editor extraordinaire, for the guiding hand and for being so easy to work with. This story really is so much better for her involvement.

Thank you to the media outlets, bloggers, reviewers, librarians, booksellers, and readers for all the wonderful support. To hear that my stories, which really are from the heart, are being so widely enjoyed is amazing.

Special thanks to Dr Meredith Frearson for very generously and patiently answering all of my medical questions. Any errors or inaccuracies are my own or due to taking creative liberties.

Finally, thanks to dear friends Carole and Ken Wetherby, Mel Sabeeney, Arlene Somerville, NEL, and WTC for all your love and support. I am truly blessed for having you in my life.

Please note: From 2007 the Adelaide International Horse Trials event has been called the Adelaide International Three Day Event and held in November. I have chosen to change some details relating to the event, including its name (it will always be the Adelaide International Horse Trials to me), date held and other details to better suit the purposes of my story, which is a work of fiction.

*To all those who love and protect animals,
especially those who rescue, rehabilitate, and
provide them with a second chance.*

Chapter One

Jessica warmed Prince up just behind the starting line. She'd studied the plan well and walked the cross-country course twice today and three times the day before. She had all the twists and turns and best places to steer Prince into the fences memorised. He wasn't as light and quick on his feet as most eventers, so if she had any chance of capitalising on her good dressage score, she'd have to keep him to a tight line. Thankfully the course was dry – a damp, slippery track made for a treacherous, slower round.

Her first Adelaide International Horse Trials. *God, I'm nervous,* she thought, *a lot more than usual.* Her stomach was churning, trying to find food she hadn't eaten. Nothing new: she never ate until after the cross-country round. Her husband, Steve, often wondered why she put herself through all this. How much fun was it if she almost made herself sick with nerves every time? Fair comment, she reckoned. It wasn't really about having fun, but about the drive to be the best you and your horse could be. For Jessica, there was no better feeling than winning. Well, that and making her father proud. She didn't like to admit it, but she was fully aware that much of what she'd done in her life and what continued to push her was all about gaining her hard-taskmaster father's approval.

And today her nervousness was exacerbated by Jeff Collins' absence. He'd been her coach as well as her father and she hadn't realised it would be this hard to go on without him. This was a huge event, so much bigger and more important than any of the others she did throughout the year – had ever done, actually. In the past few weeks since her father had passed, she'd begun to question if she was losing her edge, her guts and her determination to tackle the fences, and the will to keep up with the high standards necessary to succeed. For the first time, she hadn't had him beside her walking the course, discussing the options and choosing the best one, pointing out overhanging tree limbs, where she could cut corners, where it wasn't safe to, etc. Two knowledgeable heads were always better than one.

Yesterday, on her first walk around, she'd been sad to be doing it alone. She'd nodded to other competitors she knew, but they all tended to walk the rounds in concentrated silence. And then her feelings had turned to guilt as she'd contemplated how much she actually quite liked the silence and being able to carefully consider the many aspects to the round without her father muttering and imposing his views on her or demanding to know her every move, over and over.

Training for this event had been different, and so many times she'd doubted what she was doing. Realising just how much of a crutch her father had been had come as a shock. Now, almost daily, she had moments where she didn't believe she could do this on her own, before she reminded herself that she had always done all the riding – her father had just stood on the ground or sat on a rail – and, towards the end, in a deckchair – issuing orders and criticism.

The problem was she'd always had the comfort of knowing that if something went wrong, her dad was usually there to sort it out, to issue instructions or phone someone for help. Now she was all alone. But she had to suck it up; she was a big girl. She felt kind of liberated. She had to keep believing in herself – and Prince. He was ready, they were ready. Anyway, her father would be furious if he could see her being so insecure. He'd probably say something like, 'We didn't spend all this money and all this time, all these years, just to have you be so pathetic.' Yep, her dad had been pretty hard on her. But he'd also been fair. She wouldn't be where she was if it hadn't been for him. And her mother, before she'd died a couple of years ago.

Jessica thought about the advice her dad used to give her on competition days, and how he'd always question her instincts and decisions – sometimes over and over. It used to drive her mad. She so didn't miss that. The really annoying thing was that he hadn't actually been on a horse in twenty-odd years, so he couldn't begin to know her mount's fears, how long his stride really was, when he preferred to take off well out from a jump or go in deep. But that didn't stop her father thinking he knew best and forcing his opinion on her. And she'd learnt early on that you didn't contradict or argue with Jeff Collins. It was easier to just pretend you agreed and then do your own thing. Nonetheless, over the years she'd done pretty well. And today she would too.

Saddling up, she'd felt very sad and alone, and had wished she hadn't been so quick to urge Steve to go and play tennis.

Her husband didn't share her love of horses and competition, but he was supportive. Yet Jessica didn't like to take advantage of his kind nature and have him traipsing all over the place with her when it really wasn't his thing. In addition to his tennis and golf, he had his Country Fire Service; the CFS regularly took up a lot of time. And there was only so much someone could do.

Jessica watched as the horse before her went through the start gates and approached the first fence. Her heart was pounding and felt high up in her chest, as usual, but she also had a lump lodged in her throat that was threatening to upset her breathing. Normally her dad would be there just off to the side. While she never saw him scurrying across the course to keep watch on her, it was always a comfort to know he was out there somewhere. She was starting to feel quite melancholy and found herself gasping. God, she really had to pull herself together.

Jessica took a few deep breaths and patted the neck of the large bay thoroughbred-warmblood cross beneath her. He was still calm and didn't seem too affected by how tense she was. But she had to get herself together; she was the one in charge. Prince had to follow her direction; if her messages were mixed or indecisive over jumps this size, it could end in disaster and serious injury – for one or both of them. It was a warm day with little breeze, so she'd also really have to keep on him to up the pace, stop him slacking off.

'Righto, mate, that's us. Let's do this,' she said, gritting her teeth and turning him towards the starting area as her number was called. Her heart flipped, but she gathered up her reins and stared down the course at the first jump – a nice solid log – twenty metres away.

'And ten seconds to go,' the starter called.

Jessica tightened her reins and applied more leg to wind Prince up like a spring ready to go. He responded perfectly: head up, ears pricked, his powerful hinds well underneath him.

'... four, three, two, and go!' the starter said.

Jessica gave Prince his head as they leapt across the start line and bounded towards the log. She stared hard ahead, feeling the length of Prince's stride below her. She tightened him up around eight strides out from the jump so she could carefully count her last four strides and shorten or lengthen him so he'd be placed to take off perfectly. The type of jump determined where she placed him, except with the first, where she always tightened him up a lot more so as to leave nothing to chance. Prince's approach and leap over the first obstacle usually gave a good indication of how the whole round would pan out. If he was unsettled and a bit spooked by spectators or the shadows, and hesitated at all approaching the first fence, she knew she'd have a battle on her hands to keep him focussed. She always held her breath until they were safely on the other side and on their way to the next fence.

Today she let out her breath and relaxed a little as they landed beautifully and headed on to the hay bales.

'Good boy,' she whispered.

They bounded along, Jessica picking her track just as she'd walked it. She continued to count her last four strides into each obstacle in her head, adjusting Prince as she went. He was responding perfectly. A third of the way around and she was still clear and travelling well.

But Prince's breathing was more laboured than she would have liked, and he was sweating more heavily than usual. It was a tough course, and her first at this higher standard. She had to do her best to keep him up and energetic. No matter how hard she pushed him, though, he didn't seem to have any more pace to give. He was moving along okay, not so tired that she'd pull him up and retire, but she certainly wouldn't be anywhere near the top of the leader board at this rate unless everyone else bombed out. All she could do was her best to keep them safe and go for a clear, slow round with time penalties.

The water jump was next. Around the jump was a sea of colour. *Jesus, look at all the people. Crikey. Concentrate, Jess!*

Did Prince have the legs to go straight through or should she go the safer, longer route? It was coming up fast. She was through the trees and on the approach and had to make a split-second decision. She hesitated, her mind clouded. Prince was on track to go right through. She gathered him up, but it was too late – she'd missed the first of her four strides. Three, two … Shit, she wasn't going to make it. He was half a stride out and badly placed – too far for one stride on such a fence and too close for him to get an extra one in. All she could do now was just hope to hell he'd get her through this. She gave the horse his head, grabbed onto the martingale strap with both hands, sat back in the saddle and held on tight with her legs. She'd let them down.

He leapt. But not high enough. Among the sound of flapping leather and the heave and grunt of the big horse beneath her, she heard a collective intake of breath from the crowd. *Oh shit. Shit!*

There was an almighty thud as the tops of Prince's legs hit the solid timber of the jump.

Everything became a slow-motion whirl as the horse struggled over, Jessica still in the saddle and clinging on. Then she could feel them tipping sideways, falling. It was deathly quiet around them.

A loud splash shattered the eerie silence. Jessica felt herself hit the water, and then the heavy weight of Prince was on her. *Ow! Oh Christ.* She wanted to scream, release some of the agony in her leg. But if she opened her mouth she'd probably drown. Her helmet was full of water. She was too heavy. It was all too hard. If Prince was dead on top of her, she'd rather be dead too.

She closed her eyes.

Chapter Two

Jessica felt the weight leave her. She lifted her water-filled helmet, coughed and spluttered, spat out a mouthful of mud. She wiped a filthy hand across her face to try to clear her vision and her fuzzy mind. She thought she could see that Prince was upright, standing nearby, but the angle she was at and with her brain playing tricks on her, she wasn't certain of anything, except that she was in a shitload of pain. *I've got to get out of here. I'm holding everything up.*

'Ow! My leg!' she screamed as a bolt of pain seared through her when she tried to sit up. *Holy fucking shit, that fucking hurts! Shit, I didn't swear out loud, did I? Oh fuck, who cares? This fucking hurts! Jesus Christ.* She felt sick.

People were calling to her to stay where she was. She knew now she couldn't move if she wanted to. There was the pain, but she also didn't seem able to thread enough thoughts together to put her limbs in the right place. She stared around the crowd, dazed. Everyone looked really worried. She examined herself from her awkward, half-curled position. At least her leg seemed to be at a normal angle.

And then panic gripped her. Where was Prince? He wasn't still in the water with her. That was a good sign. Was it? She tried to cast her eyes around her. She'd seen him on his feet, hadn't she? She couldn't remember, couldn't focus on anything but the pain.

She could feel the cold water in her boots, so she couldn't have broken her neck or back. She wriggled her fingers. Fine, too. She would sit up. But when she tried to prop herself onto her right elbow, an excruciating pain shot down her right side.

'*Ow!*'

At least she could now see Prince. He was standing, his head hung, being held by one of the officials in a hi-vis vest, over by a tree. When she concentrated, she could see he was resting a back leg. Shit, how badly hurt was he? She put her hands to her head and began to cry – loud, racking sobs. She needed her dad.

'It's okay, love,' the man holding Prince called. 'I've had a good look. He seems fine, just a couple of scrapes. And he'll be a bit stiff and sore tomorrow …'

Had a good look? How could he have, it'd only been two seconds, hadn't it? Though she'd also swear, if asked, she'd been lying there for half an hour. Time was doing weird things.

Jessica tried to focus on the two people in green overalls who appeared beside her – a male and a female paramedic. She felt bad about them having to get in the muddy water to tend to her. And she felt bad for the organisers now she'd stuffed up their timing for the day. God, she had to get out of this and let them reopen the course.

'It's okay, I can get up,' she said. At exactly the same time she wondered, *Can I?* Feeling very shaky, she put both hands down to hoist herself up. And then realised she couldn't feel her feet.

'No, you don't.'

'But I'm holding them up.'

'Too bad, young lady, you're hurt,' the male paramedic said gruffly, then added in a more gentle tone, 'If you move you'll just make things worse. Please let us do our jobs and take care of you.'

Jessica nodded.

They asked her question after question. They peered into her eyes with a light, poked and prodded her. She had trouble following what they were doing and saying. Her leg was now throbbing.

'Here, suck on this. It'll help with the pain,' the female paramedic said, and pushed a hard, green, whistle-shaped plastic object between her lips. It was a little like what she'd seen in the movies. Jessica took a deep suck. Bloody hell, it tasted awful! Sweet, sickly, slightly fruity – they didn't mention that in the movies! But the instant warm feeling that flooded her body was worth enduring the dreadful taste. *Actually, it's growing on me.* It was starting to remind her of the Juicy Fruit chewing gum she'd loved as a kid. *Man, that's good shit!* She felt all woolly and cosy, and the pain became a dull, barely there, ache. She'd found her new best friend. She felt herself relax. They could do whatever they liked to her now.

A stiff collar was put around her neck – just as a precaution, she was assured – and then, on the count of three, she was lifted out of the water and onto a hard board.

'Please don't cut my boots off,' she said as they carried her to the ambulance. But the words that came out were so slurred it was no wonder they looked at her and frowned with confusion. Oh well, what's a grand for another pair? She was alive and Prince didn't look too bad. Well, he was upright. She held on tight to her new green best friend. She was beginning to feel quite okay. Perhaps she wasn't too seriously hurt after all.

'Just lie back and relax.'

Jessica felt she had no option but to comply.

'But I need you to stay awake,' the woman added, as Jessica closed her eyes and let out a deep breath.

Damn. They didn't half want much. She felt so sleepy. She opened her eyes and looked around to try to distract herself from the sleepiness trying to claim her. She saw that the man holding Prince had brought him up as close as he could get without being in the way. Jessica could see the course vet was having a good look at her horse. The man holding Prince gave her the thumbs-up signal.

She tried to lift her hand to wave back and offer some sort of gesture of thanks, but it was too heavy. And her brain was struggling with basic thought and battling exhaustion. God, she was tired. And sore; the pain was masked, but there was enough of a feeling to tell her she'd done some damage. At least she hadn't broken her neck – if she could feel pain down her right side all the way to her foot, she couldn't have broken her leg or have serious spinal damage, right?

She noticed a few familiar faces gathered around Prince – fellow competitors who had been before her in the draw and their strappers; someone would make sure Prince was looked after. That was the great thing about the horse community: they were all fiercely competitive, but they all banded together when necessary. And was that Zoe and Lucy, two of her young pupils, standing over there too? Poor kids, having to see this.

Jess was loaded into the ambulance and the doors banged shut behind her.

★

The trip in the ambulance seemed to take just moments – or maybe it was an hour? Jessica was in no state to know, or care. But with the event being in the city's parklands and less than a kilometre from the Royal Adelaide Hospital, it was more likely just a few minutes. She was wheeled into an open area with cubicles divided by curtains, and hoisted onto another gurney. The paramedics wished her all the best, and said goodbye. She thanked them in a mumble. She tried to apologise for their wet, muddy attire, but they were gone. She hoped they had a change of clothes in a locker somewhere.

Left alone, Jessica returned to worrying about Prince. When she tried to picture the accident, her mind went blank. She was able to relive their take-off, with Prince failing to fit in the extra-small stride, but was unable to recall the actual fall and the horse being on top of her in the water. She really hoped they hadn't lied to her about his injuries so she wouldn't worry. What if he had to be put down? Jessica began to sob. Oh, God, he'd looked so forlorn.

She chided herself into getting a grip. He'd been upright and on all four legs. He was probably just a bit bruised and feeling sorry for himself. And exhausted – he'd managed to get around half of his first international two-star cross-country round.

Jessica wondered who might have sorted out her gear and taken Prince home. She wished she knew what was going on. She felt naked without her mobile. And her wallet – wouldn't they need her Medicare card? Oh well, perhaps her full name and date of birth would do. But of course they had all her details – they were on the medical armband each competitor was required to wear. She relaxed slightly. Someone would call Steve, her listed emergency contact, and he would be by her side as soon as he could. Though, he was at least an hour's drive away. Had someone phoned him already? Was he still at tennis? Tears began to sting.

Her best friend, Tiffany, was her second emergency contact. But today she was off competing at Burra – miles away – and would have her phone off or not with her for most of the time.

Jessica blinked back the tears. She needed someone beside her to tell her everything would be okay. She had to keep it together. But she was frightened, and so lonely. More tears prickled, and a few slipped out and down her cheeks.

Jessica felt a wave of pain roar down her right side and promptly burst into sobs. She'd never felt so utterly alone and helpless. She realised she'd lost track of her pain whistle – hadn't sucked on it for ages. She looked around and down. Suddenly the thought of the pain returning was quite terrifying.

She found the whistle clutched in her hand, lying on her chest. Thank God she still had her little friend. But how long would it help her? She took a suck and firmly told herself to pull it together. There was no blood or protruding bones that she could see; she was probably only bruised and suffering from shock. All of this was most likely just precautionary and part of event procedures to comply with their insurance cover.

'Hi, I'm Anna,' said the nurse who had materialised beside the bed, dragging the curtain closed behind her with a long whoosh and metallic zing.

Jessica tried to say hi, but her chin was too wobbly and her voice came out as a croak. She thought she probably should be embarrassed to be blubbering like this, but then decided the nurse would have seen a hell of a lot worse in her time.

'Are you in pain?'

'Just feeling sorry for myself,' Jessica finally managed with a grimace of a smile.

'You're allowed. I hear you've had half a tonne of horse on top of you, you poor thing,' she said. 'You're damned lucky to still be here, let alone conscious. Now, first up, I'm going to get these wet clothes off and get you warm. If you're not already, you'll be cold soon. And I'm afraid we're going to have to cut your boots off. And they look so expensive. I need some heavy-duty scissors, back in a sec.'

Jessica nodded, feeling a new wave of tears threatening.

'The ambulance guys said your horse got up okay. Thank goodness for that,' the nurse continued when she reappeared with a large pair of what looked like dressmaker's shears. Jessica nodded. Tears poured down her cheeks again. She didn't know what had set her off this time; she'd known her boots would have to be sacrificed and had thought she'd already come to terms with it. She looked down at them, wondering what damage they were hiding. Now she was thinking about it, her boot felt really tight, like, *excruciatingly* tight. The sooner it was off, the better. She hoped it wouldn't hurt.

'Such lovely boots – what a waste. I feel terrible doing this. Hopefully they're covered by your insurance,' the nurse said as she began to cut.

Jessica mumbled and tried to make a mental note to remember to look into their contents insurance, but she was suddenly feeling very queasy. She felt the bile rise.

'I think I'm going to be …' Too late. She only just managed to turn her head to stop the vomit from going down her front. It went onto the floor instead. Her throat burned from the acid and the absence of anything else in her stomach.

'Oh God, I'm so sorry,' she groaned.

'It's okay. Someone will clean it up later. It's my fault; I should have made sure you had a bowl first up. You might have concussion. Do you think you lost consciousness?'

'I don't think so, but it is all a bit of a blur.'

'You might need a CT scan. We'll see what the doctor says when one turns up. Not sure when that will be.'

The nurse went back to work on her boot. Jessica could feel the movement of every snip. It didn't really hurt, but did feel uncomfortable. She hoped the nurse wasn't doing any more damage to her leg. She looked away; she didn't want to see anything gory when the boot came off.

As she studied the geometric pattern on the curtain, Jessica felt time starting to do weird things again. One moment she felt like she'd been in the hospital for hours, but the next it was as if only seconds ago she and Prince had been making their way around the course. And she'd been doing so well. A touch slow, but clear. *Damn it!*

Jessica heard the words, 'Just over here,' and then the ashen, worried face of Steve appeared.

'Steve,' she whimpered.

'Oh, God, you poor thing,' he said, coming up alongside her and putting his hand to her face. Tears welled again. 'How are you? Are you okay? What happened?' He was babbling; a clear sign he was way out of his depth.

'I'm okay,' Jessica reassured him. 'Anna, this is my husband, Steve,' she said to the nurse who had finished removing her clothes – Jessica thought she'd never been so embarrassed in her life, if she could remember it happening – and had draped a hospital gown over her. Jessica hoped when they moved her for X-rays someone would remember to do up the back of her gown if she didn't. Anna was now covering her with a blanket, being careful to leave her injured leg free. Jessica couldn't bring herself to look down at her leg; the cool breeze on it compared to the gentle warmth over the rest of her told her it was uncovered.

'Hi there,' Anna said, accepting the hand Steve offered. 'We won't know the extent of her injuries until she's had X-rays, and possibly a CT scan, and seen a doctor.'

'CT? Shit – that sounds serious!'

'It's too soon to know anything much yet,' Anna said, 'but Jessica being so coherent is a great sign.'

'Where's Prince? Who rang you?'

'Prince is with Tash and Donald Roach. It was Tash who called me. Can I get you anything?' he asked, looking around helplessly.

'She's nil by mouth until we can make absolutely sure she doesn't need surgery,' the nurse warned without looking up. *Surgery? Jesus.* Jessica felt sick to the stomach at the thought. There probably wasn't anything left to vomit up, but that hadn't stopped the pure bile from burning its way up her throat and out her mouth the first time.

'I think the boots probably saved you from a lot more serious injury,' Anna continued.

'Steve, how bad does it look?'

'It's fine. Seriously. There's no blood or anything. Not even any swelling.'

Jessica loved that Steve was there holding her hand, providing assurances, but at the same time she suddenly wanted to be left alone to go to sleep. And she wished the nurse was one of those surly, silent types, not Little Miss Chirpy. God, there was so much going on around her; beds being wheeled in and out, people bustling about. It was like Rundle bloody Mall. A slightly overweight man pushing a yellow bucket with the handle of a mop appeared, mopped her sick up, didn't acknowledge her apology to him, and disappeared, all in the space of less than thirty seconds. Did he just wander around looking for sick his whole shift? How did he know he was needed right there, right then?

It was all quite exhausting.

A young doctor appeared in a white coat with a stethoscope draped around his neck. Jessica almost giggled at how clichéd he looked. *Great, they sent the intern*, she thought, taking in his young, boyish looks.

'Hi, I'm Doctor Grant,' he said, picking up the chart Anna had just put down. While Doctor Grant was reading, mumbling to himself and nodding, Jessica was trying to work out if Grant was his first or last name. Oh, what did it matter? She relaxed back into the mattress, too tired to care. She could hear Nurse Anna and Doctor Grant talking around her, but it was as if she was underwater; she couldn't make out precisely what they were saying.

And then he was right beside her, touching her leg, poking and prodding her stomach, and asking questions. She answered them all as best she could.

'I don't think there's too much damage done, but we'll know for sure after your X-rays. I'll see you a bit later,' Doctor Grant said, with a friendly hand on her shoulder. He was smiling warmly down at her. He nodded and offered a smile to Steve, and was then gone.

Chapter Three

Jessica was desperate to go home. She was in an overnight stay area, not a proper hospital ward, in the closest bed to the corridor, separated from the other patients by curtains. It was really just like the initial casualty area, perhaps not quite so busy. She'd barely slept a wink thanks to the glaring light in the hall outside the room and the pokes and prods and assessments they'd given her at regular intervals, not to mention the trotting in and out to do the same for everyone else in the room – if there was a door, it was never closed. The Panadeine Forte she'd been given had helped her snatch some sleep, but each time, she'd woken with a start, fighting for air and feeling like she was back in the filthy water trying not to drown.

She'd suffered many a sleepless night thanks to competition nerves, but never had she experienced nightmares like last night's. A few times she really had thought she was drowning. She shuddered, recalling how terrified she'd been. Hopefully when she got home to her own bed they would go away. Yes, she was just unsettled, she told herself forcefully.

God, she wished Steve would hurry up. She'd urged him to go home yesterday, get a decent night's sleep and bring her some clean clothes in the morning. Until he arrived, she was stuck here in this scratchy hospital gown with the knotted ties poking into her lean back and bum. At least someone had tied them for her along the way. She couldn't remember when.

She looked down at her injured lower leg, which was now a lovely shade of purple. The nurse who'd put the cast on had sworn her to secrecy – the lighter fibreglass casts in the wonderful array of colours Jessica had had to choose from were only meant to be for kids. Apparently the public health system preferred adults to lug around the old-fashioned plaster that would only stay bright white for a matter of minutes rather than bear the extra cost of brightening up an injured person's life. Jessica hoped the nurse, whose name she'd forgotten, wouldn't get in any trouble. She wasn't sure how leaving with her leg looking like a beacon in forbidden purple could possibly go by unnoticed. The colour was so loud it was practically shouting.

Her injuries had turned out to be minor – just her right ankle fractured in two places – but she'd had to stay overnight to let the swelling go down before a cast could be applied. Apparently her needing to wee and being able to – God, how bloody awkward, embarrassing and downright awful were bed pans for women? – was a very good indication all was well, according to the new nurse tending her. Anna had long since finished her shift, said goodbye, and wished Jessica and Steve luck before going home.

Doctor Grant had been back to check on Jessica after the X-rays and had pointed out, while shaking his head slowly with wonder, that she had got off very lightly. And didn't Jessica know it? There were plenty of stories about riders being killed when their mounts had fallen on them – either from the force of being crushed under a horse or having the hooves of a creature struggling to its feet do irreparable damage to internal organs or the brain.

But Jessica couldn't shake the feeling of embarrassment of having fallen right in the middle of the water jump, the jump that always attracted the most spectators. And, God, there had been hundreds of people sitting there – not to mention the TV cameras. Probably best she'd had to be carted off in an ambulance; if she'd had to walk out she might have died of humiliation! She was relieved she hadn't seen any news coverage of the event – the media loved showing the thrills and spills. Bad news is good news.

A jolt of fear went through her. What if Prince was distressed about being in a foreign stable? What if he hadn't had his regular nightly feed? He'd be out of sorts. She told herself to get a grip, she was getting hysterical. It was she who was out of sorts if her routine got out of whack – Prince was much more easy-going. He was probably savouring the attention Tash and Donald Roach were no doubt lavishing on him, and enjoying the company of all of their horses.

By all accounts, Prince really was fine. That was the main thing. But all that work down the drain. It would take a lot to get back to where they'd been after a few months being laid up. Maybe she could get someone to keep Prince on track while she was in plaster? It would cost a fortune, though, and that was money they really couldn't spare. She wouldn't be able to instruct either, she suddenly realised, so there wouldn't be any cash coming in. Prince would definitely have to be turned out, along with Beau, the youngster she was bringing up. God, and just when he had been coming along so well too. Beau was sure to be pining. She racked her brain for a time in the last four years since having them both when they'd spent a night apart. She tried to calm herself down; she just had to get home and sort it out.

Jessica shifted her weight. Damn, she was aching all over. It was as if Prince had actually been tap-dancing on her in his studded shoes. She lay back and stared up at the ceiling. *Where the bloody hell is Steve?* Her leg ached something wicked, but she wanted to avoid painkillers as much as she could – the last thing she needed was diarrhoea when she couldn't bolt to a bathroom. While much of the day before was a blur, she could clearly remember Nurse Anna warning her of the most common side-effect of the pain-killing tablets she was being given.

She turned her head at a rustling sound and was surprised to see Doctor Grant enter. Was he still on the same shift or a new one? He seemed a little more tired and uptight than the day before as he inspected the nurse's purple handiwork. He pronounced it a job well done and handed Jessica a packet of Panadeine Forte, saying, apologetically, that if she needed more pain relief, she'd have to see her GP. Then he said he'd made an appointment for six weeks' time for her to come back to have her plaster off, and to contact them if she had any problems in the meantime.

'Right,' she said, nodding and trying desperately to take all the information in and keep the details straight in her mind.

He handed her an envelope, wished her all the best with her recovery, and left with a wave of his hand.

'Thanks, for everything,' Jessica called, but he was gone, the door closing with a click behind him. Now they finally close the damn door!

*

It seemed to Jessica that she had been waiting for hours after Doctor Grant left, tapping the covers on the bed with her fingers and fiddling with the woven design on the pale pink cotton cellular blanket covering her, before the door to the hall opened with a whoosh, and in strode Steve.

He took his dress Akubra off and pushed a hand through the top of his hair to lift it up a bit. To Jessica's well-trained eye, it meant he was harried. Something had gone wrong. Or perhaps it was just that his morning schedule had been disturbed and now his mood out of kilter. Steve would've had to get up extra early to do his morning run around the stock – or perhaps he was waiting to do it when they got home. Either way, the change would have him a little antsy. She'd be agitated too, if the situation was reversed and her schedule was so dramatically changed. It was one of the things they had in common and one of the reasons they worked so well together: they both enjoyed being structured and well organised. People would say they were obsessive, but for them it worked.

He came over to the bed and pecked her on the cheek. 'How are you this morning? Sleep okay?'

'Looking forward to getting home. And no, I did not sleep well. Did you know they wake you up every four hours to check you're not asleep?'

'Well, once we get you home you can sleep all day if you need to,' he said, kindly.

Jessica was tired, but she didn't know how she'd cope with sitting around all day, and for weeks on end – it just wasn't in her nature. She was always moving. Sometimes she didn't know where the day had gone or what she'd achieved, but she was always on the go, bustling about.

'Now, I brought track pants because I figured jeans wouldn't be wide enough,' Steve said. He was pulling clothes out of an overnight bag and was putting each piece on the bed.

Jessica struggled to get her right leg with its thick cast through the leg of the track pants Steve held up for her to step into. She leant against him and hopped a few times. It was going to be a long six weeks. She slumped back onto the bed, exhausted. What was wrong with her? She was a well-muscled, fit person, and already she was puffing.

Finally, she was dressed and they were ready to go. Steve put his hat back on, slung her bag over his shoulder, and held the crutches up for her.

'Hey, steady on, I don't want any more accidents,' he said when on her first step she nearly went head over turkey. 'Take it slow, and short steps. You don't want them sliding out from under you.'

It was harder than it looked and Jessica struggled to go slow; she was desperate to get home and make sure Beau had been fed. She didn't want to ask Steve in case he'd forgotten the horse – he'd feel terrible. And she didn't want to nag him.

'Why the hurry?' Steve asked, as he settled her into the front of the four-wheel-drive ute. He put her crutches behind her seat and handed her his hat to either hold or put at her feet before going around to the driver's side.

'You've got six weeks of sitting around ahead of you yet,' he said when they were both settled. 'You're going to have to get used to having things done for you without complaints or you're going to send us both mad.' He grinned at her.

He knows me so well, Jessica thought, offering him a wry smile and roll of her eyes.

'Laurel and Hardy were all clingy last night and this morning. It's as if they know something's up,' Steve said as he started the throaty diesel engine.

Jessica smiled, thinking of their brown kelpies. The dogs were talented and each worth at least two men. She loved that Steve was happy to treat them as part of the family, rather than much lower down the pecking order, as many farmers did. He was a blokey bloke who didn't suffer fools, but his handsomely rugged, weathered exterior hid well his kind heart and soft nature. Though he was no pushover. He was an astute businessman who was decisive and could be as stubborn as an ox when he chose to be. While his doggedness at times drove Jessica nuts, she admired his strength of character.

'And how was your night?' Jessica asked. He still looked stressed. His brow was furrowed and there was a slight blue tinge under his eyes.

'You know I never sleep well without you,' he said, pulling out of the car park.

'Oh well, I'll be there tonight. Though you might not like this alien leg beside you,' she said lightly. He'd sounded a little evasive, but she didn't want to nag. If he had something to say he'd say it in his own time. She looked out the window, feeling like so much had changed and she was seeing the world from a different perspective. She turned back to Steve.

'What?' he asked, when he caught her looking at him.

Did you happen to feed Beau? 'Just thinking how lucky I am to have you,' she said, with a smile that was meant to be warm but ended up tight.

'Are you okay?' she blurted after a moment of silence. She never had been good at waiting. 'Has something happened, well, other than the obvious?'

Steve ran a hand through his hair. 'Just didn't sleep well. Some bastard was out shooting in the middle of the night. They were pretty close because Laurel and Hardy were beside themselves. The poor calves must have been terrified. Beau was pretty uptight too – I was worried for a bit that he was going to go through the fence. And the cattle. I went out and had a look around, but by then they were well gone. I tossed Beau a bit of extra hay to settle him.' He glanced at her. 'I hope that was okay. I know it's out of routine, but I figured with you out of action it wouldn't matter too much. He liked the attention and calmed down, and seemed none the worse for wear this morning when I fed him.'

'Oh, great,' Jessica said, the words rushing out with a gasp of relief.

'What, did you think I'd forget him?'

'Well, you would've had a lot on your mind when you got home. And it was dark,' Jessica said.

'That might be, but he certainly told me. Didn't let me get halfway to the house before he was bellowing that he needed feeding,' Steve said with a grin.

'What did you give him?'

'What do you mean, what did I give him? His usual evening feed and then his ration this morning. You've got it all clearly written up on the whiteboard. I might not be into horses, but I can follow simple instructions, you know,' he said, sounding miffed. 'Sorry,' he added, patting her leg. 'I'm tired. And I don't like the idea that someone's out shooting so close to our stock in the middle of the night.'

'Did you call Tom at the station?'

'Yeah. I put in a report, but there's nothing anyone can do without a licence plate or at least a description of the vehicle. They must have been right up the back – I could only see the odd flash of light. I thought of letting a shot off into the air, but Beau was scared enough. And it's such a bloody palaver getting the gun and bullets out these days.'

'Do you think they were on our place?'

'Not sure. I didn't really get a chance to have a good look. Tom is going to take a drive around this morning and we agreed it was best to keep it to one less set of tyre tracks. Sadly, I don't think it's as easy to match prints to vehicles as those *CSI* shows would have us believe.'

'Maybe he'll find some shell casings.'

'Maybe, but that'll only help if they catch them and get hold of the gun.'

With the cost of meat it was no wonder stock theft was on the rise. There had been reports a few districts over of farmers finding pools of blood and drag marks where someone had shot a hogget or two through the fence and carted them off. Cattle were a little harder to lift, but not impossible.

Even if no stock was injured or taken, the shooting still caused damage: it stirred up the animals. Steve and Jessica's meat was known for its tenderness. They had a reputation to uphold. That was no accident; along with choosing the best breeding stock, they kept their cattle quiet by being very careful about how they interacted with them, and making contact with them twice a day. And any farmer worth his salt knew the benefits of working with quiet stock. It was also why Steve preferred kelpies over blue heelers. Kelpies were gutsy enough to cope with cattle, but weren't as aggressive and nippy as blue heelers. Border collies were too timid and were best left to working with sheep. Steve and Jessica ran a small flock of sheep – only around five hundred ewes, and really only so all their eggs weren't in the one basket.

'Do you want to call in and see Prince?' Steve asked.

'No, thanks, I'd rather get my head together and then phone and see how the land lies.'

'Fair enough.'

Jessica wasn't sure how she was going to look Prince in the eye after so badly letting him down yesterday, and wanted to put off seeing him as long as possible. This she couldn't tell Steve; it would probably sound ridiculous. Deep down Jessica knew horses weren't capable of such complex thought, but she still couldn't shake the feeling of guilt. How was she ever going to get over that?

'He really is fine, you know,' Steve said. 'Tash rang again. They've had a good look at him. He's just got a couple of scrapes down his back legs.'

Jessica nodded and fiddled with Steve's hat in her lap. Great, she'd have a physical reminder too.

'So, are you in much pain?'

'Not really. It actually feels more weird and heavy than painful,' she said, looking down at her purple plaster with slight surprise. She was overdue for another dose of Panadeine Forte. Hopefully she'd be able to hold off.

'I meant to say earlier, what a nice colour,' Steve said, smirking.

'I figured it was more practical than white or one of the paler colours. Apparently the fibreglass is much lighter to haul around than the old plaster type, though it still feels pretty heavy to me.'

As they turned into the driveway and made their way along the avenue of poplar trees flanking the gravel road, Jessica tried to think that nothing had changed and she was driving in just like any other day. Of course, everything *looked* the same – except Prince wasn't in sight – but nothing *felt* the same. It was really quite disconcerting. She looked around. She couldn't put her finger on it; couldn't put words to it even if she did want to say something to Steve. It was as if she'd been gone for months or was driving in for the first time ever. Jessica's head began to pulse with the confusion of it all.

'Welcome home,' Steve said, with a sweep of a hand as he pulled up alongside the verandah.

'Thanks.'

Beau neighed as if welcoming her and Laurel and Hardy stood wagging their bodies and tails and offering cheerful grins. It was as if they knew she was injured – normally they'd be clambering about beside the vehicle. She could only hope their respect and calm demeanour would continue and she wouldn't get her crutches tangled up in a flurry of boisterous dogs and end up sprawled on the ground with them on top of her trying to lick her to death. Oh well, she'd soon find out.

She opened the door.

'No, wait, I'll give you a hand,' Steve instructed and leapt out of the driver's side. He rushed around to hold the door, pulling the crutches from behind her seat and setting them on the ground for her.

'Thanks, I'll take it from here,' Jessica said when she had the crutches in position under her arms.

'Okay, I'll put the ute away. You go in and get yourself settled on the couch with your leg up and I'll be in shortly to get you a cup of tea.'

Jessica took ages to get up the two steps and across the verandah, the dogs loitering at a respectful distance. She sensed Steve was sitting in the ute watching her, desperate to jump out and do something to help. But other than carrying her – which she was sure he'd do without complaint if asked – there was nothing he could do. And she had to get used to moving about on her own if she wasn't going to go mad or turn into a fat blob.

As she entered the house, Jessica had the same strange, disconnected feeling that everything and nothing had changed. Did she have a head injury after all?

Exhausted from dragging the extra weight of the cast and the effort of using crutches, Jessica practically threw herself onto the closest leather couch. She was surprised at how much effort just the short trip in from the ute had taken. But she didn't have time to dwell on it because Laurel and Hardy were suddenly on the couch and curling up beside her as if that was how things were normally done. It was not. To the best of her knowledge, the farm dogs had never so much as set foot in the house, let alone sat on a couch. They'd never shown any interest in coming inside before.

When Steve came in he stopped and did a double take at the dogs on the sofa. Jessica put her hands up in a gesture of helplessness.

'I hope you two don't stink,' he said. 'And don't think you're getting morning tea. Aren't they smelly?'

She was loath to have them taken away, but couldn't ignore the fact that the longer they sat there, the worse they smelt.

'A bit; not of dead sheep, just farm dog,' she said.

'Right, you two, if you want to stay inside, you'll have to be bathed. Sorry, but you're going to have to wait a bit for your cuppa,' he said to Jessica. At that moment, Beau neighed loudly. 'Now *that* coming inside I will object to,' Steve said with a laugh. 'Seriously, does he need me to do anything for him?' He nodded in the direction of the window.

'Perhaps just open the gate and let him out into the bigger paddock,' Jessica said. Her words were light, even if her heart was anything but. Turning him out meant the loss of all the past months of hard work and progress. They'd been doing so well. For Jessica, it felt too much like giving in, like admitting defeat, even if it was beyond her control. 'But there's no rush,' she added. 'You sit and have a cuppa too.'

'I think I'd better sort those two out first, if you can wait?'

'Okay, no problem.'

'Come here, you two, bath time.'

Jessica watched Steve go into the laundry with the two dogs following and then after the door was shut, she listened to him muttering, the running water, and the whine of protesting dogs.

She smiled. Bless him. She really was lucky to have such a good husband.

She and Steve had run the farm together since getting married six and a half years ago. He was a well-established third-generation farmer and she appreciated his generosity in including her as he did; again, something plenty of other farmers didn't do. They were still as happy as the day they'd got married in front of a handful of friends and family under one of the sprawling gum trees down by the dam, with Laurel and Hardy, then just puppies, frolicking nearby. Actually, she was even happier. The romance and passion hadn't subsided as all her friends had warned it would; instead, she and Steve seemed to have settled into a harmonious existence where they fitted together so well they may as well have been pieces of a jigsaw puzzle. They were in no rush to begin a family, but it was something they definitely both wanted. Like pieces to a puzzle, they were different; had their own interests and minds. But when they were together, it was really quite magical. Sure, they'd had their fair share of conflict, but such was their mutual respect, they were good at resolving it or at least agreeing to disagree. Jessica knew it was early days – there was still the seven year itch to get out of the way – but for now she was content.

Her father had warned her against marrying someone outside of the horse world she'd been born into, saying no one else would understand the drive, discipline and commitment eventing required. Jessica didn't think she'd deliberately gone against Jeff Collins' advice, but she didn't think there was anything wrong with 'outsiders'. It was probably good to have a more balanced life with someone who wasn't as obsessed with it all as her father.

Other than Steve and the farm, Jessica's life pretty much revolved around feeding, working and cleaning up after horses, and that's the way it had been for as long as she could remember. She liked her life just as it was. Well, she didn't really know anything else, so couldn't really compare, but she was happy.

The more Jessica thought about how her accident meant her life might change, the more she yearned for her promised cuppa and perhaps a piece of cake as a distraction. She usually did a big bake every few weeks so she could have individual portions on hand. Today she had a hankering for orange cake. And boy, did she need a soothing milky tea. She was meant to be resting with her leg elevated, but surely it wouldn't hurt to make a cup of tea – and one for Steve if she made a second trip. She could spend all day resting after that.

She stood up and got her crutches in position, but she soon knew there was no way she could carry a cup of tea without spilling it everywhere. The realisation that she wouldn't actually be able to carry anything except in a bag dangling from her teeth or in a backpack dawned on her. Damn it, she was completely bloody helpless! And her stupid leg was now hurting. And she was tired. She didn't even have the energy to get a piece of cake from the freezer and put it in the microwave. It was going to be a long six weeks.

Chapter Four

Steve had gone out after lunch, this time to check the sheep, and was still out when their silver four-wheel-drive wagon and float made its way carefully up the driveway. A dual-cab ute followed close behind. Jessica checked her watch – Tash had called to say she'd return Prince at two o'clock and she was right on time.

She struggled up from the sofa, dislodging the dogs, and grabbed her crutches, before slowly making her way to the door. The dogs still seemed to understand they were to take care; there was no jostling for lead position from them, no mad rush to run ahead. They ambled slowly beside her.

Tash had her hand raised ready to knock when Jessica opened the door.

'Oh, look at you, you poor thing,' she said. 'How is it? Should you be up?'

'I'm okay, could have been a lot worse.'

'Right, so where do you want him?' Clearly the niceties were over! The really serious riders, like Tash, who made a business of running stables, buying and selling horses, and instructing full time to pay their way on circuit, tended to be a little brusque. Jessica wondered if the behaviour was the competitiveness that the really top riders had to have to succeed or if they thought that if they appeared too nice and friendly they wouldn't be taken seriously. She hoped people didn't see her like that.

'Just pop him in the nearest day yard, thanks, and I'll get Steve to move him later. I wouldn't mind just running my eye down his legs.'

'He's fine, as I said on the phone,' Tash said.

No need to get defensive, I wasn't questioning your treatment of him.

'I've taken him for a lead to stretch his legs and he doesn't seem too stiff and sore. He's pulled up remarkably well. Just a few scrapes on his back legs.'

Tash turned on her heel and strode back down the steps and over to the float, where she opened the front door and reached in to undo the lead rope. She then went around and opened the tailgate and lowered it. Jessica felt awkward and helpless, but didn't feel stable enough to make the trip down the steps. She instead offered a smile and wave to the driver of the ute – William, Tash's teenage son, judging by the P plates and lack of interest in getting out and being sociable. She was rewarded with a nod and three-finger salute from the hands still on the steering wheel.

Jessica gasped as she caught sight of the large patches of purple down the fronts of Prince's back legs. That particular antiseptic spray always made things look a whole lot worse than they usually were, she knew that, but still got a bit of a shock. She preferred the amber-coloured iodine-based antiseptic products.

Tash led Prince the few metres to the yard, gave him a solid pat on the neck, unclipped his lead rope, and closed the gate. She draped the rope over the rail and strode back to where Jessica stood, now in quite a bit of pain.

'He's a nice horse,' Tash said, briskly. 'And he was going so well. He's really come along.' She paused. 'So what are you going to do – turn him out?'

'I don't really have any other option.' She really couldn't afford to send him to one of her fellow eventing competitors' stables to be kept up to standard, it would cost a fortune. And, anyway, she didn't like the idea of someone else being able to take some of the credit if she did well down the track. She'd always been stubborn and pretty independent, well, except for having her dad as coach.

'If you want to sell him on while he's at his peak, Sharon Parks is looking for something at two-star level.'

'Oh, right, well, I'm not sure I ...'

'No pressure, just a suggestion. You think about it.'

What would Dad recommend? As much as horses were for leisure, at Jessica's level they weren't really considered pets that could be kept hanging around without being useful. And she'd get a whole lot more for Prince while he was in peak condition than if he'd been turned out for a few months. Jessica hadn't even thought of getting rid of Prince before this moment, and now was in a dilemma. Just what she didn't need, when her brain wasn't functioning very well at all.

'Thanks. So much. For everything. I really appreciate it. I hope he didn't give you any trouble.' But it was just small talk – Prince was the consummate gentleman to handle and was never any trouble.

'Nope, not a peep out of him,' Tash said. She shifted her feet and Jessica wondered if she was meant to offer payment – she seemed to be waiting for something.

'Um, I'd offer you a cuppa, but I think you have an impatient chauffeur,' she said, nodding towards where hands could be seen drumming on the steering wheel of the ute. 'What do I owe you?'

'Not much, I'll do up an invoice – no rush.'

'Oh. Okay, thanks.' Well, what had she expected? Jessica and Tash knew each other and were friendly, but they were not friends. This was business, not a favour. Still, it did hurt a little that someone couldn't do something for nothing. She would have, without hesitation.

'Well, I'd better keep going. But let me know if you want to sell. Perhaps Sharon can come and have a ride here or take him for a few weeks' trial,' Tash said with a shrug.

Jessica felt a surge of annoyance – how dare anyone think she'd move Prince on so quickly. God, she hadn't lost a leg, only fractured an ankle!

'Honestly, Tash, it's too soon for me to even think about – I'm still trying to get my head around this,' she said, lifting her plastered leg slightly and nodding down at it.

'Fair enough, but you'll get the most for him while he's in peak,' Tash replied with another shrug.

Is there a sentimental bone in her body? Jessica wondered. 'Thanks, I'll think about it.' What she wanted to say was *Why the hurry – are you expecting a commission, or something?* But of course Tash would be – it was how those at the top operated. Favours were rarely done for nothing.

'Okay then, you look after yourself. Let me know if there's anything I can do for you.'

'Thank you. And thanks so much, again, for everything. I really appreciate it.'

'No problem. We all do what we do.' Tash walked over and got into the passenger's side of the dual cab and, with a wave out the window, was heading back down the drive in a cloud of dust.

Now what? She'd said she'd check Prince over, but the fact was she wasn't sure she could hobble that far, given the immense pain she was in. And she really shouldn't get in with him if she was so unstable on her feet – he only had to give her a friendly nudge and she'd be on her arse, unable to get up again. Besides, Tash had made it clear Prince was fine.

At that moment he whinnied. In response, Beau lifted his head and cantered the length of the paddock.

A few minutes later when Steve pulled up, Jessica was still watching the happy reunion, ignoring the painful throbbing in her leg and the ache in her hands from clutching the crutches.

'So he's back then?' Steve said by way of greeting as he pecked her on the lips. 'That was quick – she didn't stay for a cuppa?'

'No.'

'He looks happy enough.' Jessica knew Steve was thinking the scrapes didn't look too good, but didn't want to say anything lest he cause her more concern.

'His legs look worse than they are. Tash assured me it's super-ficial,' she said.

'Shall I put the float away then?'

'Thanks.' *And could you clean out any manure if there is any?* she wanted to say, but while she liked to keep everything in pristine condition, the sky wouldn't fall in if a small pile of horse dung was left in the float.

'So are all the stock okay?'

'Seemed fine. Anything else to do for the horses? I'll unpack it, shall I – just put everything in the laundry to sort out later?'

Jessica smiled to herself. Clearly he'd been taking note of her after-event routine. But a sizeable part of her didn't want her riding things in full view where they'd be a constant reminder of her not being able to ride. She knew she should get him to bring her saddles in to be cleaned. She could probably easily enough sit and do that, but she wasn't in the mood. Anyway, she had the next six weeks sitting around; she'd do it later. Meanwhile, the tack area of the float was as good a place as any for them to stay.

'Actually, would you just put the saddles and bridles on the rack in the tack room and lay the saddle cloths over top? And just plonk the rugs on the bench.'

'No worries.'

She waited to see if the dogs would stay with her or go with Steve before heading back inside. They went with Steve.

Jessica felt guilty about having Steve doing her work, but that was all but forgotten as she sank onto the sofa. *God, this thing is heavy to lug around*, she thought as she raised her ankle and positioned the pillows under it now she had the couch all to herself.

Just as she got settled, the pain started up – a deep, piercing throb. She checked her watch. She was allowed another lot of painkillers. And she would take some if they weren't in her handbag on the floor a metre or so out of reach. Perhaps if she closed her eyes she could nap through the pain. She pulled down the throw rug lying across the back of the sofa and spread it out over her, as her mind drifted to the events of the previous day.

Jessica wasn't one of those people who looked for the sympathy vote with long stories full of minute and gory details about injuries to herself or her horses. She figured what was done was done; you just had to get on with things. She did, however, like spending plenty of time among lots of minuscule details during post-comp debriefs with her father, Tiffany and, to a lesser extent, friends who were also competitors. They would literally spend hours going over each dressage movement, each fence, twist and turn in the cross-country and show jumping rounds – what had gone right, what had gone wrong, how to approach improvement for next time.

Today she didn't want to think, let alone talk, about any of it – she didn't want the reminder of so badly letting Prince down and bombing out and of the big hole the loss of her father had left, which in her current state might see her fall apart. So when the phone on the coffee table chirped just as she got herself to the point of slipping into sleep, startling her wide awake again, she thought she'd let the answering machine take it. She half-listened as the electronic American voice told the caller no one was home and to leave a message.

'Hey Jess, it's Tiff ...'

Jessica snatched up the phone and pushed the green button to speak to her best friend. 'Hello. Hey Tiff, I'm here,' she said, practically shouting into the phone.

'Oh God, are you okay? Sorry, but I didn't get Steve's message until way late ...'

'It's so good to hear your voice,' Jessica said. She let out a sigh and lay back further into the plush leather.

'So, how bad is it?'

'Thankfully, just two fractures to the ankle. In plaster for six weeks – well, it's fibreglass, but you know what I mean. And I'm already sick of sitting around not being able to do anything.'

Tiffany laughed. 'But darling, it's only day one.'

'Tell me about it,' Jessica groaned. 'I've got poor Steve out there emptying the float and I feel terrible.'

'Why?'

'Well, the horses are not his interest, it's hardly fair.'

'Yes, but sweetie, in sickness and in health ... I say enjoy having a wonderful man prepared to do these things without complaint – it's called love and devotion. And, anyway, you'd do the same for him. So you just relax and rest up and make the most of being a sloth.'

Jessica felt another twinge of guilt. Poor Tiffany had lost her fiancé, Todd, in a car crash a short while ago. Jessica yearned to help her friend more, but one of the things she loved most about Tiffany was her fierce independence. After losing Todd, she'd stayed with Jessica and Steve for a couple of weeks before finding a rental she could afford on her own. And, anyway, there really wasn't anything anyone could do – it was all about time. Tiffany said that herself, regularly. Jessica admired her courage and ability to stay positive. She probably would have run home to Mummy – if she still had one – and moved back permanently.

It was far too soon to even think about, but Jessica wondered how likely it was that Tiffany would find two lovely men who would adore her in one lifetime. She just hoped her dear friend would be the lucky one.

She dragged herself back from her memories. Tiffany was right: there was nothing she could do about her situation, so she might as well make the most of it. Her problem was minor compared to what Tiffany was dealing with.

'So how's the pain? Is it okay?'

'Okay with the Panadeine Forte. But that won't last long. They don't give you a prescription – just twenty tablets – at the RAH. If you need more you have to go to your GP. But the last thing I want to do at the moment is leave the house.'

'Hey, I've got some leftover – and I think another script; should still be good to go – from when I had my ear infection over Christmas. You can have them, if you like.'

'Oh, that would be great.'

'So, do you need me to come over, like right now? It's just I've managed to score a few days in the feed store. But I can ask to start late next week if you need me.' That was Tiff, as always, putting everyone else before herself – or trying to. She was so desperate for work that Jessica couldn't put her new job in jeopardy just to have some company.

'No way, don't you dare put your life on hold for me; I'm fine. Thanks, though. And what wonderful news on the job – well done, you!'

'It's only the feed store, but it's something. And the staff discount will be a big help.'

'So how did you go yesterday?' Jessica said, suddenly remembering Tiffany had had her own important event. Tiffany was passionate about dressage.

'Really well: a first and two seconds.'

'That's great!'

'Yeah, and scored high enough to qualify for the state champs. Not sure I'll be bothered going, though.'

'Even still. Oh, wow, we should be cracking open the champagne!'

'Not with you on painkillers, young lady,' Tiffany scolded playfully.

'Hmm.'

'So, seriously, is it really painful?'

'A bit at the moment; I'm due another couple of pills. But I'm more exhausted than anything else – I couldn't sleep in the hospital. I'm planning a nap real soon.'

'I'd better leave you to it then.'

'You don't have to, I'm fine.'

'I'd better go and get ready for work.'

'Oh, I didn't realise you were starting straight away.'

'I'm just doing a couple of hours' orientation this afternoon and then I start properly in the morning. At this stage Mondays, Wednesdays and Fridays, but I'm hoping it will become Tuesdays and Thursdays as well if the farmers have a good season.'

'Well, good luck with it. I look forward to hearing all about it.'

'Yeah, right, how many bags of chaff and how many bales of hay such and such has bought – very exciting stuff.'

'It's probably going to be a whole lot more interesting than what I'll be getting up to in the next six weeks.'

'Good point. Look, I'd better run. But I'm so relieved you're okay. I'll be over as soon as I can, but do let me know if there's anything you need. Other than more drugs – I'll put them in my bag right now before I forget.'

'Thanks, Tiff, that would be brilliant. And thanks so much for the call. Good luck with the new job.'

'Thanks. See you soon.'

'See ya.'

Jessica hung up smiling. A chat with Tiffany always brightened up the dullest of moods. And she couldn't help being pleased at the prospect of more pain relief without stepping out into the big wide world – her head was now pounding as well as her leg. She looked across at her handbag, wondering if she could get the end of the crutch into the strap and drag it within reach without falling off the couch. Maybe? She was just making her first attempt when Steve came in, followed by the two dogs.

'Hey, don't you dare. I'll get it,' he said, seeing what she was up to. 'So, have you managed a nice rest?'

'No, the bloody phone rang!'

'Oh, who was it?'

'Tiff. It was wonderful to speak to her, but I'm in pain, tired and cranky. And bored,' she added, pouting.

'What am I going to do with you for six weeks?' he said, putting her handbag on the coffee table before sitting down and wrapping both arms around her. It was so comforting that Jessica felt her throat constrict.

'Shoot me,' she said into his chest.

'I'm ready for a kip myself,' Steve said, ignoring Jessica's comment. He kissed the top of her head and let out a weary sigh.

'Horses are fine, float is empty and cleaned out. Is that all for now, m'lady?'

'Thank you. Yes, thanks so much.'

Steve got up wearily and went and stood beside the second couch where the two dogs were now sprawled without even the good grace to look guilty.

'Come on, you two, off,' Steve said, and waved his arm at them.

With two harrumphs they were off and lying on the hard floor – looking miffed. Steve lay down on the vacated lounge.

Jessica closed her eyes. The room was quiet except for the gentle rustle of trees, the woody melodic tone of the bamboo wind chime out under the verandah and the squelch of Steve on leather as he got himself settled. Finally he was breathing evenly, lulling her into the blissful no-man's land of neither being quite asleep nor quite awake.

After a few minutes she became aware of bells ringing and the humming of voices, but couldn't make herself concentrate. She fell into a deeper sleep.

Chapter Five

The sound of a bang registered in the depths of Jessica's mind. She didn't think she'd completely gone to sleep but now, as she started to fully wake, she realised there were no other sounds except for the heavy breathing of the dogs on the floor. She reluctantly opened her eyes, unwilling to let go of the nice relaxed feeling of slumber, though she knew it was sort of artificial thanks to the painkillers she'd taken. She actually now felt quite groggy.

She was slightly startled by movement nearby. And then Steve was leaning over her.

'Hello sleepyhead,' he said, planting a kiss on her forehead.

'Where were you?' Jessica asked.

'Just went and checked on the horses,' he said, perching himself on the arm of the couch.

'How are they?'

'All good. I brought Beau in, put night rugs on both of them, did their mixes, and put some Betadine on Prince's legs.'

God, Steve was exceeding all her expectations. Jessica had been prepared to ease back on rugging to make life easier for him.

Would it be pushing things to ask him to swap rugs morning and night?

'Oh you're wonderful. Thanks so much. But it's a lot of work.'

'You do it.'

'Yes, because they are my horses – they're not yours.'

'Well, you're dedicated to them and I'm dedicated to you, so you just tell me what you need me to do and I'll do it.'

Jessica's throat tightened. 'It really means a lot. Thanks, Steve.' If she didn't think she'd dissolve into tears, she would have hugged him. She was being ridiculous. 'How do they look?'

'The scrapes? Good – drying out and starting to scab over nicely. They really are quite superficial. And he didn't seem to mind me messing about with them. Oh, and Tiffany called again, among others. I've invited her for dinner, if that's okay.'

'Fine with me – you're the one who'll have to do everything,' she said, with a wry smile and arched eyebrows. Jessica didn't question why Tiffany had rung Steve as well as her; her friend probably just wanted to double-check with him to see if there was anything she could do, just like Jessica would have done with Todd if the situations were reversed. She swallowed down the sadness. She missed him and their happy little foursome.

'Who else called?'

'Someone from the organising committee, and Bob Oakley.'

Jessica shuddered. Bob Oakley had had a crush on her for years and had planted a long, passionate kiss on her lips while offering his congratulations at a comp a little while ago.

'Oh, and Vanessa and Andrew Birch stopped by. You didn't hear them?'

'No. What did they want?'

'Wanted to know if Prince was for sale. God, the nerve! Vultures! You'll only be out a few months.'

'What did you say?'

'Thanked them for visiting, said he wasn't for sale and that you were resting. Hope that was okay.'

Jessica stayed silent. Was this a sign she *should* be thinking about selling? No, that would break her heart.

'Well, I'd better get cracking if I'm to have something to feed you two lovely ladies. You can come over and settle yourself at the table and keep me company. We're having shepherd's pie, and you're in charge of peeling the potatoes and then mashing them.'

Jessica raised her hand to her head in mock salute before retrieving her crutches and pushing herself up from the couch and onto them. Steve waited and picked up the cushion she'd had her cast resting on, and her almost empty water bottle. Over at the table he dragged the chair out from the end and laid the pillow on it.

'Come on, you need to keep that leg elevated,' he said, patting the pillow.

Jessica felt strangely childlike as Steve placed the refilled bottle of water, a chopping board and knife, two bowls – one with potatoes in it and the other water – a peeler, a bottle of hand sanitiser and a roll of paper towel in front of her. She half expected him to wash her hands and clean her face for her and then put a tissue to her nose and tell her to blow. She almost laughed out loud at the thought, but stifled it. She was very lucky he was being so good – plenty of husbands might not have been.

She enjoyed watching Steve expertly making his way around the kitchen. Not that it was a rare sight – he often cooked. The shepherd's pie, complete with copious amounts of grated cheese on top, was soon in the oven and now Steve leaned against the bench enjoying a long sip of wine and taking a break before tackling the garlic bread while Jessica set the table – well, if that's what you could call sliding a knife, fork and spoon on a napkin across the table in the general direction of three places.

Jessica had rejected his offer of a glass of the red wine he'd opened. Tiffany was right, it wasn't wise to mix alcohol with the pain medication, confirmed by the label on the box. She didn't think her stomach would cope with the acidity anyway; she was already feeling the churning that might lead to diarrhoea. It was hard enough getting to the loo to pee without the added inconvenience of the urgency of that side of things as well. No, she'd be careful to eat plenty and keep her stomach lined. Too bad if she put on a few kilos; she'd soon lose them when she got back in the saddle.

Jessica had always been lean, but well covered. Her long legs looked good in jodhpurs and distracted from the bit of a pot belly that had always been her nemesis, but which she'd learnt to live with thanks to Steve's regular assurances that he loved her just the way she was. It had become an on-going joke between them since they'd watched *Bridget Jones's Diary* together. Steve had never meant to make her laugh the first time he said it, and was confused when she did. She'd had to explain the Bridget Jones reference, but he didn't fully get it until she made him watch the movie soon after. Now whenever he said the words, he did a fine Colin Firth impression. While it was a joke between them, Jessica had no doubts that Steve meant every word of what he said. That was another of the things she loved about him – he was real.

'What?' Steve said, catching her smiling over at him.

'Nothing, just thinking how cute you look in that pinny and how sexy your command of the kitchen is.' He'd grabbed the first apron in the top of the drawer, which happened to be a frilly, flowery one Jessica had been given by her mother as a gift at her bridal shower. He grabbed the bottom of his apron and held it between his thumbs and forefingers, and curtsied. Jessica chuckled and was looking around for something safe to throw at him when there was a friendly double toot of a car horn and headlights flashed across the window.

'Here, you can do the garlic bread for being so cheeky,' Steve said, bringing over everything she'd need. He kissed her on the top of her head before continuing to the door, wiping his hands on his apron.

Jessica paused in her chopping of garlic and grinned, hearing Tiffany tease Steve about his apron. She pictured him doing another curtsy. She turned to see Tiffany slap playfully at his arm as she let out a hearty laugh.

'Very good,' Tiffany said. 'And what's this – dogs in the house? Steve, you're turning soft in your old age.' She paused to ruffle the ears of the dogs now standing beside her.

'Guilty as charged,' Steve said cheerfully.

They'd always got on well and, like Steve had commented only a few days ago, Tiffany hadn't lost her sense of humour despite losing Todd. Jessica thought that was more about her friend faking it until she made it, though; there was a tightness behind the smile that didn't totally include her eyes. Men didn't tend to be as obser-vant as women with these things, she thought, but Steve was often the exception. Sometimes Jessica wondered if he'd seen Tiffany's pain too, and was playing along.

'Some prescription drugs and books and magazines for you, oh injured one,' Tiffany said, dumping her armful and handbag at the end of the table. 'Nothing like a bit of A-list gossip to keep you going.' She wrapped Jessica in her arms from behind and leant around to kiss her on the cheek. 'Looks like someone's got a slave,' she said, nodding at the makings of garlic bread.

'Tiffany, let me introduce my sous chef,' Steve said, sweeping his arm in Jessica's direction after placing a round pie plate with plastic tub of cream on top onto the bench.

'Thanks so much for coming,' Jessica said, holding onto her friend's arms. 'And for all the goodies.' Jessica tried not to drool at the thought of more Panadeine Forte. She liked the snuggly feeling it gave her – aside from the pain relief – and was probably getting a little too attached already.

'Are you kidding? As if I'm going to pass up free food – not to mention seeing Steve in his frilly pinny,' Tiffany said with another laugh. But Jessica could read the subtext: anything was better than sitting around in her tiny, drab rental on her own.

'You're always welcome when you bring apple pie and double cream,' Steve said.

'You shouldn't have,' Jessica said in a serious, scolding tone. She knew how tight Tiffany was doing it financially and how desperately she didn't want to have to call on her parents. They had insisted on loaning her a few thousand for the deposit on the rental, and to help with removal costs. Jessica had urged her friend to accept it – pointing out that the offer was as much about them as it was about her; helping was what parents did. Tiffany had compromised by accepting the money as a loan, rather than the originally offered gift.

'So how was the trial run?' Jessica asked as Tiffany pulled a chair out and sat down.

'Great. I know it's nothing flash but, you know, I think I'm really going to like it there – and not just because of the staff discount. The people seem really nice and it's a lot more interesting than I thought it would be.'

'That's great.'

'What's this about a new job?' Steve asked, taking the finished, foil-wrapped garlic bread to the oven. 'Why didn't I know about it?'

'I've got a few days at Millers' Fodder.'

'That's great. Well done, you,' he said, giving her a hug.

'Well, it's just three days for now, and the money's nothing to crow about, but it's a start,' she said with a shrug.

'I'll drink to that,' Steve said, pouring Tiffany a glass of wine and handing it to her.

'Thanks,' she said.

Tiffany and Steve raised their wine glasses and Jessica her water tumbler, and they clinked glasses as Steve gave a toast in his lovely, deep, velvety voice.

'To good friends,' he declared.

'Yes, to good friends,' Tiffany and Jessica responded. *And absent ones,* Jessica silently added.

'So what's the story with the dogs being inside?' Tiffany had taken a few sips of wine, put her glass down, and was now looking at the dogs snoozing on the floor.

'No idea,' Steve and Jessica said at once, and then broke into laughter.

'They took pity on Jess,' Steve said.

'And advantage of Steve while he was looking after me.'

'Well, aren't you just full of surprises?' Tiffany smiled warmly at Steve and then Jessica. Jessica winced, recognising the pain behind the smile. She really hoped it wouldn't be too long before a nice man would arrive and sweep their kind and generous friend off her feet.

They enjoyed a meal filled with light small talk and compliments to Steve for the lovely food, and then Tiffany for the scrumptious apple pie. And after Tiffany and Steve had cleared the table and stacked the dishwasher, Tiffany announced she had better go home and get an early night. When Jessica's eyes glanced at the kitchen clock she was both surprised and pleased to see it was only eight thirty – it felt more like ten thirty. She was relieved – she was fading fast and still had to have a shower and deal with keeping the cast dry while doing so.

Jessica loved showering at night to unwind, and then climbing into bed feeling fresh, relaxed and warm. But not tonight, thanks to having to wrap her leg with a garbage bag sealed with gaffer tape and sit on a cold plastic chair under the water. Peeling off the wet tape and plastic bag afterwards and carefully getting back to bed on her crutches was a struggle and she got into bed feeling clean, but certainly not relaxed.

She snuggled up to Steve for a moment, feeling the urge to take it further. They kissed passionately, adopted a closer position so the lengths of their bodies were touching. She felt him harden against her, but, as he tried to pull her on top of him, the weight and rigidity of her cast reminded her that things were far from normal. She did not feel sexy with the foreign object that was her purple fibreglass cast between them.

And now the moment was lost. Steve seemed to sense it too, because he stopped manhandling her, held her tightly for a moment, and then kissed her on the nose.

'Sorry,' she murmured into his chest.

'Don't be. It's not your fault.'

'It's not exactly sexy,' she said, rolling off of him.

'No, *it's* not, but you are. Anyway, I am pretty knackered. Not sure what I did all day, but I'm exhausted.'

'Hmm. Thanks for everything.'

'My pleasure, sweetie. I'll be doing it all again tomorrow and the day after that,' he said, rolling over to face her and smiling warmly.

The thought that she could be possibly the luckiest woman in the world brought on a rush of emotion.

'Well, goodnight then,' she said, giving him a quick kiss and rolling over to turn off her bedside lamp.

'Goodnight, you two,' she said, peering over at Laurel and Hardy, who were on the floor at the end of the bed where Steve had laid out a few old but clean saddle cloths for them. *Softy*, she thought, smiling to herself. The dogs looked up at her with hearty grins and flapped their tails a few times before settling back down again. She clicked off the light and lay down. They had plugged a nightlight into the power point by the bathroom door so there was a soft glow lighting Jessica's side of the room.

It seemed to take an age for her to get comfortable. She was normally a side sleeper, but with the cast neither side was comfortable. She lay on her back for a while so as not to disturb Steve. He'd never grumble about her keeping him awake with her thrashing about, but she knew if she didn't lie still he would be disturbed. She felt bad enough about all he had to do now she was incapacitated, without ruining his sleep as well.

She was exhausted and desperate for sleep, but didn't at all feel actually sleepy. The little snooze that afternoon had probably ruined her sleep pattern, though that should have made up for the sleepless night before in the hospital. It was so nice to smell her gardenia room scent, rather than the chemical clean scent of the hospital room.

Try to sleep on your back, she silently told herself. It did feel more comfortable than either side had felt, but she'd never fallen asleep on her back before, even after too much wine. She realised she still had her eyes open and closed them.

The sound of the dogs and Steve breathing and the far off swoosh of trees suddenly all sounded much too loud. She tried to put everything out of her mind by starting to count back from three hundred in lots of three. It was what Oprah's sleep guru recommended; she remembered reading it in one of the magazines she'd flicked through ages ago at the hairdresser. It took quite a bit of concentration – that, apparently, was the point: it stilled the busy brain from churning through the distractions and worries of life. Jessica wondered if it would work. She'd never really been troubled by poor sleep – just the odd night here and there tossing and turning before competitions.

As she counted down, got lost, found her spot again, and carried on, she could feel herself relaxing and gradually becoming sleepy. Every time she thought about the following day and the next six weeks, and how she could occupy herself, she'd stop and go back to the counting. What she needed was a good night's sleep, things would be better in the morning. It was something her dear mother used to say often, before she lost her fight with leukaemia. Theresa Collins had managed to stay positive to the end and, while that had been better than seeing her mope about and sitting in floods of tears, it meant that when the end actually came, Jessica had been stunned.

She hadn't believed for a second that her mum would actually die, despite hearing the doctors' increasingly poor prognoses, and watching her mother's gradual decline. She was utterly convinced that those in the know had it all wrong and her mum would prove it.

Afterwards, Jessica spent months in a shocked daze. Not even writing the eulogy and giving it, or watching the expensive polished box being lowered into the ground made her fully accept her mother wasn't going to be there to plait up her horses for the next event. That had always been Theresa's part in what was a true family activity. She'd never ridden, but was there with the hose and shampoo, comb and scissors, needle and thread, the hoof black. The reputation Jessica had gained for always turning out her horses impeccably had been solely down to her mum. She did okay herself, but there was a distinct difference in the quality of her horses' presentation during Theresa Collins' reign and after her death.

It was getting ready for the first event after her mother's death that had really brought her loss home to Jessica. She wasn't sure why, when she'd been doing the horses herself for the last twelve months because Theresa hadn't had the energy and was more often in hospital than not. But that evening, about two weeks after her mother's funeral, Jessica had stood on the bucket with Prince's mane divided ready to plait and, instead of continuing, laid her head on his neck and sobbed for ages. She'd briefly considered scratching from the event, but the thought of disappointing her father made her carry on as if on autopilot. Afterwards, the whole day was a blur.

Jessica felt a wave of loneliness engulf her. It was so strong that it took her breath away and caused her to gulp a couple of times. Tears filled her eyes. Oh, she missed her parents.

God, she needed to pull herself together – she was just over-tired and emotional. They were gone, end of story. Blubbering about it wouldn't bring them back. Her father would be the first one to say that – in fact had, on more than one occasion since losing his wife.

She forced her mind back to her counting, feeling her forehead pucker into a frown as she concentrated on trying to remember the last number.

Chapter Six

Jessica fought against the weight on her shoulders pinning her down. She tried to get up, but something was stopping her. Someone was calling her name and the sound was fuzzy, muffled. Her eyes flew open of their own accord. She blinked, trying to take in the scene. Steve was practically on top of her. He had a hand on each of her shoulders. She looked up at him, fear and confusion furrowing her brow.

'You had a nightmare. You were thrashing all over the place. For a moment I thought you were having some kind of seizure,' he said, letting go of her, moving back to his side of the bed and sitting up. 'You scared the shit out of me.' He rubbed his face. In the glow from the nightlight and clock radio she could see the creases of worry.

She took a few deep breaths in an effort to ease her racing heart. Remnants of the dream started seeping into her consciousness. She'd been drowning, pinned underneath Prince in the water jump. She was wet with sweat and sitting up now with the covers away from her chest she felt a chill sweep through her. She shuddered.

'Are you okay?'

'Yeah,' she said, nodding. 'Like you said, just a bit of a night-mare. Probably the painkillers messing with me.'

'Do you want to talk about it?'

'Not much to tell; I don't even remember what it was about,' she lied. She didn't want Steve to worry. No point causing him extra worry for no reason. Her whole world had been shaken up, there was bound to be a few sleepless nights and weird dreams. Though she felt a niggle inside her that suggested this was a lot more serious than a weird dream brought on by medication. She forced it down, telling herself firmly that she would stop the pain-killers and then worry about it if that didn't work. She looked around the room to try to fully shake the dream and the panic still coursing through her in the hope she might go back to sleep, and noticed the dogs sitting to attention beside the bed, looking up at her full of concern.

'It's okay guys, I'm fine, but thanks for caring,' she said, leaning down and ruffling their ears. 'Back to sleep now,' she said and pointed at the end of the bed.

They seemed to understand and disappeared, soon to be heard giving deep harrumphs and making settling-down noises. Within seconds their breathing was deep and even. *Lucky things.* She couldn't believe how quickly they'd adapted to being inside dogs, and how well behaved they were being. Jessica couldn't imagine getting back to sleep now. Actually, she didn't even want to try; that feeling of panic, helplessness, of drowning, had been horrific. She didn't want to ever experience that again. She'd have to try to stop the painkillers.

'Would you like a hot chocolate to help you get back to sleep?' Steve asked, rubbing her arm.

'That would be lovely, thanks,' she said, smiling over at him and covering his hand with hers.

As she watched him get up she stole a glance at the clock radio on Steve's side table. Two a.m. At least she could sleep all day tomorrow. But poor Steve couldn't. He was meant to be marking the calves in less than five hours.

Jessica lay back down, fully aware her heart was still racing, and ran her hands through hair that she discovered was damp and sticky with sweat. God, she needed another shower. But with all the rigmarole that entailed, she'd stay put and be stinky. She'd have to hope Steve didn't notice.

'Here you are,' he said, handing her one of the mugs he held.

'Thank you.' She smiled up at him and took the mug in both hands. She felt herself relaxing ever so slightly as the warmth of the mug began seeping through her hands. She took a sip and savoured it before saying, 'Ah, that is lovely.' It felt quite decadent to be sipping mugs of hot chocolate together at this time of the morning.

'You'd better get some more sleep else you'll be too tired for marking tomorrow,' Jessica said a few minutes later.

'Hmm, today, you mean. I'll just finish this.'

At least he would drop back off to sleep quickly.

'Mind if I turn the light off now?' he asked when he'd put his empty mug down.

'No. I need a wee, so you turn yours off and I'll put mine on.'

'Do you need a hand?'

Jessica almost laughed at the image of him actually trying to help her pee. It was different for men, who had something that needed holding up. She didn't want to laugh and have him think she wasn't being grateful. 'Thanks, but I should be fine,' she said, being careful to keep any sarcasm out of her tone.

'Well, be careful – especially with the crutches on the tiles.'

'I will. Goodnight.' Jessica leant over and kissed him before leaning the other way, turning on her light, grabbing her crutches from where they were stacked against the wall, and carefully getting out of bed. The dogs were again at attention beside her. They stepped aside and followed her to the ensuite toilet where they sat watching her. It was kind of cute, though a little weird and disconcerting.

'All done, back to bed,' she whispered to the dogs, as she hoisted herself back onto her crutches. As Jessica turned out the light, Laurel and Hardy were already curling up on the floor.

Jessica lay in the dark, desperate to relieve the scratching feeling in her eyes by getting some sleep, but fearful of returning to the nightmare and that feeling of drowning. And putting Steve through it all again. She listened to him breathing – already sleeping soundly again.

She forced herself to endure the discomfort of lying on her side; that way she was unlikely to go to sleep. She listened to the whistle of the wind through the pine trees and the faint, occasional whirr of a vehicle out on the highway. She felt sleep tugging at her eyelids and her body twitch as she gave in. She was just too tired to resist.

★

Jessica was riding that cross-country course again, checking off each jump, each twist and turn, each marker, as she went. She could feel her heart rate soar as she came around the last corner to face the water jump. Her heart leapt into her throat as Prince slowed, too much – to the point she knew he wouldn't make it. Then the sound of scraping and the feel of him twisting awkwardly underneath her as he scrambled over, and finally the crash and splash as his legs buckled and they went down.

This time Jessica somehow managed to wake before the feeling of being pinned underneath Prince and the sensation of drowning hit her. She was sweating and gasping once more but thankfully had this time managed not to disturb Steve. She forced her breathing to slow, detecting the furious pounding of her heart under her ribs. She felt as if she'd actually ridden the round.

Early morning light glowed at the edges of the nearby curtains. Around five thirty or six, she guessed. As she returned her gaze to the bed she noticed Laurel and Hardy beside her.

'Do you need to go out?' she asked in a whisper. But they stayed where they were, their expressions apparently just of concern.

'It's okay. I'm okay,' she said quietly. Jessica was surprised to see them leave and then hear their snuffling as they lay down out of sight. She shook her head with wonder. *Don't ever tell me animals don't understand human emotions.*

Seemingly seconds later, Steve's alarm went off. He raised himself with a groan.

'Good morning,' Jessica said.

'Good morning. Did you manage to get some more sleep?' he asked, leaning across to give her a kiss.

'Yep, I'm fine,' she said, forcing joviality into her voice.

'Well, I'd better get the cattle in. Do you mind waiting an hour or so for breakfast? I'll come back once they're in and before Gary arrives. I don't want to hold him up.'

'I'll be fine. You go. Can I help at all?'

Steve paused, thinking. 'I don't think so, since you can't drive.'

Jessica felt a whole new rush of guilt. Today was one of the major days on their cattle-raising calendar – the marking of the calves. And she was unable to contribute, thanks to an accident that happened while she'd been playing horses. It meant Steve had to get someone else in to do what she should have been doing. He hadn't mentioned if he was paying Gary, or if he was planning to return the favour in manpower; either way it was a cost. They had insurance for him in the case of sickness and being out of action for any significant length of time, but they'd dismissed it as not being necessary for her.

'We'll be right, won't we, dogs?' Steve said cheerfully. The dogs leapt to attention.

'See you in a bit,' he said when he was dressed. He came around to her side of the bed to give her another kiss.

Jessica began to get up. She really would feel guilty if she was still lazing around in bed while Steve was out working.

'No, stay here for a bit. Get some more sleep. If you're still here when I get back, I'll bring you your breakfast.'

'That would be nice,' Jessica said, knowing full well she'd be up the minute she heard his ute leave.

Today she was going to actually do something. Starting with … Starting with what? What could she do that was useful? She ran through a list of chores, discounting each as she went. She couldn't change rugs – she was too unstable on her feet to heft them over the sixteen-hand-plus horses. She couldn't carry anything while on crutches, so feeding them was also out. She could open the gate and let them out, but they couldn't be let out until they were fed. God, it was all so bloody frustrating! She belted the bed with her fists. She could probably manage taping a plastic bag onto her leg and taking a shower, but the last thing she needed was to slip in the wet and fall and crack her head while no one was around.

Jessica looked around the room for inspiration. She'd stay in bed as instructed if there were a TV to keep her from getting bored, but there wasn't and she was bored already. She needed to get up and get dressed. Yes, that was one thing she could do. And she could probably even manage a sponge bath with a face washer. And then she'd go over and get the feeds mixed at least. Surely she could carry the light plastic tubs with their moulded soft handles in her teeth? She'd give it a go.

Feeling significantly better now she had some direction, Jessica set to. Her leg was giving her grief, but she couldn't take the painkillers on an empty stomach. Anyway, she had to toughen up and cut back. She dragged some clothes on and then made her way outside where the chill in the air reminded her that the toes on one foot were only protected by a sock. It was a clear, still morning and in the distance she could hear the ute's engine and the dogs barking as the cattle and their calves were rounded up and brought into the yards. A cloud of rich red-brown dust on the horizon to the east told her they were just over the rise.

Prince and Beau had their backs to her, their heads up with ears forwards, keenly interested.

'Good morning, boys,' Jessica called, making her way over to where they stood in the day yards. They turned to look at her, and each let out a loud neigh.

While Jessica would have liked to tell herself they were happy to see her, she knew they were more likely to be excited about what she represented – someone to feed them and give them their freedom. She leant on the rail where the two yards met and gave them some attention while resting from the short journey, which had proved both exhausting and extremely painful. Every movement felt like a bone-splintering jolt right up through her plastered leg. She was even puffing and hot under her layers of clothes. Not only was her left leg aching from taking all the weight and her right from being fractured, her hands were sore from gripping the crutches. *God, how the hell am I going to do anything?*

She thought about just returning to the house, but the horses had started pacing, clearly sure their feed was nearly there. She couldn't let them down now. Well, she had to try. Luckily, they hadn't got bored and playful and tossed their empty feed tubs around and into the middle of the yards – the tubs stood near the fence; Jessica could probably reach them from where she was if she stretched.

With each of the brightly coloured plastic tubs beside her, she now had to get them inside the feed shed for filling. She couldn't roll them because they were too flexible and the moulded handle meant they weren't round at the top. Could she get down low enough to the ground to lock her teeth onto a handle? She tried it. No, she couldn't, and fear shot through her as she only just managed to stop herself from overbalancing and falling flat on her face. Broken teeth were the last thing she needed. She scowled at the buckets and then at the horses, who seemed to find her antics amusing: they were contorting their top lips, tossing their heads up and down, and giving the occasional snort.

'Yes, bloody hilarious,' she muttered.

So how the hell was she going to get them fed? Was there a way, or would she have to go back to the house and wait for Steve? The thought annoyed her – Jessica Harrington née Collins had never given up anything in her life without giving it a decent shot.

Right, there had to be a way. She gasped and gritted her teeth as sharp pain shot up her plastered leg. She pushed it aside and focussed on the task at hand.

She considered trying putting a tub on her head, but they were far too deep; she wouldn't be able to see where she was going. Jessica had the fleeting thought that if she did manage to get the tubs to the feed shed there was no way she'd get them back with the horses' feeds in them. She dismissed it. At least having the feeds portioned, ready for Steve to give out would be a help. And she would feel a sense of accomplishment as well as less useless. Boy, did she need that! She was damn well going to get these bins over and into the feed shed if it killed her!

There was nothing for it but to pick them up and throw them, and hope they went in the right direction. They were robust enough to stand up to the horses tossing them around. She picked the first one up but, fearful of overbalancing, could only throw it a little way in front of her. But that was better than nothing. She picked the other one up. Prepared for how it would feel this time, she managed to toss it further.

Finally, sweating, cursing and heaving, Jessica had the two tubs inside the shed and up to the old chest freezers they kept the feed in so mice and other creepy crawlies couldn't get in and contaminate it. She sat down on the drawbar of the float. She was exhausted and her leg was killing her. And, she thought, looking down at her watch with horror, it had taken her twenty minutes just to get this far. She'd divvy up the feeds and then go back to the house. The horses would have to wait – this trying to be useful was bloody tiring and painful!

Jessica had just finished mixing the feeds when she heard the ute drive up, dogs barking from the tray. They always got excited when working with stock, and took a while to come down. Meanwhile they let everyone know of the fun and excitement they'd had, and how helpful they had been.

'Steve,' Jessica called when she heard the ute door close, 'can you please give me a hand?'

Steve appeared at a run, followed by Laurel and Hardy, who bounded over to where she was having another rest on the front of the float. Steve looked momentarily shaken until he'd cast his eye over her. He put a hand to his brow.

'God, I thought you must have fallen or something,' he said, a frown etched in his face.

'No, I'm fine.'

'What have you been up to?' he asked in a scolding tone, despite knowing the answer as he was now looking down at the tubs. 'You should have your leg up. I said I'd do this when I got back.'

'I was trying to help.'

'How did you get the tubs in?'

'Threw them.'

'You silly duffer,' he said, kissing her forehead and wrapping his arms around her. 'Thanks for doing what you have. Are they ready?'

'Just need to add some water and mix it through.'

Jessica had hoped to surprise him by having it all ready and being back in the house, but he'd arrived before she'd worked out how to get water from the rainwater tank. The large plastic jug she normally used would be impossible for her to handle.

'I hope you didn't take painkillers on an empty stomach.'

'It's okay, I didn't.' *But I'm beginning to wish I had.*

'Well, you go back to the house and I'll deal with those two hungry beasts. Night rugs off, day rugs on, and Betadine on Prince's legs? Anything else?'

'No, that's perfect. Thanks so much.'

'Go on then, off you go,' Steve chided. 'Dogs, go and see she does as she's told.'

Jessica didn't need to be told again. She was now in so much pain she wasn't actually sure how she would make it back to the house, but she'd have to find a way. And she figured she could almost justify spending the day resting. With each hobbling step she thought about the comfort of the couch, the breakfast and the pain relief awaiting her, and managed to put her crutches in front of her feet and her feet in line with them enough times to get her there.

Inside, she practically collapsed onto the cold leather. After staring at the blank screen for a few minutes, she turned *Sunrise* on.

'Seriously, Jess, you've got to rest up and keep your leg elevated. Doctor's orders, remember?' Steve said when he came in around ten minutes later. 'Now, toast and vegemite?'

'Yes, thanks.' Jessica watched as Steve bustled about. She noticed him regularly glancing up at the kitchen clock. Every time he did, she felt a stab of guilt. Gary would be here any minute. She wanted to say, *You go, I'll sort all this out*. But of course she couldn't. She couldn't so much as get a cup of tea and carry it back to the couch on her own.

Steve delivered her toast. Between bites, Jessica watched surreptitiously as he ate his breakfast standing up, snatching bites here and there, or carrying a piece of toast around and holding it between his teeth while he got the bits and pieces out of the fridge to make his lunch.

Finally he placed his small Esky and a thermos near the door. He brought over another thermos and two bottles of water and put them on the coffee table in front of Jessica. Next he went to the cabinet below the TV and took out all the DVDs and placed them in several low piles on the table.

'There's a ham and cheese sandwich in the fridge for you. I'll let you get up for that,' he said. 'Okay, is there anything I've missed? I won't be back until late this afternoon, early evening. Though if you need me, call. I hate leaving you like this,' he added, standing beside her, looking torn.

'I'll be fine,' Jessica said, trying to sound upbeat. 'I'll just sit here like Lady Muck and work my way through movies and books.' But inside she was already lonely, pining for him. Jessica swallowed. She was being silly; usually she and Steve spent most of their time apart. It would be different if she had Laurel and Hardy for company, but they'd chosen to stay out in the back of the ute – they had meaningful work to do, and knew it. They couldn't be more different to the dogs who'd been lazing around inside yesterday.

'Right, so you're sure you'll be okay? You don't want me to phone Raelene from next door and see if she can come over and keep you company?'

Had he read her mind? 'Darling, I'll be fine. You just go.'

They heard a car horn – Gary signalling his arrival. He would have seen Steve's ute still parked beside the house.

'Well, call if you need me,' he said, kissing her before striding to the door.

'Okay. Have fun,' she called.

'You too.'

Jessica looked around her. Bless Steve, he'd thought of everything. She poured coffee from the thermos into her mug and sipped as she thought about all the hours looming ahead of her. The only way she'd keep sane was to plan her time a little.

She really had to rest, so she might as well give in and stop fighting it. *Think positively*, she told herself. *All this time to do nothing. Think of it as a holiday.*

Jessica tried to remember when she and Steve had last had a holiday – actually left the farm. They had honeymooned six and a half years ago and Jessica's parents had moved in to keep an eye on everything. Having a holiday off the place was such a major undertaking that it was easier just to stay home. It wasn't fair to put their whole stockholding and livelihood in the hands of anyone else. And it was really too much responsibility to place on friends, though plenty had made the offer. Sadly, now neither of them had family who could step into the breach. So, instead of formal holidays, they tended to do the odd weekend away – usually coinciding with travelling for one of Jessica's horse events or a stock or clearing sale that Steve wanted to attend. They had also been known to go camping for a week or two and had done so a few times with Todd and Tiffany, but never further away than would allow Steve to do a daily check of the property and stock.

Friends and fellow farmers regularly had digs at them about their fastidiousness. While they always laughed them off, the truth was they were proud of their standards. They wouldn't be where they were if they ran a slack operation – like many who jibed them did. Not that they would ever point that out; each to their own, and all that.

Right, I'll watch Sunrise *until it finishes. Then I'll … I'll what?*

She wondered if she should log into her Facebook account – apparently that sucked up lots of time. She'd only recently created an account, mainly to appease the many friends and acquaintances who had been urging her to for years now. She was one of the few people alive who could use the internet but wasn't on Facebook every day. The few times she'd logged on, all she'd seen was stupid posts from people announcing they were off to walk their dogs, or which restaurant they were eating at, etc. It was really quite annoying. Who cared what you were doing any moment of any day? As it was, she lost quite a bit of time between Googling and online shopping, which she happily did quite regularly. But aimlessly browsing shopping sites for the next six weeks could be very dangerous. Perhaps best to leave the laptop alone.

So, after *Sunrise* she'd watch a movie or start reading one of the books Tiffany had brought; she'd see how she felt. Then at noon she could eat her sandwich and that would be the morning dealt with. She'd worry about filling the rest of her day later.

Feeling a little better thanks to her planning, Jessica snuggled down into the cushions, turned the sound up, and pulled the throw rug over her.

Soon she was seeing but not really watching the show and gave in, closing her heavy eyes. *Just a short nap*, she told herself, as she sank deeper into the cushions and pulled the blanket up to her chin. Before long the voices of the presenters became a far-off hum.

Chapter Seven

Jessica's eyes opened suddenly. It looked like *The Morning Show* was wrapping up. Soon the midday movie would be starting. She tried to remember the last thing she'd been listening to on the television with her eyes closed. *Surely I can't have slept that long?* Though she hadn't really been fully asleep; she'd been aware of the hum of the TV in the depths of her mind the whole time. Hadn't she? She checked her watch. As she registered the time, the pain gnawing in her leg served as an additional reminder: she could have another lot of painkillers right about now with her lunch.

As Jessica retrieved her crutches and hoisted herself up, she felt a little surge of satisfaction that she'd managed to while away three full hours. And she hadn't even had a nightmare. That was the good thing about it. She made her way to the kitchen bench.

Or had she? Slowly, snippets came back to her. She had been riding a cross-country course on Prince – *the* cross-country course, she realised with a sigh. But she'd woken just before the bend into the approach to the water jump, sparing her from reliving the fall and the drowning feeling. Hopefully it was a sign the bad dreams were behind her.

Jessica opened the fridge to retrieve the ham and cheese sandwich in its zip-lock bag. There was a bright pink post-it note on top bearing the words, 'Enjoy! Ring me if you need me. Lots of love, Steve.' Tears welled unexpectedly in her eyes. *Clearly overtired*. She turned her head and wiped first one side of her face on her shoulder and then the other.

As she sat slowly eating the sandwich, Jessica felt a wave of loneliness engulf her. No, it couldn't be loneliness, she told herself; she was a strong, independent woman and she and Steve spent plenty of time apart. Anyway, he was only over at the yards. But telling herself that just added to the guilt and frustration already consuming her. She wouldn't feel nearly so bad if it had been a car accident, or something unrelated to horses.

Steve would say an accident is an accident and that what was done was done, and she might as well accept she was out of action for a bit and enjoy some rest. As would Tiffany. But Jessica just wasn't cut out for sitting around – she missed her horses and her students already. It gave her such a thrill to work with them week after week and help them improve, no matter what level they were at. One of the younger ones, Katie, had started off as such a nervous rider and Jessica had been tempted to tell her parents that she didn't think riding was the right sport for their daughter. But Katie had persevered and was now, in less than a year, starting to even tackle low jumps. A couple of her pupils were quite advanced competitors and keeping the training up was critical. Jessica didn't like that she'd be letting them down, as much as she didn't like the idea of not being able to work with her own horses.

Perhaps when the pain subsided in a few days she'd be able to hobble about without crutches and do the feeds and rugging.

Maybe she could even supervise some students. If she hadn't been feeling so tired and out of it, she could have managed a bit of bookwork. She should probably force herself to do it, but couldn't muster the required effort. She was already turning into a couch potato.

Oh for goodness' sake, it's day two of six weeks. You've got a good man taking care of you and picking up the slack. You're allowed to relax and take some time out. The words sounded very much like Tiffany's. Jessica sighed. It wasn't as if she had much choice right now.

She finished her sandwich and poured herself a cup of coffee from the thermos. As she sipped, a strange calmness came upon her. What if Tiffany was right, and everything – good and bad – happened for a reason? Could her accident have been a way for the universe to stop her in her tracks?

Both Tiffany and Steve had been worried that she hadn't grieved enough for her father. They'd now stopped saying anything about it, but Jessica had detected odd glances between them since. She wasn't sure what they expected her to do. Carrying on was what she knew – Collinses didn't drop their bundles and sit crying in corners. Jeff Collins hadn't when he'd lost his wife, and Jessica had followed his lead. She'd simply and silently sobbed in the confines of the loo for a few nights before firmly telling herself tears didn't solve anything.

It was something her father had driven home plenty of times since she'd started riding, after every fall, after every poor dressage test, cross-country and show jumping round. She'd be upset and he'd say, 'Just get back on', or 'You'll just have to do better next time', depending on the situation. He would have been furious with her at losing concentration this time and presenting Prince at the fence so badly. Forget her injury, Jeff Collins would probably only have let her off the hook if she'd ended up in a wheelchair for life.

Jessica tried to tell herself she was being too hard on him, and heard her mother's voice clear in her head: 'Don't speak ill of the dead.' But a newsreel of memories of minor injuries began rolling in her mind, starting with the time she'd fallen while training over the huge Irish bank he'd put in.

She'd known her arm was broken when she'd hit the ground – the snap had been so loud she couldn't believe her father hadn't heard it too. She'd screamed in agony, but what had he done? Thrown her back into the saddle and told her to do it again – properly this time. And with the pain and shock making tears stream down her face, blinding her, she had done as she was told.

Twice more she'd had to go through, and could barely stand when she'd finally got back to the stables and dismounted. She shook uncontrollably. She was twelve. She'd felt her 'snivelling like a girl' had been vindicated later that night when her mother brought her home from the hospital in plaster, but there was no apology from her father. 'What doesn't kill you makes you stronger,' he'd said with a shrug more times than Jessica could ever have counted.

It had been his mantra. He'd also been fond of regularly reminding her about each of the Olympians who had gallantly carried on with their cross-country rounds while seriously injured. And of course he'd been right. Jessica Collins was well known for her robust, fearless nature out on course. She'd learnt, thanks to her father's tough love, to rise above the pain. And to conquer the fear, after being made to go around their course of jumps at home plenty of times with her eyes closed, without stirrups or without reins.

He'd been a hard taskmaster, but he'd got her to where she was. Jessica couldn't help thinking, though, that she wouldn't have a busted leg if he was still alive – she probably would have been more focussed.

At least she hadn't been part of a team and hadn't let anyone down but Prince and herself. Well, and her father. She wasn't at all religious and didn't really believe there was a heaven where everyone who had died was lying about stretched out in deckchairs like at a resort, watching the goings-on down below on earth. But she did have the uneasy feeling that Jeff Collins would know she had let him down. He had always seemed to know everything.

Here she was breaking the number one rule: Always get back on the horse straight away. Sure, she'd had no choice, but that didn't mean the rule wasn't broken. And when she could get back on, would she have the necessary drive to do it alone after such a setback? What if her whole riding career had pivoted on her dad's presence? Oh God, how was she going to carry on successfully without him by her side?

Tiffany and Steve would say Jeff was still there. And while it might be true to some extent, he certainly wasn't standing there yelling at her not to be a wuss and just face up to the damned jump!

Shit, what if this is it? What if this is the sign to stop riding? There would be a huge hole in her life. Horses were everything to her – they weren't like a motorbike that you took out when you wanted a ride; they made up a sizeable chunk of her whole existence. Jessica couldn't even conjure up an image in her mind of not having horses.

She shook her head. No, she was being melodramatic. She was tired, overly emotional, probably still in shock for all she knew, and on pretty heavy painkillers. It was all messing with her mind. She needed some decent sleep and when the pain subsided she'd feel less useless. Meanwhile, she'd put on a happy face – fake it until she made it. The flashing light on the phone handset caught her attention. Maybe not to the point where she could be bothered returning calls though. It was nice that people cared enough to call, but why did they think hearing about how well a particular rider had done would make her feel better when she'd bombed out?

She decided to play the too-injured-to-do-it card and ask Steve to make some quick, polite phone calls on her behalf. According to friends, if she was on Facebook, she could put a note up and let everyone know in one hit. That wouldn't exactly pass her mother's test of good manners, but it would be something. Though she had very few 'friends' on Facebook, anyway. Perhaps she'd send a group email.

She sat up straight, suddenly remembering again the few pupils she had booked in for instruction. She sighed. She'd have to get Steve to call them too; she was in no condition to supervise those kids, let alone teach them anything.

*

Jessica was woken from her nap by the sound of a vehicle pulling up out front. It was about the right time for it to be Steve, but she remained where she was in case it wasn't and the visitor noticed her through the window. Bored and lonely she might be, but she still really didn't feel up to being sociable.

No one came to the door and a few minutes later she heard a whistle and Steve calling the horses by name. Jessica struggled to her crutches and went over to the large window to see what was going on. She was just in time to watch Steve standing at the day yards holding up a tub and the horses cantering over. She found herself genuinely smiling for the first time that day. She loved seeing their manes flying, their heads held high and their ears pricked as they came on command. The sound of their hooves thundering across the paddock was wonderful.

Often the horses would come to a sudden halt just before hitting the electric fence, their hooves leaving skid marks. And there had been plenty of times they'd turned and raced off again, prancing, bucking and rearing, and burning off excess energy before settling in for the night. While she enjoyed the spectacle, Jessica didn't like that it caused them to sweat under their rugs. Usually she'd put a dry under-rug on to ensure they couldn't catch a chill from staying in a damp one. Steve wouldn't be expected to know that. She put her worry aside – it was cool, both horses were in peak fitness and had only done a short canter from the other side of the paddock. Steve rubbed their heads as they tucked into their feeds before starting on their rugs.

She was back on the couch as he came in, followed by Laurel and Hardy, who hopped up on the couch beside her. She was half expecting them to be smelly, having been in the yards with cattle all day. The dust of stock yards always had a distinct smell – a mixture of dirt, dung, animal sweat and a faint trace of chemicals. Sheep smelt slightly different – they had a greasy lanolin scent and their dung was less pungent than cattle's. But no offensive odours wafted up from the dogs.

'How was your day?' Steve asked from the end of the small passageway, just as Jessica opened her mouth to ask him the same question.

'Quiet, fine. How about you?'

'All good. Gary says hi and wishes you a speedy recovery. And the good news is these guys didn't find any corpses to roll in,' he said, nodding in the direction of the dogs. While he sounded relatively upbeat, Jessica could see and hear the weariness he was carrying. 'But I need a shower before I do anything; I'm filthy. Won't be long.'

And exhausted – you look exhausted. She felt terrible that he'd put in a full day with the stock – tiring enough in its own right – and then had to come home, see to her horses and get their dinner organised.

Later, working her way through the delicious meal of steak, chips and salad he'd prepared, Jessica cringed at how drawn Steve looked, and how slowly he moved. She so badly wanted to lighten his load. Making phone calls was one thing she could physically do, and should do … She hated herself for her pathetic selfishness, but the thought of phoning people, having to talk about her accident, hear their sympathy, listen to their own war stories, compare notes, filled her with an almost paralysing dread. She nibbled on her lip and worried about how to ask Steve to do it instead. She was getting dangerously close to taking advantage of him and his kind nature.

As she and Steve settled into bed that night, Jessica silently prayed – to whomever, whatever – that she might have a calm, restful sleep free of nightmares.

'I think you'd better get a little vitamin D tomorrow,' Steve said, breaking into her thoughts. 'It's going to be twenty-two and sunny. I don't want you getting sick, or osteoporosis, or anything. I'll set you up out on the front deck.'

'Okay, good idea,' Jessica said. But she was thinking she didn't want to be out there and visible if anyone decided to pop in. She wondered briefly if her newly acquired aversion to human contact was normal, but tossed it aside.

'Hey, can I ask yet another favour?'

'Sure. Anything for you, my love.'

Jessica could barely look at him. 'Could you return some phone calls for me? I'm really not up to speaking to anyone else about how the event went and how happy they were, or otherwise, with their performances.'

'Why don't you just send some text messages, that way you won't have to talk to them?'

Because I don't want to. 'Could you do it? Please?' she said, knowing she was pouting like a sulky teenager, but didn't care. She really didn't want to talk to anyone beyond Steve, Tiffany, the horses and the dogs right now.

'Fine. I'll call or text everyone tomorrow before I go grocery shopping.'

'You are the best husband in the entire world,' she said, forcing herself to bestow a beaming, grateful smile upon him. 'Well, goodnight then.' She gave him a kiss. He pulled her to him for a brief, tight hug before kissing her on the forehead and releasing her.

'Sleep tight. No nightmares tonight,' he added.

'I hope not.'

Her painkillers were already doing their thing and making her woozy. She'd have liked to not need them, but she wouldn't have been able to sleep with the splintering pain working its way up and down her leg. She hoped she wasn't about to become addicted. Who was she kidding? She was one of the most strong-willed, determined people she knew, not that she was feeling anything like that at the moment. She was just enjoying the nice, cotton-woolly feeling of pain relief.

Chapter Eight

Jessica woke feeling like she hadn't had any sleep at all. Her eyes were gritty and burning, and her throat felt tight. When she reached for her crutches to make her way to the loo, she felt like she was carrying around the lead apron they used for X-rays.

Steve rolled over to face her as she hefted herself back into bed and pulled the covers up.

'You must have slept better,' he said, 'no nightmares.' A statement, not a question.

'Yeah, better thanks,' she lied. If she used fewer words it wouldn't feel so bad. She really didn't like lying to Steve, but she also didn't want him worrying. He didn't need to know she'd woken maybe a dozen times through the night, gripped with fear, her heart racing. And if she'd managed to keep from tossing and turning and waking him up, well, so much the better. He was too busy to be dragging around tired eyes and weary bones. She just hoped the heaviness in her own eyes wouldn't be as bad as she feared it might look in the bright light of day.

Snippets of her dreams filtered into her consciousness. The same jump had appeared over and over, always with the same consequences. This time she'd seen not only Prince fall but Beau – and he was nowhere near competing at that level – and every other horse and pony she'd ever ridden, one by one.

Steve got out of bed and when Jessica made to follow suit, he said, 'No, you stay here. I'll do the horses and then come in and get you breakfast. No arguments.'

Bless him. She smiled as she watched him dress.

'Right, come on, you lazy gits,' he said, slapping a hand on his leg as he left the room. 'We're not having you peeing in the house.'

Jessica watched the dogs reluctantly get up – complete with groans – and trot after their master. She thought for the umpteenth time how amazing it was that they'd so quickly adapted to life inside, and hadn't had one mishap on the floor. For farm dogs they made pretty darned good house dogs.

She lay back and closed her eyes, but she was a morning person and now she was wide awake, she was unlikely to get any more sleep, no matter how tired and groggy she felt.

It would be nice to be able to stay here in her jammies and not bother getting up at all. But a part of her knew if she did that, her mind would go over and over the nightmare, making her tense and unhappy and she didn't want Steve coming back to that. Their relationship was already at risk of changing thanks to her accident and how useless she felt. She sighed, threw back the covers and got up.

She was settled on the couch, engrossed in a story about the merits of age-defying face creams on *Sunrise* when Steve and the dogs made their noisy entrance. Immediately Laurel and Hardy leapt onto the couch and curled into position, their total confidence making Jessica smile as Steve stood nearby and shook his head in mock consternation.

'How are the horses?' she asked.

'All good. Only another five days weaning them off their mixes and then they're turfed out, right?'

'Hmm,' Jessica said.

'Jess?'

'Yep, sounds good.' During the night, as she'd lain awake, she had pondered keeping their feeds going a while longer. The thought of selling Prince and perhaps even Beau had lodged in her mind and been nagging at her. She knew it really wasn't wise to make decisions like that when she was tired and emotional. And she was only going to be out of action for six weeks. Only six weeks! The last two days had felt like a month already! Though, really, six weeks was only one farrier visit – nothing in the scheme of things.

She really needed to stop worrying about them, didn't actually need to do anything about them. But there was a nagging inside her that told her she did have to make some decisions. Perhaps it was just guilt at imposing on Steve. Sure, looking after Prince and Beau would be less onerous without feeds to mix, but he'd still have hay to put out and rugs to change. She didn't want them looking like unkempt hairy beasts, regardless of what she decided to do.

Perhaps it was something else. The expense? Yes, but something more.

Tiffany would say that unless she got a clear sign of what she was meant to do she should stay the course. Just sit tight.

Or was Sharon Parks showing an interest in buying Prince the sign – that and the fact she was out of action? Jessica gnawed at the inside of her bottom lip.

'Are you okay?' Steve asked, putting a mug of coffee and plate of vegemite toast in front of her, startling her slightly.

'Sorry?'

'You were miles away.'

'Hmm.'

He brought a second mug and plate over and sat down on the opposite couch. 'What's got you so thoughtful?'

'Are you okay with doing the horses? Honestly?'

'Jessica, it's fine. I'm fine,' he said. Jessica detected definite lethargy to his words. She didn't feel any better for his response. Though what did she expect? That he'd be all beaming and crying, 'I love doing the horses, what are you talking about?'

'Don't you go making rash decisions,' Steve warned, before taking a long sip from his mug. 'I'll admit I won't be getting into horses myself any time soon, but I'm happy to do it, as I've said a million times. In sickness and in health, remember?' He smiled. 'So stop those cogs turning. Now,' he went on, changing the subject abruptly, 'I was serious about you getting some vitamin D while I go and do groceries – unless you've changed your mind about coming along?'

'No, thanks,' Jessica said, shaking her head. *And I'd rather not be out on the verandah as an invitation to anyone driving past, but I will do it if it makes you happy.* She was quite astounded at just how antisocial she was feeling.

Jessica, with Steve's help, soon found herself settled out in the sun on the front verandah with a book and everything else she might need. The gentle breeze made it far too chilly for shorts and a T-shirt but her left track pants leg was rolled up to above her knee and her long sleeves were pushed up to her elbow in the hope of getting a few rays of sunshine. She waved to Steve as he drove away, and continued watching his ute making its way down the driveway.

As he turned out onto the public dirt road and headed towards the highway, she felt a pang of sadness take over her whole body. Loneliness? Surely not; he was only going to be gone a few hours. Or perhaps what she was feeling was a little depressed. Well, she certainly wasn't feeling 'up' so, technically speaking, that would be it.

Oh for goodness' sake, you have nothing to be depressed about. You have a wonderful life, an adoring husband and good health. A broken leg is just a temporary condition, a minor setback. You'll be back on the horses and in top form in a matter of months.

She looked over at Prince and Beau grazing in their paddocks. But instead of a fierce longing where she'd picture herself making her way around her arena and practice fences, she felt nothing more than when she gazed upon the cattle or sheep: it was a lovely, calming sight, but nothing more than that. With the sheep and cattle she always felt a certain pride in their condition and of course appreciated their value to the farm's bottom line. Right now, staring at the horses, she felt nothing more than scant affection.

Was this another sign to give them up? The money would be useful. Steve wanted to add another bull and two rams to their holding soon. And she knew he'd love them to start a family; the money could come in handy if she got pregnant. Babies cost a lot, didn't they?

She wasn't feeling at all maternal – had never gooed and gaaed over babies or small children, nor felt the strong desire to have one of her own. But she did think it would be nice to have children to one day take over everything they'd worked hard to achieve. And while she didn't yet feel that burn of cluckiness she kept hearing other women speak of, she did keep coming across articles online and in magazines warning women not to leave it too late. She was coming up to thirty-one and the practical side of her said it'd be best to do it all before the age when the tests for at risk and older mothers kicked in.

But if she had a baby, she wouldn't be able to keep up her training and competition schedule, not with a little one in tow. And there were the months of pregnancy before that when she couldn't or shouldn't ride. As hard as it would be to part with Prince and Beau, it would be the right thing to do if she and Steve decided to start a family.

She felt a slight sense of panic at the thought of not being in horses any more – the one constant that had been there through every major event in her life and proven such a great source of distraction from any pain. If she was having a grief-stricken day, she only had to get out there on the arena and focus on her dressage moves or do some jumping and she was okay again.

Could she survive without that? Jessica wasn't sure she could go cold turkey, but it would be a waste to have such well-bred, valuable horses just wandering around in paddocks doing nothing. And surely it wouldn't be fair on Prince or Beau, either; they both seemed to love to work hard and please her.

She had the fleeting thought that she could get herself a cheap, quiet old hunter to potter around on after the baby was born – perhaps even join the hunt club that already used their property as part of their run. But deep down she knew she would never be content with anything less than the best and what she was used to. Jessica Harrington née Collins was a horse snob. *Nothing wrong with being discerning and having high standards*, she told herself.

Fine, some people liked the challenge of taking some scrubber horse without any serious breeding and getting it to do reasonably well in the basics and lower level comps. But that wasn't Jessica's thing, nor had it been her father's. Only the best conformation and breeding had ever done for the Collinses of Collins Park, and while they started from scratch with their horses, they worked hard to get them up through the ranks as quickly as possible. Those who couldn't hack the pace and crumbled under the pressure were sold on without too many qualms. It was business.

One of Jeff Collins' mantras had been 'Sentimentality has no place.' Which was how Jessica, despite having a lot of affection for Prince and Beau, could even think of parting with them without a rush of heartache or tears.

And while she liked the thought of someone else taking Prince and Beau on to excel while she concentrated on giving Steve the family he wanted, her fierce competitive streak didn't want to see it or hear about it. And she wasn't about to let her insecurity stand in the way of what had the potential to be a considerable amount of money; Prince was at a high level and Beau was doing well in his own right. And Jessica had got them there – well, with considerable help from her father before his passing. She could live with that kudos.

Jessica found herself wondering if her few fleeting moments of apprehension in recent competitions were signs she'd had her day. A few times lately, she'd felt the slightest bit of a falter at seeing some of the jumps, though not such a strong feeling that she couldn't banish it with a shift of focus or stern word. Her father would have been so disappointed in her.

Not that she believed too much in signs – didn't let herself. If she gave in to that sort of scattered thinking she would look for them everywhere and never stay focussed. It would be like giving in to the fear, and she might as well throw in the towel and waste all the years and money her parents and she had put into chasing her dreams. Her aim had always been to represent her country, hopefully at the Commonwealth or Olympic Games. And while she'd had so many setbacks along the way – horses not making the grade, or being injured or getting sick; eventing was tough on everyone – Prince was finally looking like the one to get her where she wanted to be.

Jessica closed her eyes and tried to picture herself riding cross-country again. It was daylight and she was wide awake, so there was no fear of the drowning nightmare frightening her. In her mind, she rode the course. But as she came around that last bend and imagined herself preparing to approach the water, her heart rate rose significantly. Suddenly she was gasping for air and gripping her chest. The dogs beside her got up and sat to attention, looking up at her. They whined. There was a sharp pain in her chest. She still struggled for air, her breathing too quick and shallow. *It can't be a heart attack. It's just an anxiety attack. You're fine. Just breathe.* Jessica pulled her jumper up over her face in the hope it would act like a paper bag.

She started to calm down and was soon able to take a few big, gulping breaths. She leant down and began stroking the heads of the worried dogs, slowly and rhythmically. Gradually the pain in her chest dulled and then disappeared, and her heart rate returned to just above normal. She was okay – weary, but okay.

She sat feeling stunned, like when her father had rung to say her mother had died. *I'm never going to be able to approach a water jump again, am I? I'm never going to ride cross-country again, because every course has a water jump.* Then her mind went completely blank and still. She could hear birds chirping, the quiet whoosh of cars out on the highway, the gentle slap of the dogs' tails on the timber below them. But other than these observations, she had nothing else going on in her head.

Jessica felt as if she'd been punched in the ribs. She was no longer fighting for breath, but there was an ache, not too dissimilar from when she'd been dumped by her first boyfriend in year eleven. He'd just casually said with a shrug that he liked Mia Stevens more now. Jessica had stood there blinking with the same ache deep within her.

She needed Steve. He always knew how to calm her down, how to make her feel loved. She'd had plenty of boyfriends since Paul Bowman, but Steve had been different from the start, even if it had taken her ages to believe his assurances that he wouldn't leave her. They'd never sat down and discussed previous relationships at any great length, agreeing that what was important was theirs – the past was done; the present and the future were what warranted thinking about. When it came down to it, what you needed was someone who quietly and calmly supported you – even if they didn't agree – someone you could safely navigate the choppy waters of life with. Jessica was beginning to see that the tough love approach of her father wasn't quite all it was cracked up to be. Sure it had toughened her up, but thank goodness she hadn't married someone like him. She felt safe, taken care of, with Steve. Right now she craved to be wrapped in the arms of her kind, rational, gentle but strong husband and hear him say what she was feeling was normal and that whatever decision she made would be the right one. And that's what he would say, wasn't it?

God, everyone will think me a complete wuss, giving up eventing after only one major accident. The Olympians over the years who had got back on and competed with dislocated shoulders and broken bones had really set the bar high. But there it was, the key to it all: they'd got right back on, straight away. Their adrenaline had kept them going and ensured their confidence remained intact.

She could probably build hers up again if she could have had her father by her side. She'd trusted him implicitly and had needed him to drive her beyond where she thought she could go. There was no one out there she trusted that much. Maybe she could try to find herself a new instructor, someone to take her father's place. But she knew there was no one on earth who'd be willing to push her like he had. And anyway, the cloud of litigation that hung over all instructors these days meant there was always an understanding that they couldn't bully you into anything. For Jessica to get back to where she had been and over her fear, she'd need that motivation – a lot of it.

If she could block out the pain, could she ride in plaster? Probably, but that might do more harm than good – to Prince, not her. She had him so finely tuned she'd totally muck him up with one leg feeling so different. And the additional weight of the plaster would unbalance her.

She sighed. The best she could do was to pay someone to keep him in work at a reasonable standard, even if the thought of someone else messing with him irked her. And she really didn't think they could justify the cost. What a bloody mess!

Jessica's heart pounded slowly but forcefully behind her ribs. *I'm done*, she thought. She took a deep breath. *The horses have to go.* A lump rose into her throat and a wash of tears filled her eyes then began spilling; first one at a time and then in a rush, down her cheeks. She leant forwards, put her head in her hands and sobbed.

It was the dogs burrowing under her arms, their wet noses tickling her skin, that finally stemmed her tears and brought her head back up and into the daylight. She couldn't help smiling weakly at them. She dragged her sleeves down her arms, wiped them across her face and then reassured the dogs she was okay, would be okay.

She looked up at the horses wandering the paddocks, grazing, not a care in the world. She'd miss them, she thought, her throat catching again and a fresh batch of tears gathering, but they wouldn't miss her — as long as they were fed and well looked after, they would be fine.

When the sun went behind a bank of clouds, highlighting the chill in the air, Jessica went back inside, where she and the dogs settled onto the couch. She turned on the television, more for its soothing presence than anything else. With a heavy heart she picked up her latest *Horse Deals* magazine to start trying to get a good idea of what price to put on her horses.

Chapter Nine

Jessica was dozing with the *Horse Deals* magazine and a notepad and pen on her lap when Steve arrived home, the sound of the front door banging shut startling her slightly.

'Hi,' Jessica called.

'Hi,' he replied, looking a little flustered, 'Sorry I took so long. I'll just get everything unloaded.'

After making a number of trips back and forth between the ute and the kitchen, dumping green eco-shopping bags, he kissed Jessica hello. 'Sorry, took a lot longer than I thought it would. But I do come bearing gifts – well a loan, actually,' he said, producing a handful of DVDs. 'From the library,' he explained, handing them to her.

'Thanks.'

'Hey, what's this?' he asked, nodding at her lap where the pad of paper was sitting on the closed magazine. He seemed perplexed. 'You looking at buying another horse?' He was used to seeing her flick through the magazine each month, but not post-its poking out from pages, and certainly not a pad bearing notes and figures.

'No, selling two,' Jessica said quietly, and continued examining the DVDs, pretending to read the blurbs. Part of her hoped Steve hadn't heard her. Saying it out loud caused a lead weight to drop in the pit of her stomach. It was the right decision. She knew it was. But that didn't make it any easier.

Steve sat down on the couch opposite. 'Why?'

'Because I'm never going to be able to ride cross-country again.'

'That's being a bit melodramatic, isn't it? It's only a fractured ankle.'

'Not when the very thought of a water jump gives me night-mares. Literally.'

'It's been your dream since you were a kid – you can't give up. Not like this. You're just having a crisis of confidence. Quite under-standable. You've probably got some minor post-traumatic stress.'

'It's too big to deal with on my own,' Jessica said, knowing she was being vague and petulant, but unable to stop herself.

'What about seeing a psychiatrist or a psychologist, or someone; get some professional help.'

'But Dad was always there ...'

'Well, he's not now. But I am. You tell me what I can do to support you and I'll do it. I can stand there and yell at you all you like.'

Jessica rolled her eyes at his attempted joke. She wasn't in the mood. 'There's a bit more to it than that.'

'I know, I was kidding. I'll swot up, read all your books. I'll be your coach.'

Jessica shook her head slowly. 'It wouldn't be the same. I appre-ciate you wanting to help, I really do. But I know I can't do it without Dad.'

'Thanks a lot for the vote of confidence!'

Jessica's heart lurched. But she didn't know what to say. It was the truth. No matter what Steve did, it would never be the same as having her father coach her. He was too kind, for a start. Tears welled in her eyes.

'I'm sorry,' Steve said, leaping up and going over to her. The dogs got off the couch and he sat down, wrapping his arms around her, holding her tight. 'But it's frustrating. I love you. I'm here for you. You don't have to go it alone. I'm trying to help, to stop you making the biggest mistake of your life.'

'I know. And I'm sorry, but I've just got to face reality.'

'And anyway, since when has Jessica Harrington née Collins ever used the word "can't"?' Steve said, sounding genuinely aghast. 'You can do anything you put your mind to. You're just spooked and in pain. Like I've said, don't make any rash decisions. You don't need to make *any* decisions, just enjoy some downtime and get better.'

'We could use the money.'

'Of course we could; we can always use more money. But I'd rather it not be at the expense of your happiness.'

'Perhaps this is all a sign to start trying for a baby.'

'Oh. Right. Well, that's a little from left field,' he said, clearly caught off guard. 'Maybe it is time, but it doesn't mean you have to give up your passion. And certainly not right now. Plenty of your fellow competitors have kids.'

'But wouldn't you worry about something happening to me – something serious?'

'Darling, I worry about something serious happening to you every time you get on a horse, let alone head off with the float. But it's your choice to ride, and I'm not about to stand in your way.'

'Well selling them is my choice.'

'But why? And it had better not be because you feel guilty about having me do the feeds and rugging, because that would be a cop out. I'm fine doing it.'

'Look, I honestly don't see myself ever having the guts to ride cross-country again – especially on Prince.'

'You've got Beau. Just do dressage on Prince.'

'I don't want to do just dressage.'

'Can't you drop Prince back a few levels and work at getting your confidence back?'

'And admit defeat? I'd be the laughing stock.'

'And giving up horses altogether isn't admitting defeat? How is it any different? It's still giving in to your fears.' He was clearly becoming exasperated. 'Obviously it's totally up to you, but you've had horses since before you could walk, and I know for a fact you'll be miserable without them.'

'But I can't do it without Dad,' she said again, tears welling, her chin beginning to wobble.

'Of course you can,' Steve said.

'I can't even picture myself riding cross-country without breaking into a sweat. And Prince and Beau are too valuable to just have sitting in the paddock doing nothing.'

'And you really wouldn't want to do dressage or show jumping?'

'No, but even if I did, they're good all-rounders, but not perfect for either discipline on its own.'

'Sorry, I just don't get it. What you're saying is it's really all or nothing?'

'I guess I am.'

'But hang on, don't you sometimes use Prince during lessons, for demonstrations?'

'I'm giving up instructing too.'

'But you love working with the kids. And they love you.'

'I can't instruct someone to do what I wouldn't do myself – that would be completely hypocritical. Anyway, there are plenty of good instructors around.'

'I suppose if you did regret it you could get more horses down the track. But parting with Prince and Beau?' He shook his head. 'I couldn't part with Laurel and Hardy. They're family.'

'Don't make me feel worse than I already do. It's hard, but it's business.'

'No, it's not, not from where I'm sitting,' Steve said. 'All I can see is you throwing in the towel too easily. Quite frankly, I'm wondering where the gutsy girl I married, who was here three days ago, went. How many times have I heard your father yell, "You're all right, just get back on"? Spraining your wrist seriously didn't stop you.'

'I got kicked; it wasn't a fall. And it wasn't a water jump. All cross-country courses have a water jump.'

'So I get out the front-end loader and build you some smaller versions to work with.'

Jessica's heart went out to him. He was trying so hard to help. It was lovely he cared so much, but there was really nothing he could say to convince her. She'd made up her mind. He wasn't the one having the nightmares.

The phrase 'things happen in threes' came to her and Jessica suddenly realised she'd had three signs: the fall and injury, the offer by Sharon Parks to buy Prince, and her nightmares and the anxiety attack.

'Your mind's made up, isn't it?' Steve finally asked after a few moments' silence. The television flashed bright and dull as it went about its business, the sound on mute.

'Yes. The money will be helpful. We could be looking at around fifty grand.'

'Gosh, that would be helpful,' Steve said, inadvertently swayed. 'But, honestly, no money is worth seeing you unhappy. And I think you will be. I'm certain of it. But, ultimately, it's your choice,' he said. 'Cup of tea? I certainly need one.'

'Yes, thanks. So who did you see in town? Any goss?'

'Not really. Saw Tom Rankin, Sebastian Jones and Jack Green outside the newsagent. They're all worried about the long-term weather forecast – saying we're in for another drought.'

'Are you worried?'

'No more than usual. Though I am thinking we might hold off from getting a new bull and rams and get in extra feed instead. I put in the order we discussed, but I think I'll do some more calculations and phone back in the next few days.'

'We'll be able to do it all if I sell the horses.'

He stood. 'That's your money, not the farm's.'

'But what's mine is ours. I'd like to help.' Jessica saw his jaw tighten ever so slightly. He was as stubborn and proud as she was – he wanted to do it alone – though he wasn't dogged or stupid enough to knock back her money if it meant insulating the business against hard times. And while they were doing okay now, things could turn around very quickly. She knew taking the help would be a pretty bitter pill for him to have to swallow. Just as much as her using farm money to buy horses would be for her, she realised. She wanted to throw her hands up in the air at the mess she'd made of everything.

'What does Tiffany think of you totally going out of horses?' Steve asked over the roar of the kettle.

'I haven't spoken to her about it.' She felt a pang of annoyance and almost snapped at him that she was quite capable of making her own decisions, thank you very much! But he had a point. Since meeting Tiffany, Jessica hadn't bought a pair of horse boots or reins without at least discussing it with her.

She knew Tiffany would side with Steve on this, but she also knew Tiffany would understand better than most. Tiffany had had a serious fall show jumping at pony club as a kid. While it had ended up not being serious, for a while they had suspected she'd injured her spine. It had really put the wind up her, and it was why she stuck to the lower levels of dressage, the safer sport. They'd often discussed how their confidence was diminishing with age, and how much harder the ground looked and felt with each passing year.

'Oh well, it's not like you can't get more horses later if you change your mind,' Steve said again, as if trying to convince himself. He was looking out the window at the horses as he waited for the tea bags to steep. 'But I like those guys,' he added wistfully, 'especially now I'm getting to know them so well.'

You're really not helping, Jessica thought. She had to keep her mind on the money, and the fact it was selfish to have such good, well-trained horseflesh going to waste in the paddock. Her father would have been totally with her on that front, but furious with her for tossing it all in so easily after all the years they'd put in. *I probably wouldn't have had to resort to this if you were here.* Damn him for dying and leaving her.

It was best she sent her life in a totally different direction – motherhood. Making a family with the man she loved. Part of her hoped she'd fall pregnant quickly to prove this was the right thing to do, another was quite terrified at the prospect of being responsible for something so small and fragile.

Chapter Ten

Steve went out to do his rounds, as they called them; a quiet drive around checking the stock, troughs and fences. Jessica thought she wouldn't have minded going along with him and sitting in the ute to break the monotony of being inside on the couch. But Steve had marched out, throwing, 'Just doing the rounds, be back in a bit,' over his shoulder. And he'd called the dogs to accompany him.

He'd been distracted since her bombshell about the horses, and seemed almost angry. He often was when perplexed or worried about something: his forehead would crease into a frown and his eyebrows would lower, making him look decidedly cranky. In the early days, it had taken Jessica ages to learn to correctly read him. Far too many times she'd accused him of being angry at her when he was merely confused or thinking something through.

She knew Steve was worried about her and her decision. Hell, *she* was worried about her and her decision! But she didn't see any other logical course of action. Steve would see that in time. Hopefully the jittery feeling would leave her soon too. Meanwhile she had to swallow down all the sadness and put on a happy face. It was the right thing to do.

Keeping all her gear was a good idea. She could almost picture herself with small children, teaching them to ride, taking them to pony club, plaiting up small ponies for shows. She loved teaching the handful of students who had come to her over the years and could see how much more it would mean to be introducing her own children to the world of horses. Jessica felt the tiniest glimmer of excitement. Yes, perhaps this really was a sign of the new phase in her life – motherhood. Was she becoming clucky? The emotion wasn't that strong, but she was feeling a little buoyed.

Jessica got up and went over to the window and watched the horses grazing. Her stomach seemed to grow full of lead once again and a sadness she hadn't felt since losing her mother overcame her. God, could she do this? Really? Tears welled and then started to spill. She would have put her hands to her face, but she had to keep hold of the crutches supporting her. She dipped her head and sobbed. She knew she should look away; distract herself, but another part of her mind said if she cried enough tears now, let them all out, when the time came to say goodbye she would be able to stay strong.

Twenty minutes later, a few tears were still trickling down her cheeks. She hadn't even cried this much over losing her father. And this thought brought another flood and a sharp stab of guilt. Jessica felt her knees go weak and was grateful for the crutches that stopped her crumpling to the floor. It's what Steve and Tiffany had said numerous times while expressing their worry over what she was putting herself through: she *had* been trying to outrun her grief over her father's death by keeping herself busy and focussed.

Slowly she made her way back to the couch. Maybe she shouldn't give up horses; if she did, she'd have all that time to think, to regret her lost goals, to miss her parents – to feel sorry for herself.

Exactly. She was just feeling sorry for herself. She needed to buck up. Someone would give the horses the home they needed. She had to forget them – she had new goals now. The money would help the farm significantly if drought set in, as forecast. And the sooner she sold, the better the price; in twelve months, or even six, there could be a glut of good horses for sale as people tightened their belts. She was doing the right thing; she just had to hold her nerve.

Some time later Jessica heard the ute come back. But when Steve hadn't come in after a few minutes, she looked over the back of the couch and out the window.

He was on the phone, clearly agitated; pacing back and forth and running a hand through his hair. *Gosh, what's happened?* she wondered, starting to worry. Then he was nodding, calmer. He stopped pacing, stopped fussing with his hair, and slid his phone back in his pocket. He rubbed the ears of the dogs in the back of the ute and swept an arm in command, encouraging them out of the tray.

She lowered herself back onto the leather and turned up the sound on the TV.

'How's the patient?' Steve said as he came in. Jessica noted the weariness in his tone.

'I'm fine,' she said. 'How's everything?'

'All good. I sure hope they've got it wrong about the long-term forecast of drought. But we'll be right,' he added as if reminding himself. It was his mantra, and everything usually did turn out okay in the end, not that they hadn't had their ups and downs and share of hairy moments.

This time they definitely would be fine, Jessica knew. No matter how hard it would be to say goodbye to the horses, deep down she did feel good about being able to make a considerable financial contribution to their enterprise. Steve's male pride wouldn't totally love it, but he was a smart enough businessman to take help where it was offered.

She watched Steve making tea for them, itching to ask who he'd been talking to on the phone.

She was still teetering between asking him and admonishing herself that he'd tell her when and if he wanted to when she heard a car arrive outside. She didn't get up to look, only clutched her mug of tea, silently willing Steve to get up from the other couch and go. He did. He put his mug down on the coffee table and eased himself to his feet. He was still weighed down by something, Jessica noted, and she felt a stab of remorse that she might be the cause. 'No pain, no gain' swept into her mind, but left just as swiftly, leaving her nodding in agreement and staring down into her milky tea.

'What's this I hear about you selling up and getting out of horses?' Tiffany's voice was loud as she stepped into the lounge area.

Jessica looked up, stunned, and took in her friend's navy blue shirt with orange Millers' Fodder logo. So that's who Steve had been on the phone to. Tiffany had that just-dropped-everything look about her. Jessica stared at her friend, unsure what to say.

'Well, is it true?'

Jessica nodded as she prepared herself to speak.

'I'll just leave you two to talk,' Steve said quietly. Jessica watched as he went into the bedroom and came out with their clothes hamper. She felt a new rush of affection for him and then, as he closed the laundry door behind him, a new ache of guilt at causing him to worry and for upsetting their generally harmonious life. The accident and last few days really had shaken things up.

'Why? What's going on in that brain of yours?' Tiffany asked, more kindly now as she settled herself onto the couch. Laurel left Jessica's side and hopped up beside Tiffany. *Thanks very much, traitor.*

Jessica told Tiffany all she'd told Steve earlier. It really did make sense – even more so on the second telling. But that didn't ease the pain inside her when picturing how sad and lonely she would feel, saying goodbye and then looking out at empty paddocks and day yards.

She knew Tiffany had every right to turn around and tell her that it wasn't what her father would want, that she was being a victim. But Tiffany didn't say any of that. She sat through Jessica's explanation of what she was thinking and feeling, occasionally nodding, but more often shaking her head slowly and pursing her lips. Then, just as Steve had before her, Tiffany tried to offer alternatives, halfway measures. When Jessica told her of the nightmares and being fully convinced she couldn't ride cross-country again, she made the suggestion of concentrating on dressage, despite knowing Jessica's disinterest in it, that it just didn't give her the buzz cross-country did. Tiffany then pushed the angle of getting counselling.

It wasn't that Jessica didn't believe in counselling; she'd heard it had done wonders with many sports people. She just didn't see the point in paying a fortune to be told she was giving up too easily and letting her fear win. She didn't want someone to tell her there were other good coaches. There were, plenty, but none with the skills of Jeff Collins. Her dreams were over, she just had to face up to that. And she had. She was.

'You've really thought this through, haven't you? There's nothing I can say to change your mind?' Tiffany said finally.

Jessica shook her head. 'My mind's made up. It's hard – and it's probably going to get a lot harder – but it's what I have to do. It's what I *feel* I have to do.'

'Okay. Fair enough, I suppose,' Tiffany said with a deep sigh. 'I don't agree, and for the record I think you are going to regret it. But it's your decision and, as your friend who loves you very much, you have my full support.'

Jessica felt a huge weight she didn't even realise she was carrying leave her.

'And if you do regret it,' Tiffany continued, 'you can always get back into it later. You're keeping all your gear, right? At least for now?'

'Yes.'

'Good. Well, all I can say is I hope you'll make me an honorary aunt very soon.' She offered her friend a warm smile tinged with sadness.

'I'm sorry Steve dragged you out here.'

'He's worried about you, Jess. So am I.'

'I know.' *I'm worried about myself,* Jessica wanted to say. She did feel a certain relief at having made a difficult decision, and had the sense of being in control again. But she couldn't ignore the suspicion that she was standing on a slippery slope with no way back. Hopefully it was just the pain and the medication messing with her. She was sure she'd start to feel better when the horses were gone and she could put the decision behind her.

Jessica heard the washing machine fill with water before the laundry door opened. She hoped Steve had thought to scrub the breeches she'd worn for the dressage portion of the competition clean by hand before putting them in – the ones from the cross-country had been cut from her and had ended up in the hospital bin, she supposed – before realising it didn't matter;

she'd never be wearing those breeches again. With that thought a fresh lump lodged in her throat. She forced it aside. *Just the fear of change.*

'Can I get you a cuppa, Tiff?' Steve asked, entering the lounge area.

'That would be great, thanks. Can I have a hot chocolate, please? I'm all caffeined up for today.'

'Sure, no probs. Jessica, another?'

'Hot chocolate for me, too, thanks.'

'Would you like me to do the negotiating for you and organise everything?' Tiffany asked as Steve rattled away in the kitchen and Jessica sat stroking Hardy.

Jessica looked up at her friend, a new rush of affection and deep gratitude flowing through her. 'Would you?'

'I just offered, didn't I?'

'That would mean so much, you've no idea.'

'I'm not saying I agree,' Tiffany warned, 'but I did say I will support you.'

Jessica thought her offer went way beyond mere support, and was truly grateful to have such a selfless friend. Especially when she had so much going on in her own life. 'Oh God, Tiffany, you've no idea what a weight off it would be,' Jessica said, letting out the breath she'd been holding. If she could have got up easily to go over and hug her friend, she would have. Instead she put her hand out, which Tiffany took and squeezed.

'So, these are the amounts you're thinking of putting on them?' Tiffany said, picking up the pad of paper Jessica had put on the coffee table. 'Do you want me to phone Sharon Parks and Vanessa and Andrew Birch first and see if they're serious and still interested? And would you rather not be here when they go, or do you think you'll need the closure? It's entirely up to you.'

Jessica's head was spinning. This was happening very quickly. But that was a good thing – it showed it was meant to be, right?

'Thank you so much,' she said, holding onto her friend's hand tightly.

'You'd do the same for me,' Tiffany said.

I absolutely would, Jessica thought, but stayed silent and nodded.

'Here you are,' Steve said, putting steaming mugs in front of them on the coffee table. He touched Hardy on the hind legs, said, 'Off you hop,' and sat in the newly vacated space beside Jessica. He looked defeated. She knew he'd eventually understand, he just needed time to adjust. *Don't we all?* And when their baby arrived, he'd probably forget all this drama in his delight at finally being a father.

They laughed, watching Hardy climb up beside Tiffany and on top of Laurel, who eventually, reluctantly, made space while letting out a loud harrumph.

'So how's the world of feed and associated supplies?' Jessica asked.

'Good. Busy. All the farmers are buying up in bulk. Apparently there's talk of next year being dry. What do you think, Steve?'

'Looks that way.'

'Well, if you want extra hay, you'd better get it ordered. They've got three trucks coming in in the next few days, but they're saying the price might go up after that because they're running out locally and will have to start trucking it in from over the border.'

'I did an order this morning, but I'm thinking of adding more to it. Thanks for the heads up.'

'No worries. I didn't see you. I was probably on my coffee break.'

'Barry served me. Maybe being prepared will mean I won't need it. They're saying next winter will be wet, but this spring will be dryer than average. Goodness only knows – just sounds like their usual each-way bet to me.'

'Isn't that farming, generally?' Tiffany said with a cringe. 'And life, for that matter,' she added with a laugh.

'Yeah, pretty much.'

They made small talk about the current racism and substance abuse scandals gripping the AFL until Tiffany announced she'd better get going. Steve tried to convince her to stay for dinner, but she said she had a lot to do. And it really was only four in the afternoon – far too early even for an early dinner.

'Right, so you're absolutely sure about this?' Tiffany asked, pausing after picking up the sheet of prices Jessica wanted for each of the horses.

'Yes. And thank you so much. You've no idea how much it means …'

'I know,' Tiffany said, waving Jessica's words away with the paper in her hand.

Steve got up to see their friend out. Jessica knew he would express his disappointment to Tiffany again. But this time she knew Tiffany would defend her, tell him that she didn't agree, but would support her since her mind was clearly made up. They'd most likely share a rolling of the eyes and comment that when Jessica's mind was made up there was no budging her – or something along those lines.

Jessica wasn't unsure about her decision being the right one – she really didn't see an alternative – but she did feel uneasy about actually parting with Prince and Beau. She wondered about taking Tiffany up on her offer of being there when they were loaded. Steve could take her away for the day so she wouldn't have to see them leave. Or would the closure gained through being there be better for her healing process?

She really had to have more faith. Look at what Tiffany had been through and she remained relatively cheery and easy-going. This faith in the universe she held onto really seemed to work. Thanks to being raised by stern, pushy parents – especially her father – Jessica was prone to trying to control things. Jessica Harrington née Collins knew it was unlikely she'd ever be described as easy-going.

As she listened to Tiffany's ute start up, she vowed to not let Tiffany and Steve down. She wouldn't prove them right, either; she'd focus on the next phase of her life: getting back on her feet and having babies. And she'd do it all with a smile on her face and a cheerful disposition.

Chapter Eleven

Jessica woke feeling refreshed. No nightmares. *So there!* she silently declared, feeling vindicated. She tried to recall any dreams she might have had and came away empty-handed. Giving up the horses was the right decision. A big part of Jessica already knew she would regret it – horses were such a big part of her life, and always had been – but if she filled that void with a baby she'd be fine. She was relieved to be without the gravelly eyes or slow heaviness that had dogged her for the past few days. Even the pain in her leg had lessened, she realised with slight surprise; it was just a dull, manageable ache.

'Good morning, gorgeous girl,' Steve said, leaning over and kissing her. 'I hope you slept as well as I did.'

She smiled at him. The night before, determined to prove all was well after their serious discussions, Jessica had fought the awkwardness and romance-killing nature of the rigid cast on her leg and insisted she and Steve make love. Steve had tried to assure her he was fine to wait, but she needed the reassurance of their closeness. Later she felt guilty for faking her orgasm; she'd been unable to ignore her leg feeling completely wrong and the big decision she had made.

She followed Steve out to the horses and leant on the fence to watch him tend to them, as much to show Steve she was fine as to prove it to herself. It would be hard, but no pain no gain, as her father would have said. She wasn't sure if the sentiment really fitted here, but shrugged the thought aside. Better that than getting all choked up and teary, as she would if she allowed herself to dwell on it.

She patted their sleek, strong necks and the horses nuzzled her, a little more affectionate than normal. Did they somehow sense what was coming? How could they? She was just seeing things that weren't there. Nonetheless, their deep brown eyes and long lashes got to her and a lump caught in her throat.

'I'm cold, I'm going back in,' she said, and gave a shudder before turning and hobbling away back to the house. Her sad heart pounded away beneath all the layers she was wearing and the slight awkwardness she felt at lying to her husband caused heat to break out across her chest.

Back in the house, Jessica escaped to the bathroom to give herself a little pep talk to get her through. While she feared looking at empty paddocks and lonely stable yards sometime soon, she hoped Tiffany wouldn't take too long to find a buyer or two, and have Prince and Beau removed. Oh, it hurt just thinking their names. Then the current torture could end and the healing process begin. She tried to ignore the little voice deep inside her that questioned whether she was feeling so bad because it was not the right thing to do.

But it is, she countered forcefully. *I can do this.* She looked into the mirror. *I'm strong. I wouldn't have got to international two-star level without being strong. This is the right thing to do.*

Her phone beeped as she settled herself on the couch. A text from Tiffany: *No go with Sharon P. Txx* Jessica shook aside the disappointment – it would have been good to have the business so easily and quickly dealt with – and distracted herself with morning TV. She planned to while away the rest of the day with two romantic comedy DVDs, punctuated by lunch. Along the way she'd actually do something useful and fold the clean clothes when Steve brought them in off the line. *It's going to be a good day.*

A little later, over her sandwich – this time Steve had boiled eggs and made a creamy, lightly curried filling before heading out to help Gary down the road with tailing his lambs – she gave in and logged in to Facebook. Tiffany, bless her, had already put up a few lovely photos of Prince and Beau standing together, under saddle, and in action, captioned with enticing descriptions. The post had been shared four times, twenty people had liked it, and twenty-three people had posted comments. The last few visible comments were simple questions: 'Why?' 'What's happening?' 'What's going on with Jessica?' 'Why is Jessica Harrington selling up?' The notifications symbol on Jessica's private profile was showing twelve, and there were four messages.

She closed the laptop, put it on the floor and pushed it just under the couch so as to be out of sight and temptation. While she desperately wanted to know how things stood, she didn't want to read any gossip or speculation about herself. And, anyway, Tiffany would be dealing with genuine enquiries via her own private messaging. She wished she'd asked her friend to discuss every-thing with Steve and leave her out of it altogether, but that would be completely passing the buck, which wasn't fair on them. And not on herself either.

This was her decision and the least she could do was have the guts to discuss it like a rational human being when called upon. *It's business*, she told herself. She rubbed the ears of the dogs beside her.

Steve was right – what she was doing was the same as selling Laurel and Hardy. They were family – more so now they were inside dogs and a constant presence. The reality was she was selling her best friends, friends that had done well by her. But the horses meant so much to their operation financially. Money wasn't everything, but it sure helped. She could always get more horses later. And this concession helped ease her mind a little.

She put the second movie in and forced herself to concentrate on it.

★

Three days later, Jessica hadn't heard anything more from Tiffany about the horses, just the odd text message checking on her and her leg and quips about how many bags of chaff or bales of hay she'd sold.

Jessica had managed to refrain from looking at Facebook again. She'd become a bit DVDed out and thanks to Steve had a new hobby: jigsaw puzzles.

Stretching out before Jessica on the large coffee table was a two-thousand-piece puzzle where a field of multi-coloured tulips was slowly coming together. He'd borrowed it from the library when he'd returned the DVDs. Jessica just hoped all the pieces were there and she wouldn't have to face the frustration of ending up with an empty space after all her effort. She'd become quite keen on jigsaws, and was really looking forward to tackling the next box – a complicated cityscape of London.

When she tired of jigsaw puzzles she thought she might get Steve to get her some knitting needles and wool and, with the help of Google, she'd teach herself to knit. It would be lovely to have some baby blankets and cute little outfits ready to go. Perhaps being organised would make her hormones surge and she might begin feeling clucky.

She shook her head – she was getting way ahead of herself. Being organised was one thing, but she was being ridiculous – she'd only stopped taking the pill a few days ago. She'd been on it for years and it could take ages to get pregnant, by all accounts. She really hoped her body would be more compliant. Nonetheless, the last thing she wanted was to jinx things by being presumptuous and too prepared.

★

Steve announced on Monday morning that he was taking Jessica out for the day – no arguments. He would drive them over to Mannum for lunch at the new café that had been getting great reviews. Jessica was momentarily excited – she hadn't left the property since breaking her ankle just over a week ago, as she hadn't felt up to making small talk with people she knew. There'd be less likelihood of bumping into people she knew in another town. Hopefully.

But her excitement left her almost as quickly as it came, causing her pulse to race. Today was the day: the horses were being picked up. A boulder settled in the pit of her stomach and bitter, burning bile gathered around it. She'd made it very clear to Steve and Tiffany that she didn't want to be there when the time came; didn't want to stay goodbye; Jessica felt making the decision itself was as good as saying goodbye. And there was no point dwelling, making herself and everyone else uncomfortable with a stoic show of no tears – or worse, floods of tears.

She showered, made an effort to dress up a little – wearing a long skirt to hide her cast – and put on a cheery disposition despite feeling nauseous, nervous and jittery.

In Mannum, Jessica barely tasted the three-cheese soufflé that Steve raved about, or the warm apple strudel with thick double cream and freshly brewed coffee. But she forced herself to nod and contribute her own not as enthusiastic appreciation of the meal.

They wandered the main street, slowly making their way through the art gallery and home wares and interiors, antiques and bric-a-brac shops. Jessica needed regular breaks and Steve chattered constantly, clearly trying to keep her spirits up. She joined in on autopilot. They even wandered through the baby and children's wear shop, something they had never done before, holding up the tiny, cute garments and raving about how precious the things were. It was evident they both wanted to buy something but seemed to agree it was too soon.

Jessica found herself muttering her thanks to the friendly shop assistant and going back out into the street to look at the range of mobiles hanging in the front window. She stared at the shapes and bright colours, thinking about what was going on at home. Had it happened yet? Had she made the right decision in not being there and saying proper goodbyes? Had she made the right decision, full stop?

She was distracted by Steve's presence beside her, his arm draped around her shoulder. He held a brown paper carry bag out to her with a gentle half-smile. Jessica frowned and wanted to hand the bag back, tell him she thought buying baby things would be bad luck – clearly they hadn't been of the one mind after all – but his nod of encouragement made her take a cautious look inside.

She drew out a plush, chocolate brown bear and hugged it to her. It was all she could do not to burst into tears. Bless him. She smiled sadly at him before touching his shoulder. If she hadn't been on crutches, she would have thrown her arms around him. Steve carefully hugged her, the bear between them.

'He's gorgeous. Thank you,' she murmured into his shoulder as her husband stroked her hair. They broke apart and Jessica reluctantly placed the bear back into the carry bag and handed it to Steve. As much as she could feel the bear's comfort flooding through her and didn't want to let him go, a grown woman clutching a bear in the middle of the main street of a country town was sure to raise eyebrows.

Jessica was exhausted and nodded off a few times on the drive home. She hadn't spent so long on her crutches before and now she seemed to ache all over. The pain was quite dull, and while she knew she could do with only half the recommended dose of medication she liked her emotional pain being masked too. She'd take a full dose when they got home.

Tiffany's ute was beside the house as they drove onto their property. She emerged and greeted Steve with a sombre 'Hi,' and a quick peck to the cheek before wrapping her arms around Jessica.

'Thank you for everything. You've no idea,' Jessica croaked before she burst into tears. Tiffany erupted too and the two women clung to each other.

After a few moments Jessica pulled away and wiped her face as she bent to pat the dogs, who had appeared beside them.

'Are you okay?' Tiffany asked, full of concern.

'I'm fine,' Jessica replied heavily. 'I'll be fine.'

Tiffany stayed for a cuppa, but it was clear to Jessica that she wanted to be elsewhere. Fair enough, it must have been a fairly harrowing day for her as well – not to mention all the negotiating she must have been doing this past week.

As Steve saw Tiffany out, she said, 'Should show up in the account by tomorrow – if not, let me know.'

That night Jessica went to bed with a heart so heavy she thought she might never be able to get out of bed again. But her conscience was relatively clear. Steve had filled her in on some of the details from Tiffany: both horses had gone to a wonderful stable – horse people Jessica had a lot of respect for. She knew that hearing about them doing well, or not, would wrench at her, but for now this was good news in bleak circumstances. She wasn't sure why, but she was pleased Sharon Parks wasn't Prince and Beau's new owner.

Jessica pushed through her tiredness and broken heart to again make love with Steve. The whole time she felt hollow, not comforted at all despite enjoying the feel of them entwined. But she kept her mind on the prize: planting the seed for a baby, a distraction, a new life. She hated herself for her dishonesty and almost wept when Steve went out to get them a glass of water. But she had to toughen up; the last thing she needed was to bring Steve down as well.

Chapter Twelve

The week passed slowly for Jessica. Gradually she and Steve were settling into a new routine: she inside the house amusing herself and doing whatever chore she could manage, and Steve doing everything else. At least now he was free to concentrate on running the farm again without the added burden of the horses.

Jessica spent most of the days trying not to look out the window at the paddocks where Prince and Beau had grazed, nor across at the purpose-built stable, feed and tack shed that housed the horse float. Steve quite often used the float for moving stock, so it would stay on the property as a constant reminder. She knew she'd have to face sorting through all the remaining rugs and grooming gear – a veritable mountain accumulated and inherited over her and her parents' lifetimes – and do some culling one day. Folding up her breeches from the dressage competition and adding them to her drawer of riding clothes had nearly done her in. She'd said she'd keep all her gear, but she hadn't really meant it. She had just wanted to appease everyone – have a bit of an each-way bet. If only Tiffany was the same size, she could have had it easily dealt with. Tiffany had helped by taking the feed for her own horses, so that was one less thing to think about.

She really had to start bucking up. But not today – today she was going into town with Steve and, while he pushed the grocery trolley up and down the supermarket aisles, she was going to pop into the haberdashery shop that sold wool and knitting supplies. She'd seen all the DVDs she wanted to, completed enough jigsaws to last a lifetime, and couldn't seem to concentrate on reading for long. She'd decided knitting might be the answer to staving off the boredom that threatened with each new morning. She'd marked the day she was due to get her plaster off on the calendar and each night she put a cross through the day just finished. Only twenty-six sleeps to go. Only! It seemed like a lifetime away. Meanwhile she would try knitting – not baby things, just some simple projects to learn and practise with. She'd decided on a scarf for Steve, and then one for her – she might have them done by the time winter came around again in eight months.

They had just parked and got out and were ready to go their separate ways when Jessica heard her name called. She turned around to find one of her pupils coming towards them.

'Jessica, wait up,' the girl said, waving her arm.

'Hi, Molly.'

'Sorry to hear about your accident. How's the leg?'

'Thanks. Getting there. How's school?'

'School's school,' Molly said with a loose shrug. 'Hey, when can I start having lessons again? Tiny's been doing great.'

'That's good to hear, but sorry, Molly, I won't be able to instruct you anymore.'

'Oh. But why? It's only a broken ankle, right? I heard you'd sold Prince and Beau, but that won't stop you instructing – why would it?'

'I've given up riding altogether.'

'But instructing isn't riding – well, it doesn't have to be.'

Lost for anything more to say – what was there to say? – Jessica just shook her head and frowned.

'But you're the best instructor I've ever had,' Molly wailed.

'I'm sorry. And it's lovely of you to say, but I'm sure …' Jessica wanted the ground to swallow her up. This girl with her open face marred by confusion and disappointment, standing there in the street, on the verge of tears was heart-wrenching.

'What about not giving up when it gets a bit hard?' Molly pleaded. 'That's what you're always saying.'

'I know. And I'm sorry, Molly, I really am.'

'Why? That's what I don't understand,' Molly said, her bottom lip quivering. She turned and fled down the street, leaving Jessica feeling helpless and very guilty, on the verge of tears herself. She wondered why too. Damn being so emotionally fragile! Steve put his arm around her and she leant in, grateful for his comforting embrace. They broke apart and turned when Jessica's name was called again.

'Jessica! I hope you're happy – you've broken my little girl's heart.' Big, burly Tom Baines, Molly's father, strode towards them.

Oh shit. People in the street stopped talking and turned to stare in their direction. Jessica felt her face and neck flush.

'Dad, don't,' Molly pleaded quietly, blushing a bright shade of beetroot. She hung her head and stared at her feet as she twisted them back and forth, the stance every embarrassed teenage girl had down pat.

'I'm sorry, Tom,' Jessica said.

'Not sorry enough to continue instructing her, though, are you? You know she's been in tears all week? Hope you're happy.'

'*Dad.*'

Jessica looked down at her own feet.

'No, thought not. Selfish, that's what you are,' he said, pointing an angry finger at her.

'Hey, now come on, mate,' Steve said, stepping in front of the man, who practically dwarfed him. 'That's not fair. Jessica's going through a really tough time.'

'It's all right, Steve,' Jessica said, putting her hand on his arm.

'Come on, Dad, let's just go, pleeeease,' Molly said, tugging at her father's arm.

'One day when you have kids, maybe you'll understand,' Tom said over his shoulder as he let Molly pull him down the street.

Jessica nearly crumbled at the look Molly shot her: a cross between white-hot hatred and sympathy. Thankfully everyone else in the street had returned to their business.

'Wow,' Steve said. 'I didn't see that coming.'

'No,' was all Jessica could say. She was shaking so much she had to lean on the bull bar of their four-wheel drive for extra support.

'Are you okay?'

She nodded, and was just opening her mouth to speak when another voice cut in, this one old and scratchy.

'I never thought I'd hear about the daughter of Jeff Collins giving up so easily. Unbelievable. And gutless. Thought you were made of sterner stuff, my girl.'

Jessica closed her mouth and stared, stunned, at the old man as he drove past on his motorised scooter. He was one of the old pony club stalwarts she'd known since she was a toddler. He and her father had butted heads many times.

'Good to see you too, Bill,' she finally managed, but he was long gone.

'Jesus,' Steve said, running a hand through his hair. 'Sorry, I was a bit useless, but I was too shocked to speak. What is wrong with people?'

'Nothing you could have done. So, shall we get on?'

'If you're still up to it.'

'Absolutely,' Jessica said, a lot more enthusiastically than she felt. She needed to stay true to her form of putting on a strong façade, regardless of how she actually felt.

The woman in the haberdashery store, which Jessica had never set foot in before, seemed very excited when Jessica told her she'd like some advice on knitting when she had the time – the store was surprisingly busy. Jessica was happy to wait and take some minutes to try to pull herself together; she was still feeling shaken. How embarrassing to have been accosted like that in the street with the whole town watching! Her mother would have had kittens. At least she was too shocked for any tears to form. Really, what business was it of anyone's how she lived her life? She did feel kind of guilty about letting Molly down, but it wasn't like the kid had been with her long term – she'd only had around a dozen lessons. And she was easy enough to work with – she'd find another instructor she liked. Maybe even one day it might be Jessica, but not right now. She felt terrible about letting anyone down, but when it came to her students it couldn't be helped. She needed to have a new, totally different focus now. Well, that's what she was telling herself.

Gradually the shop emptied. Each person had nodded and smiled hello and she'd replied in the same fashion. She particularly liked that not one of them spoke to her. Finally it was Jessica's turn to be served. She put the knitting needles and yarn she'd chosen on the counter and chatted with the woman ringing up her purchase about her plans for the scarf. The woman showed

Jessica how to cast on and knit a few stitches, though Jessica didn't really think she had the hang of it. She'd go to the YouTube tutorials she'd found when she got home and watch them again, though she promised the saleswoman she'd come back for advice if she ran into trouble. She felt quite good about being at least a little informed.

She handed over her debit card for processing, barely taking in the rather large total of her purchases. *Gosh, no wonder everyone buys acrylic, made-in-China jumpers.* But she didn't really care about the cost, she just wanted to get home before anyone else bailed her up.

★

Following lunch, Jessica settled in with her knitting, only having to tell the dogs twice not to touch her wool after she'd caught them looking playfully at the ball that had dropped from her lap and run a short distance across the floor. For dogs that didn't play games like fetch and didn't even own tennis balls, they were showing far too much interest in chasing her wool. After being told, 'No. Sit. Leave it,' the well-trained dogs had lain either side of the ball with their heads on their paws, eyeing it, clearly waiting for the object to move.

Jessica took pity on them and brought the ball of wool back up to her lap.

Now that she was actually knitting, she wasn't sure it was the distraction she'd been looking for. She'd got the hang of the plain stitch – sticking the needle in the right spot, pushing it through, wrapping the yarn around it, and slipping the loop over the end of the other needle, and doing it all again – she didn't have to concentrate too much and her mind was beginning to wander …

to her students. She'd enjoyed instructing, would really miss them and seeing their improvement week after week. Her thoughts drifted on, settling on Prince and Beau and how they were faring. Hopefully they were coping better with it all than she was. Far too often her stomach would clench and a ball of sadness would engulf her, tears threatening. While she knew she was putting on a good front, the truth was she felt like she was dying inside. Not unlike losing her parents all over again, but at the one time.

She couldn't tell Steve; all she could do was keep up with her façade and hope she'd soon start to get over it. If she opened up about her feelings, he'd track down the horses and get them back. And now they'd used a big chunk of the money – which had come through as promised – for stockpiling feed, that option was gone. And she'd never be able to choose Prince over Beau if it came to that. Anyway, it wouldn't be fair on the new buyer, and she'd be putting her reputation as a fair person to deal with in jeopardy. Not that that really mattered now she was no longer in the horse world.

Suck it up, Princess, she told herself, wishing she really could just snap out of it.

Jessica's mind moved to the future, when she was out of her cast and off her crutches. What would she do with her time then? This sitting around knitting and being housebound was fine while she had the excuse of her ankle, but then what? She would have all those hours she'd spent with the horses to fill in. She tried to push the thoughts aside. Tiffany would say to just let the universe deal with it; that the right answer would turn up at the right time.

Perhaps she *should* resume her instructing – increase the number of pupils even. She could do that while pregnant. And she certainly had all the facilities. Well, except she'd probably need a horse or two to keep her hand in and give the odd demonstration on. And acquiring new horses would completely defeat the purpose of her having gone through all this grief, and prove to everyone that she had acted too hastily. She wasn't ready to admit to that just yet, and she wasn't totally convinced she had done the wrong thing. But she was terribly sad about not seeing Prince and Beau move slowly around the paddock, and not being able go out and stroke their lovely long faces and look into their deep brown eyes.

She sighed heavily and forced herself back to her knitting, holding it up when she got to the end of the row. She'd done about two centimetres. It was satisfying to see her scarf growing – far too slowly for her liking, but growing nonetheless. Only around one hundred and eighty centimetres left!

'How's the knitting going?' Steve asked as he took his boots and then his coat off near the front door. 'It's getting longer,' he said, nodding with approval.

'Hmm. Very slowly. I'm not sure I have the patience for this.'

'This was in the letterbox.' Steve pulled out a white envelope and handed it to her. She frowned slightly at the Eventing South Australia logo on it. She hadn't withdrawn her membership; was just going to not renew when it came up next year. This must be something about her accident.

She prised the envelope open, slid out the crisp, folded letter, and smoothed it flat. Her mouth dropped open – she'd been included in the South Australian state team and was required to be at a training session at Naracoorte in five months. What? How could this be? She'd bombed out of one of the major selection events. Her heart began racing. Her brain fought to understand.

'What is it?' Steve asked.

Jessica ignored him. She knew the committee did selections throughout the year based on results. The availability of team members and their mounts would have to play a big part as well.

Horses and riders were always getting injured and sick and then recovering. Perhaps she'd been selected on her previous scores, or through someone else's misfortune. How or why didn't really matter now.

She let out a deep sigh and handed the paper to Steve, who was now perched beside her and looking very worried. One of her dreams had come true. This was what she'd been working towards for years. She should be leaping up and down and demanding that they open champagne to celebrate. But all she felt was sick. And angry and disappointed in herself. Why couldn't they have informed her a few weeks ago? Before she'd quit the sport and sold her horses.

'Shit,' Steve said, quietly as he read. 'So what do we do?' He laid the paper gently on the coffee table.

'Reply "thanks, but no thanks", and include an explanation, I guess,' she said, shrugging her shoulders. She looked composed, almost nonchalant, but it was an act that drew on all of her strength of will and acting skills. If she could have run, she would have – to the bathroom to throw up. Acid rose from deep in her stomach, biting painfully.

'But it's what you've been dreaming of for so long.'

'Well, it's over now. It's too late.'

'No, surely not. Can't you …?' His voice trailed off but he was clearly becoming frustrated.

'No, Steve,' she said firmly. 'It's over. I'll write to them and explain.' A mere formality, since everyone in South Australian eventing would already know the truth.

'Sometimes I don't think I know you at all,' Steve said with a heavy sigh, shaking his head slowly.

'You can't be more disappointed than I am.' *In myself.*

'So bloody do something about it!'

'Like what? I can't exactly phone up the new owners and say I've changed my mind, can I?'

She could see that was exactly what Steve was thinking, and his pause before speaking again confirmed it.

'No, I suppose you can't.'

'And the reason I sold them is still there anyway. Being selected for the team really doesn't change anything. I've still lost my nerve, remember? And don't suggest counselling. We've been over that.'

'Okay,' Steve said with a deep, resigned sigh. 'I'll get you a cup of tea.' He got up slowly. Jessica knew he wanted to fix this; it's what Steve was good at. But there was nothing to be fixed – there was no longer an eventing combination of Jessica Harrington and Collins Park Prince, no Jessica Harrington in the world of eventing, full stop. She knew it sounded melodramatic, but she really did feel like a big part of her had died.

She returned to her knitting, taking much more time and care with each stitch than she needed to, determined to show Steve she was fine.

'I guess I should at least be celebrating that I made the team,' she called.

'Yes, it's a huge achievement. You should be very proud of yourself. *I'm* very proud of you.'

'Thanks,' Jessica said to both his comment and the arrival of the steaming mug in front of her. But there was no talk of getting a bottle of something bubbly from the fridge. They always had a bottle of sparkling wine on hand; it was an unspoken pact they seemed to have made early on in their relationship – to keep something on hand for celebrating or commiserating, because life was too short to not drink good wine. Anyway, her selection was as much down to her father as herself, and without him being here …

It's the way it's meant to be, she told herself. But it didn't make her feel any better. She'd totally let him and herself down by not placing Prince correctly and causing the fall, and not having the guts to face her fear and get back in the saddle when her leg healed.

If only she had the justification that she was pregnant. Perhaps she was; she hadn't used one of the three pregnancy test kits she'd picked up after buying knitting supplies. Thankfully the pharmacy had been empty and she hadn't been accosted by any of the local gossips and quizzed on her purchase. Worrying about that had meant she almost hadn't ventured in.

Despite knowing a few weeks off the pill was probably not nearly enough time to get pregnant, she got up, declared, 'Sorry, need a wee,' and went to the bathroom to do a test.

A few minutes later, Jessica was staring at the negative test. She'd known it was a long shot, but still felt totally bowled over with disappointment. She put her head in her hands and waited for the tears. None came. She sat there for a few more moments, hoping the sadness that was making her whole body ache might ease.

Jessica wanted nothing more than to curl up on the floor and be sucked down the drain into the molten core of the earth.

Chapter Thirteen

Jessica and Steve were silently engrossed in their own activities later that afternoon – Jessica plodding along with knitting and Steve browsing a stock magazine – when the phone rang. Steve answered it when Jessica showed no interest.

'Steve speaking … Hey, I'll just get her. It's for you. Tiffany,' he said, holding the phone out.

Jessica scolded herself for the feeling of annoyance that swept through her. She wasn't exactly enjoying her knitting, but she was on a mission, and the interruption was unwelcome.

'Hi Tiff,' Jessica said, laying the phone on her lap and pressing the speaker button. She resumed her knitting. 'What's up?'

'Are you okay?'

'Yes, fine, why?'

'What is that noise – that clicking sound?'

'Knitting needles. I'm knitting.'

'You're what?'

'Knitting. A scarf for Steve.'

'Since when do you knit?'

'Since this afternoon when I bought wool and knitting needles. I needed something to do. If I watch another DVD or infomercial I will go mad.'

'Sounds like you already have.' Tiffany paused, then spoke hesitatingly. 'Er, congratulations on selection for the state team.'

'Thanks. How did you find out?'

'It's in this month's Equestrian SA news – the email came in last night.'

Jessica let out a groan. Of course the team announcement would be in the newsletter.

'So, are you okay? Really?'

'I'm fine.' She didn't sound convincing even to herself. 'Really, I'm fine.'

'You're allowed not to be.'

'Well, I am.'

'Great. It's a huge achievement. I hope you're letting yourself indulge in a little pride. Your dad would have been very proud.'

Hmm, actually, I don't think anything short of being a fully fledged member of the Olympic team would have garnered much high praise from Jeff Collins. But she kept the words to herself. Tiffany would agree – she'd seen and heard Jessica's father in fine form plenty of times – but would tell Jessica to stop being so hard on herself.

'So, what's up with you? How are Brandy and Storm going?'

'Oh, okay. I don't have a lot of time left to work them with this earning a living caper. I'm so tuckered out when I get home it's all I can do to get them in, rugged, and fed. Maybe when daylight saving starts again.'

'That's good,' Jessica said, concentrating more on her hard plastic needles. She quite liked their industrious sound. It was probably driving Steve mad, but he'd be too polite to say anything.

'Do you fancy coming along and watching me on Saturday? It's the club championships.'

Jessica immediately saw what her friend was doing – trying to get her out of the house and improve her spirits. 'I can't strap for you, so there's no point.'

'Not to strap, obviously. To watch. Moral support.'

'I can't, Tiff.'

'Oh. Okay.'

Jessica felt bad for letting her friend down, but she really couldn't face horse people yet. Especially now, thanks to her news. Actually, she didn't think she could face any more than one or two people at a time, full stop – especially after being bailed up in the street. A jolt of fear shot through her as she pictured the mass of people who would be attending the dressage day. Jesus, was she becoming agoraphobic? She put the thought aside. No, she just wanted more of her own company for a while longer.

Jessica could feel Steve's worried gaze on her. She silently thanked the knitting for letting her pretend it needed her attention.

'I'll be sending lots of positive energy,' she said to Tiffany. It sounded lame, but it was the best she could do.

'Thanks. Well, I'd better get going. I just wanted to make sure you were okay with the announcement. I'm sure if you wanted to, you could …'

'I'm fine. I do appreciate the call, though, thanks,' Jessica cut in.

'Okay, then. Well, you take care.'

'You too.' Jessica pushed the button to end the call.

'Why did you lie to Tiffany?'

'I didn't lie.'

'You told her you can't go to watch her at dressage.'

'I can't. I can't face all those people staring at me and talking behind their backs: "Oh, poor Jessica Harrington." "There she is, did you hear she sold her horses because of her fall only to find out she made the state eventing team?"'

'So it does bother you?'

'Of course it bothers me. But it was my decision and it's done.'

'Well, you're going to have to face everyone sooner or later.'

Jessica kept her eyes on her knitting. *Not if I never go to another horse event – and why would I, when I'm no longer involved?*

'She's your best friend, Jess.'

'She understands.'

'I don't think she does. I'm sure she was gutted. And after all she's done for you these past weeks.'

Jessica knew he was right and the guilt niggled at her, but it seemed small in the scheme of just how bad she felt about herself and her life.

'I'll go with you. We can park on the ring and you won't even have to get out of the car and talk to anyone, if you don't want to.'

'You go, Steve, but I don't want to.'

'Jessica, not everything's about you. Tiff's your best friend. She clearly wants you there for a bit of moral support – she called especially. How could you be so selfish and cruel? After all she's done for you.' He glared at her, shook his head, got up, and silently made his way to the kitchen.

Jessica cringed. If she thought about it, she could probably only count on one hand the number of times she'd had that particular searing expression bestowed upon her. God, it was all so hard. She was having a bad enough time dealing with her own disappointment in herself and holding that back from consuming her while keeping up her 'I'm fine' façade. She sighed.

'All right, if it means that much to you, I'll go,' she said.

'Don't do it for me,' Steve said, head buried in the fridge.

Jessica put down her knitting, picked up the phone and pressed redial. Tiffany answered after a few rings.

'I'm so sorry,' Jessica launched straight in, 'I'm being a selfish, unsupportive cow. Steve and I will come along on Saturday.'

'Oh, that would be nice,' Tiffany said guardedly. 'But don't feel you have to; I've been plenty of times on my own. It's just another comp.'

'It is not – it's your club championships. I'm so sorry. I'm far too wrapped up in my own crap right now. You're right; the team announcement did hit me for a bit of a six. I only got the letter today.' She looked up to find Steve watching her from the kitchen sink, tea towel in hand.

'What? Oh! You poor thing. Jess, you have every right to feel weird about it – even angry at yourself. Just don't dwell on it and let it drag you down. You made the decision based on how you felt at the time. You can always change your mind – woman's prerogative and all that,' she added with a laugh, trying to ease the tension.

'I'm just feeling a bit sorry for myself and need to snap out of it. Thanks for being such a good friend. I'll be fine. Sorry I won't be able to strap for you, but I'll be there cheering you on.'

'Thanks, Jess, I really appreciate it. I'd better go, I've got dinner on the stove.'

'Okay, see you Saturday.'

Jessica hung up and threw Steve a look that said, 'Happy now?' and resumed her knitting.

But her conversation with her friend wouldn't leave her. Damn this knitting making her think a little too deeply. If only she could get rid of the blackness inside her and return to being a good friend, wife – person. She felt as if she were trapped down a well and couldn't climb out, couldn't find the energy to even try. She knew it sounded melodramatic, but she really did feel that her life was empty and meaningless. Even worse, it was largely her own doing.

Jessica fleetingly wondered if she should take Steve and Tiffany's advice and see someone about how she was feeling. They'd probably only tell her she needed to find something to look forward to and she had that – a baby – she just didn't actually feel all that positive about it.

If she let herself, she might feel good about her financial contribution to the farm and ensuring they wouldn't have to worry about feed for next year. But if she thought about that, it brought her right back to having given up Prince and Beau, and riding – the one thing that actually made her feel whole. The one thing she'd been good at, the one connection to her father she'd severed.

Oh God, what a mess. Again Jessica expected tears, but it seemed the façade she was trying so hard to keep up was working. At least something in her life was.

Or maybe she'd just run out of tears for now.

Over dinner, Jessica made a special effort to be gushing with her praise of Steve's meal of warm chicken salad and crispy-skinned baked potato. It wasn't difficult, it was one of her favourites in his repertoire. Tonight, though, she hardly tasted it. And every mouthful sat heavily in the pit of her stomach that had felt full before the first bite.

Steve was subdued and, as Jessica watched him, she wondered if he was tired and picking up on her sombre mood, or if he was genuinely upset with her. Usually he shrugged a disagreement off quicker than this. What if this was the beginnings of the seven-year itch? What if she was sending their marriage into a downward spiral by not hiding her true feelings well enough? She thought she'd been doing so well at keeping it together. Clearly not, if it was affecting Steve and, in turn, them. But they were stronger than that, weren't they? She'd have to work even harder. Their future depended on it.

That night they made love again. It was the last thing Jessica wanted to do, and she suspected Steve felt the same, by the perfunctory way he responded to her. They were making a deliberate effort. For the first time ever, Jessica had insisted on turning out the light. She was suddenly feeling self-conscious about how untoned she was becoming – even a little flabby. She didn't want Steve to see but, more importantly, she didn't want to see herself. She'd have to take up running or something when she got the damned cast off.

Their kiss goodnight was tense. Or was she reading too much into it, being paranoid? They had both read enough articles that said once the intimacy stopped, the marriage was pretty much dead in the water. And for them to have sex less than three times a week would surely be the death knock.

She couldn't dwell on it – she didn't have the brain space. She turned her mind to the letter she would write to Eventing SA, giving up her place in the team. At least someone else would get a call-up thanks to her withdrawal. That was something. The idea should have made her feel better, but it didn't. She wanted to hang on to her place now she'd finally got it.

But she'd given it up the day she'd walked away from horses, gutlessly thrown in the towel after twenty years of work. *Idiot!* She lay awake, staring at the ceiling listening to the dogs and

Steve breathing quietly and evenly. There really was no going back now, was there? She'd look more of a fool if she publicly declared her change of heart.

Her role now was to give Steve the children he wanted. He'd waited long enough, been patient with her long enough. It was the least she could do.

Chapter Fourteen

Jessica felt quite uneasy leaving the property, not just because she was going off to face all the inquisitiveness of the horsey set, but also because she'd practically become a hermit. She liked being cocooned at home and now dreaded leaving the property. She wasn't sure why really, except she felt safe there. From what threat, she didn't know either. She was emotionally fragile and felt better able to cope on her own or just with Steve and Tiffany. She hadn't even accompanied Steve to town since being accosted by Tom Baines and Bill Smith.

She cursed her heart rate rising as they drove to Tiffany's club championships. It wasn't as if anyone could say anything worse than had already been said or make her feel worse than she already did. If only she could ask Steve to turn around and take her home. But that would cause all sorts of questions and she was trying so hard to appear normal, unaffected by her grief. Perhaps if she hadn't had Jeff Collins as her father she might have been able to swallow her pride, admit to a mistake and put an end to this torment. She probably wouldn't have made the stupid, kneejerk decision in the first place! *Damn you, Dad!*

Lately whenever she thought about him, she got angry. This was all his fault. If he'd been at the comp, she wouldn't have been distracted, wouldn't have let Prince down. Her father's death certainly had set off a horrible chain of events, like knocking over a line of carefully placed dominoes. And if it wasn't for his blatant dislike for dressage as a sport on its own – he'd thought of it as a 'necessary evil' – then maybe things would be a whole lot different. She stopped herself letting out a loud harrumph and folded her arms tight across her chest.

'You okay?' Steve asked from the driver's seat beside her.

'Yep. All good.'

'Tiffany will really appreciate you being there.'

'I know. And it's fine. Really.'

She wanted to say, *It's not about that*. But that would open a big old can of worms. She stared out the window, trying not give in to the few tears filling her eyes or the desire to bang her head hard against the car door. She wished she could stay angry, but her anger was always followed by the hollow feeling of guilt that then settled in her stomach as an aching ball of sadness.

'How was she feeling about it?' Steve asked, clearly trying to keep Jessica talking and from sinking into the silence that seemed to be her default position these days. Had she once been considered chatty? Had she noticeably changed these last few weeks to those around her? So what if she had? She had a lot on her mind.

'Okay.' Jessica had rung her friend the night before to check she didn't need them to do anything and to tell her they were bringing a picnic lunch. 'She's a bit concerned about her lack of preparation now she's working. But you know Tiff, not *that* worried.'

'Yeah. I'm sure she'll do fine.'

'She can only do her best, and she will.' They were just words. Jessica longed to believe them. If only she was as easy-going as

Tiffany. Jessica had often both cursed and been impressed by her friend's laid-back attitude to riding and competition – sometimes she downright envied it. Tiffany did it all for fun: missed a comp if she didn't feel like going; didn't ride when the weather was too hot, too cold, too windy, too rainy. She hadn't had a Jeff Collins standing in the arena bellowing at her not to be a wuss. But perhaps if she had, Tiffany wouldn't still be at the same standard she'd been at for the last five years. Jessica regularly was both in awe of and frustrated by her friend, who seemed content to be mediocre. Tiffany could be so much better, but she didn't appear to care. Jessica hated her critical thoughts and kept them to herself – though she did try to gently urge Tiffany on.

If she was to be honest, now she was in such a different place and headspace, her overwhelming feeling towards Tiffany and her riding was envy. She particularly envied her closeness with her horses. Tiffany would never consider selling Brandy or Storm for any reason – even though to Jessica they were just creatures that had been rejected from the track or hadn't made the grade for someone else; nowhere near as well-bred or as well put together as Prince and Beau. Perhaps that was the difference. The thought made her guilt bloom again. *God, stop being so catty!* Jess shook it aside. She was being a bitch, lashing out, no doubt brought on by feeling sorry for herself. She hated herself right then. But it was true that Tiffany was a bit of a sucker for a lost soul. It was probably one of the things that Jessica loved most about her: she was a genuinely kind, generous person through and through. Tiffany was her best friend. And Jessica was going to watch her ride because that's what friends did. And she would enjoy it – or at least pretend to.

She felt Steve's hand give her thigh a gentle squeeze. She patted it and smiled across at him. 'Thanks for taking me.'

'My pleasure.'

'I hope you realise you're going to be bored out of your brain.'

'Not with the latest Lee Child to read I won't.'

It was actually quite nice to be going out for the day. And the weather was perfect for it: sunny, but not too warm. It would be just right for sitting in the cosy car. And Steve had put together a wonderful picnic. Unlike Jessica, Tiff didn't suffer nerves to the point they stopped her eating.

Forty minutes later they pulled into the showgrounds, where four dressage arenas edged in white were set up. Jessica tried to gulp down the flurry of butterflies that started up in earnest every time she pulled into an event and then settled as a knot of tension in her belly. They fluttered harder when she saw the horses being worked out the back in the warm-up area. She reminded herself she wasn't riding and had nothing to be nervous about, then sighed and settled back into her seat. She hadn't even realised she'd moved to the edge of it. God, she'd almost forgotten how jittery she used to get before competitions, and that was mere weeks ago. She really didn't miss that. Had it all been worth it? 'Yes,' Jeff Collins would have said, and Jessica would have agreed. 'No way,' Tiffany and Steve would say. Her father's obsession with being the best, winning, meant Jessica had always been ravaged with nerves. It was now clearly so ingrained, such a part of her makeup that she couldn't shake it even now he was gone.

Her heart felt as if it had stopped and her blood ran cold as her attention was caught by one of the horses in the workout area. No, it couldn't be. *Of course it could.* But was it? Was that Prince over there being worked? If not, this horse had a very similar stride. Her heart stopped and then began beating a slow, painful tattoo against her ribs. She hadn't considered she might see her horses here – had forgotten that most other eventers did straight dressage as well. But you wouldn't bring a horse to compete after just owning them a few days, surely? Well, she wouldn't. You needed time to settle, establish a good, solid partnership. She found herself holding her breath as the horse came around the circle. *Come on, show me your face.*

Finally, it did – and it had a big white blaze. Phew. Jessica opened her mouth and breathed in deeply, but had to force herself to carefully let out her breath and not draw Steve's attention.

'Where do you think we should park?' Steve asked, looking around as their vehicle crawled forwards.

'Sorry? What's that?'

'You were miles away. Where should I park?'

'Oh. There's Tiff,' she said, pointing to where Tiffany was frantically waving them over with both arms.

'Brilliant. Looks like she's got prime position for us.' They drove around the arena to where Tiffany had set up several buckets to save them a park beside her ute and float. She gathered the buckets as they pulled in.

'Hey, you guys!' she called through the window Jessica had wound down. 'Great to see you.'

Jessica felt a surge of emotion. Tiffany was beaming, clearly so pleased they'd come along. How could she have thought of letting her down, even for a second?

She got out and carefully made her way across the uneven gravel, getting a fright each time her crutches slipped off the larger stones or sank into soft areas. She felt a little jittery as she hugged her friend and then followed her around to the side of the float where Brandy and Storm were tied up.

'Careful, you're not stable on your feet yet,' Tiffany warned.

'Tell me about it,' Jessica said with a groan.

'Well, I don't want to be responsible for more injuries if one of those two boofheads gives you a nudge and sends you flying.'

Jessica didn't need to be told twice. She was keen to not touch them anyway. If she did, the gorgeous smell of clean horses, feed and tack she could already detect might be her undoing. These scents were as alluring to horse lovers as the finest designer eau de parfum was to the rest of the population. She stood back with Steve and watched as Tiffany put her helmet on and then put the bridle on Brandy. But she was still too close. She silently groaned with a mixture of pleasure, regret and disappointment. She hadn't set foot in the barn since the horses had left. Oh how she now ached. She couldn't resist taking a deep whiff, despite knowing it would make her sadder. She breathed in the mixture of clean horse, leather, soap, boot polish, hairspray and enamel. Oh, how she'd missed that.

'Okay. I'd better be off.' Tiffany's voice shattered her reverie and brought her back from the sadness threatening to swamp her.

'Good luck,' Jessica and Steve said in unison.

'Thanks,' Tiffany said cheerfully, and leapt into the saddle.

They watched as she trotted off and then got back into the car. Despite feeling a little self-conscious, Jessica pulled out her knitting. She was no longer doing it out of enjoyment, only determination to get the project finished.

As she watched Tiffany warm up and then enter the arena for her first test, Jessica had to fight to stop herself rocking in time with Brandy's stride. She had a habit of 'back-seat riding', moving this way and that, clenching her thighs and lower legs, curling and uncurling her hands as if tightening and releasing the reins – most horse people did. Today, though, she had to be different. She wasn't meant to be interested. But even the relatively green Beau would have held his own among these horses. If only she was interested enough in dressage as a sport on its own. Could she make herself be interested? She doubted it. Not now. Anyway, she was only being swayed by feeling left out – her competitive nature was trying to take over. She was on another mission now.

'Are you missing being out there?'

She looked down at her hands. They were busy knitting. Was Steve just making conversation or had he noticed her back-seat riding?

'Hey? Oh. No. No way.' It wasn't an outright lie. She was missing being part of the action, striving, doing her best, pitting herself against the other riders, making her dad proud … 'I certainly don't miss the nerves,' she said.

'I never got why you'd put yourself through that.'

'No, I know you didn't. Sometimes I'm not sure I did either,' she said with a laugh. Another lie. Of course she knew why she regularly put herself through hell emotionally and physically – bloody Jeff Collins. She was really starting to resent him. Annoyance surged again. She wished she was at home, alone. The need to express her anger – throw something, yell, scream – was overwhelming. She wanted to shout at him, at the memories of him, to leave her alone, that dying meant he no longer had a voice, could no longer control her. But the larger-than-life Jeff Collins wasn't one to be quiet. He'd been such a big presence for her, more than just a father. Hopefully, without the horses bonding her to her memories of him he would fade into the background and she would get some peace. Oh how she wished she was pregnant and had that to distract her.

She vowed to be a whole lot kinder to her own child if he or she chose to ride horses. That was another thing: Jessica's child would have the choice she hadn't. Another jolt of disappointment passed through her. She ignored it and focussed on watching Tiffany make her way around the arena doing okay movements – okay but not great. Jessica would have encouraged her to push Brandy into a tighter frame. But Tiffany wouldn't ask her opinion and Jessica wouldn't offer it, despite the frustration at what she could see almost killing her. They'd agreed early on to disagree and not let their views interfere with their friendship. Jessica knew she was bossy. She couldn't help it. Luckily she was nowhere near her father's level. She bloody well hoped not, anyway! If she were, she wouldn't have had any students. Though she did still subscribe to the 'make that damned horse do it' school of thought rather than just having fun and enjoying the sport as seemed to be more the approach these days. The cost in time, fuel, equipment, etc was too much for it to be all about fun. She was beginning to see Tiffany's point, however, that it was no different to people going on holidays: a lot of expense for a head full of memories and a few hundred photos. It was the experience, the journey, not necessarily how well you did, that counted, though winning was fun too.

Jessica gritted her teeth. *Damn you, Jeff Collins, you did not have it right! I will not be the tyrant to my child that you were to me.* She sighed, rested her knitting on her stomach, and looked down.

'Are you okay? You're not feeling sick from the painkillers are you? Are you hungry?' Steve said, looking at her with concern.

She smiled at him. 'No, I'm fine. All good, thanks. Except for just realising that I far too closely resemble my mother – and about twenty-five years too early!' She suddenly recognised that was exactly what she was doing. Theresa Collins had always sat in the car and knitted, crocheted, or completed a crossword while Jessica rode and Jeff kept a close eye on proceedings. 'Oh God, too funny. Kill me now,' she said, laughing. It was the first time she'd genuinely laughed for ages. It felt good, but was fleeting.

'I'm keeping well away from that one,' Steve said, grinning cheekily. He leant over and pecked her on the cheek before returning to the book on his lap. Jessica resumed knitting while staring straight ahead, watching Tiffany ride.

There was a knock on Jessica's window, startling them both. They smiled and nodded politely to Amanda Smith, dressage club president and general busybody.

'Hi Amanda,' Jessica said.

'Don't tell me you've crossed to the dark side,' Amanda said with a smirk.

'No, just here to watch Tiff. Actually, I've sold the horses. Haven't you heard? I'm out altogether.'

'Oh. Really? I thought I heard something along those lines, but I didn't believe it. I said, "No, that can't be right."'

'Well, it is. Better believe it,' Jessica said, forcing brightness.

'God, I'd never thought I'd see you knitting!' Amanda cried, as if only just noticing what Jessica was doing.

Jessica stayed silent, rather than retort rudely.

'What are you going to do with yourself?'

'I'm not sure, I'll worry about it when I'm out of plaster and my ankle has healed.'

'Oh, of course. How's it going?'

'Getting there.'

Amanda's name was called over the PA system along with a message for her to return to the office.

'Well, that's me. See ya.'

'Bye.'

Several other people came by during the afternoon – some kindly asked after her health or murmured with sympathy about her accident and timing regarding her squad selection, others had a dig at her for selling up her horses, while others still remonstrated with her for not giving them first right of refusal. Thankfully by then Tiffany was there to step in and say the sale was her doing.

Jessica had managed to stay pleasant to all, but by the time Tiffany had been presented with her two seconds and two third-place ribbons and they were ready to leave, she was exhausted, depressed, and was silently vowing to never venture out in public again. She so did not miss the cattiness and nosiness so many excelled at. Had it always been like that, or was it that she was a lame duck and they were picking on her because she was considered weak?

'Tiffany did well considering she said she hadn't had much chance to practise,' Steve said as they made their way home.

'Hmm. She seemed happy with how she went.' Jessica would have been very disappointed with seconds and thirds.

Chapter Fifteen

Jessica woke feeling excited, but also a little apprehensive. Today her life would finally get back on track – her cast was coming off. She really hoped her leg would be healed okay. Her last two weeks in plaster had seen her relatively pain free and able to hobble around the house without the need for crutches. She'd spent long stints outside sitting with shards of sun cutting across her one bare leg and hands, knitting frantically, trying to finish the scarf before her plaster came off and her life could start again. She'd decided she wanted a clear demarcation point between the dreadful six weeks with her broken ankle and the rest of her life – hopefully a wonderful new phase.

Jessica had laughed when she'd presented Steve with his scarf, telling him he'd better take good care of it because there wouldn't be another one – ever. She hated the bloody thing; hated knitting full stop. She still liked the colour – so did Steve – and had to admit she'd done a pretty good job for a first attempt: there were no holes, the edges were nice and straight all the way along, and both ends were the same width. But never again.

He'd teased her good-naturedly, saying, 'Oh and here I was thinking I could count on you to keep us through the next drought with your new cottage industry.'

It had been a rare moment of lightness between them, Jessica realised with a bit of a jolt. It wasn't that they'd argued or stopped making love or being affectionate, but now she thought about it a little deeper, there had been a shift in their relationship. Was it the seven-year itch, as she had feared, or was it solely of her doing? If she had to put her finger on it, she would say Steve was ever so slightly wary around her; as if he was being guarded with his words and actions. This made Jessica sad. And, yes, it was her doing. She had changed since breaking her ankle and giving up the horses. He was merely responding to her.

She thought she'd done a good job of hiding her true feelings, but clearly not a good enough job. Even sadder was the fact she didn't know how to bring him back to her, how to put things right between them.

She pictured his eyes lighting up when she told him she was pregnant with their first child, and felt a little better. But she didn't have that news to share.

Oh, well, at least today she would be properly back on two feet and they could return to some semblance of normality. Jessica ignored the voice in her brain telling her that there was no normal to return to – horses had been her normal.

Her ache for the horses and sadness at seeing the empty paddocks and lifeless stable yards hadn't improved; if anything it had become more pronounced. She'd just got better at hiding her emotions. Well, she figured she must have, as Steve no longer looked sideways at her with a slight frown as if wondering when she was going to crack and melt into a puddle of tears. He'd seen her survive Tiffany's dressage day and that had been a big, confronting step. And while she'd been shaky, she'd got through it okay. She just had to keep on putting one foot in front of the other, keep moving forwards.

Jessica thought the pain tablets probably went a long way towards keeping her together. She'd stopped taking them at night not long after the accident and had been carefully rationing them for use during the day. She hadn't been in any serious pain since the first few days, but the slightly dreamy, pillowy feeling that hung around while under their influence was something she was unwilling to give up. Soon she would have to, though; she had just a couple of tablets left. Perhaps if she did physio when she got the plaster off she'd be justified in asking a doctor for more pain relief. Part of Jessica hoped she would be refused and forced out of her slight addiction. Another part, an even bigger one, was terrified of having to get through without this additional support.

She sighed. She had to believe that everything would work out, as Tiffany was always saying – she really had no choice.

Perhaps without the codeine she wouldn't feel so down, so physically heavy. The only thing that had kept her getting out of bed in the mornings was maintaining her façade and not admitting she'd made a terrible, hasty mistake giving up Prince and Beau. She'd come so close to crumbling, but the thought of 'Then what?' seemed to stop her.

A number of times she'd sat down to try to write a simple letter to Eventing SA explaining her situation, but hadn't managed more than the date, her address, her member number and *Dear Sir*. It didn't matter – the original letter had called for responses in three months, and news would have made its way right around the horse industry – her withdrawal in writing was a mere formality.

The dogs had even decided she didn't need them anymore, and had started spending most of their time outside again. She still often marvelled at how they'd quickly become house pets in her time of need. *Don't tell me they don't share human emotions*, she'd said to herself more than once while shaking her head in wonder at them. Laurel and Hardy too had become subdued, as if in sympathy, since the horses had left. They still wagged their tails, but their silly grins didn't seem as wide and carefree as they once had. Jessica suspected she was reading signs that weren't there.

She really hoped she'd be back to normal straight away once out of plaster; she wasn't sure she had the inclination for masses of physio. She'd read on the internet that one of the best ways to get over an ankle injury was to just walk – one foot carefully in front of the other. That was what she'd do, and worry about physio later if need be.

Last night she had put the right shoe – the mate to the one she would wear – by the front door so it wouldn't be forgotten. It had come to her in a flash as she was cleaning her teeth – she'd go in wearing one shoe, but come out needing two. How embarrassing if she came out with one bare foot! She wondered how many people had left the hospital and crossed the car park with a bare, cold foot.

Steve had also insisted on propping the walking stick her father had needed after a fight with one of the young horses beside the door. Jessica wasn't sure they had to go that far, but accepted she didn't know what to expect. They needed a fact sheet on what happened after getting out of plaster, she thought, staring out the window – deliberately looking at the large dam and catchment away from where horses once stood.

They were going to a little café in Hahndorf for lunch afterwards, which would be nice, but would also signal the end of Steve being with her during the day. She often found herself wondering how he used to manage to fill his days out on the property or in his sheds. She never quizzed him on it – it was a deliberate attempt to not be like her mother, who had practically interrogated her father most nights when he came in, demanding to know how he'd spent each minute of his day away from her.

'I'm just being interested,' would be her response when he got sick of it and bellowed at her. And that would always be the end of it for that day and perhaps the following few. Her parents were a bit of a fiery pairing and many times, Jessica had been surprised and shocked at the words that could come from her quite mild, but sometimes stern, mother. She suspected that her father might have been unfaithful at some point and was glad she didn't have the proof to tarnish her respect for him – and for her mother for staying. Though, equally, she didn't like knowing that now she'd never be sure.

If Steve was ever unfaithful to her and she found out, she'd have the locksmith around faster than she could yell, 'Get out!'

'You're off in another world – whatchya thinking about?' Steve asked, placing two mugs of coffee beside her and taking his seat at the table. Jessica looked up and smiled and, as she did, realised she could have got their breakfast – she was pretty mobile again. But here she was, still Lady Muck being waited on. Steve wasn't backwards in coming forwards; he would have said something if it bothered him.

'Just thinking how strange it is that Mum would interrogate Dad on where he'd been and what he'd done. Why do you think that was?'

'That's a bit random, isn't it?' He sipped his coffee. 'No idea, dear. Probably something she was insecure about.'

'Yeah, but why?'

'I don't know. Maybe her parents left her somewhere once and she had abandonment issues as a result,' he offered with a shrug.

'Hmm.' That sounded better to Jessica than what she'd conjured up. She bit into her toast.

'Are you excited about getting your cast off?'

'I'm excited about being able to shower properly. And it'll be good to be fully mobile and independent again.'

'Well, you probably won't feel totally fine straight away. I'm sure you'll still have to take it a bit easy for a while – get the muscles and tendons and everything going again.'

That hadn't even crossed her mind. She'd only been thinking about the bone being healed. But she'd be fine – Steve was just underestimating her previous high level of athleticism and fitness. She'd bounce back just fine, and quickly.

They parked the car in the hospital's multi-storey car park and made their way up the street – which was a lot steeper than Jessica would have ever believed – and around the front to the ED entrance so they didn't get lost in the maze of corridors.

Jessica felt queasy and jittery, as she always did when she walked into any hospital – they all smelt and looked pretty much the same. It was too much of a reminder of what she'd lost; of having to say goodbye to her mother and then, just a few months ago, her father. She felt a little shaky on her feet and was glad she'd chosen to use the crutches rather than hobble.

She fleetingly wondered if she'd feel differently when she went into hospital to have her first baby and decided she'd probably feel exactly the same: nervous, apprehensive, sort of queasy. Though she suspected there would be a hefty dose of proper fear, not just mild anxiety.

She sat down in the waiting room and opened the shiny new *Woman's Day* Steve handed her from the newsagent bag he'd carried along with her handbag, the bag with her right shoe in it and the walking stick. Jessica had just scanned the contents page and decided on a story when her name was called. That was a good sign! Despite having an appointment, she had figured on sitting here for the next few hours. She looked up and returned the young, heavy-set nurse's broad smile.

Sitting propped up on the bed in the examination room with her legs stretched out before her, Jessica had a flashback of the last time she'd been in a similar position – six weeks and two days before. She almost gasped when she remembered the pain. Her heart rate rose and she had to force herself to take a deep breath.

'It's okay, nothing to worry about; you shouldn't feel any pain,' the friendly nurse said kindly, patting her cast.

Jessica knew the thing that looked like a mini angle grinder they used to remove the casts couldn't actually cut her – it wasn't a sharp blade but a disc that somehow vibrated and cut only into the rigid material – but apparently Steve didn't: his eyes were bugging out of his head. He looked from the nurse to the device and back again, no doubt trying to ascertain the level of shake in her hand and how safe his wife's leg was.

Jessica almost laughed; his expression was priceless. She listened intently to the nurse's explanation and watched the demonstration to prove the appliance posed no danger – more for Steve's benefit than her own. He gradually settled back into the chair he was in, appearing to accept what the nurse said.

The nurse put a face mask on just before turning on the appliance and sending fine fibreglass dust into the air. *What about me?* Jessica wanted to ask.

Jessica watched as the two lines down each side of her leg were completed – it seemed to take an age – and then the split cast was dragged open.

'God, it stinks!' she said, and almost gagged as the odour of sweaty, unwashed flesh overpowered the sickly smell of hot fibreglass. 'Sorry,' she said, wincing, to the poor nurse, whose nose was a lot closer to the source than her own. Perhaps that was the reason for the mask.

'It's okay, quite normal. Just like a sock that's been worn for six weeks straight,' she said cheerily.

Yes, but who wears a sock for six weeks straight?

'Gosh, stinky,' Steve said, wrinkling his nose and clearly attempting to be polite.

'Oh God, it gets worse,' Jessica said, now settling her gaze on the thick, matted hair on her leg. 'That is disgusting!' It came as a huge shock. She'd been dutifully keeping her good leg and her armpits hair free, but hadn't given a thought to what her leg would look like after being covered up for six weeks. *What, did you think the hair would just not grow?* she heard a voice inside her head say. Well, yes, actually, she probably had thought that. She certainly hadn't thought about being greeted with this sight.

'Don't worry; I'm quite used to it,' the kindly nurse reassured her when she saw Jessica's horrified expression. Jessica was still too stunned by what she was looking at to respond.

Perhaps even worse than the hair was the feeling the leg didn't seem connected to her. She could see her toes wriggling, but it was the strangest experience, almost out of body or something. She couldn't actually feel them. It was very disconcerting.

'Now, all the muscles are wasted from being inactive for so long so it's going to feel a little stiff for a few weeks – possibly up to another six weeks. But you just need to slowly build them up again. I'll just get rid of this mess and then I can show you some exercises.' She folded up the cloth, trapping all the dust and debris, and put it on the trolley beside the cutting machine.

Jessica performed the exercises the nurse showed her – it was excruciating, but she did her best to not let on. She was pleased

Steve was there to take it in too, as she was feeling sick to her stomach, really quite out of kilter, and barely able to think past how weird she felt. Was she actually going to throw up?

'Are you okay?' the nurse asked, looking with concern at Jessica, who was now feeling cold and clammy under her clothes. She'd probably gone pale. Her head was even feeling light and starting to spin. *God, what's happening to me?*

'Actually, I feel a little ill.'

The nurse handed her a plastic disc with a plastic bag attached – a disposable sick bag, Jessica surmised. She held it to her mouth. But she wasn't actually feeling nauseous, she decided, just weird. She relaxed her arms.

'You can take that with you, just in case,' the nurse said.

Steve looked pale and worried.

'She's fine,' the nurse reassured him. 'It feels weird because the brain is talking to the muscles and everything in the leg but the leg isn't responding how you expect it to. And it all feels different. It's just a bit of a disconnect; very normal. Just see a physio if you have any problems or, if you're really worried, come back in. Did you bring another sock and shoe?'

Steve pulled them out of the bag and handed them over.

Jessica stayed silent, concentrating on breathing and trying to feel the muscles in her leg and making them move. She got very little response and what she did get ached and grated, making her sure she would need the sick bag. The nurse had the sock and shoe on her foot before Jessica realised she could have, should have, done it herself.

'Right, you're good to go,' the nurse said, pulling down Jessica's track pants leg and giving her foot a pat. 'Swing your legs over the side and hold the bed while you carefully lower your weight. Take it slowly.'

Jessica forced herself to comply, but she was terrified. What if it couldn't support her, this leg that looked to be half the size of the other one, a mere twig? The sick feeling in her stomach intensified in a wave as she felt her bad foot make contact with the lino. Everything felt shaky. Jessica winced. Steve leapt up and was beside her in an instant. Soon she had the nurse holding one arm and Steve holding her other. She was standing. But for how long? She felt very unsteady.

'Now take a small step forwards,' the nurse instructed.

Jessica tried, but achieved nothing more than the hobble she'd managed in the cast. God, this wasn't what she'd expected at all. Tears sprang to her eyes.

'Are you okay?' Steve asked.

Jessica nodded slowly.

'You're fine,' the nurse assured her, 'it'll just take time. You're not in any pain are you?'

'No, I don't think so,' Jessica said. What she was feeling wasn't actually pain, was it? No, it was more an uncomfortable, grating feeling.

'You'll probably experience quite a bit of aching and discomfort as the tendons and muscles start to stretch again. Just take it slowly and carefully at first – the soft tissue needs to come back into action. Well, good luck,' the nurse said, taking off her gloves, signalling her job was done and they were expected to leave.

So that's it, Jessica thought, and imagined she now knew how a baby bird felt being turfed out of the nest. Within moments the trolley had been wheeled out and they were alone.

'Righto, just lean on me on this side and use the stick on your good side,' Steve instructed, handing her the walking stick he'd hooked over the chair he'd been sitting on. Thank God he insisted on bringing it.

In the car, she fought the desire to weep. This wasn't how it was supposed to go at all. She really had expected to be able to skip out of the hospital. She stared down at her leg that was still practically useless. It barely felt attached, part of her – almost like it was prosthetic: visible but not feeling truly belonging to her.

'Are you okay?' Steve asked, patting her thigh.

'Yep, all good,' she said, forcing out a smile.

'You look a bit pale. Would you rather skip lunch and just go home?'

'No, I'm fine.' She wasn't really fine, and she really did just want to get back home and throw herself onto the couch or into bed. But she had to keep up the act she'd been working so hard at. And Steve had been saying for ages how much he'd been looking forward to trying this café and their signature dish, osso bucco. It was the wrong season and weather for it, but too bad. She just hoped for Steve's sake they still had it on the menu and hadn't switched to more summery dishes.

'How's the leg feeling?'

'A little weird.' It was probably the most truthful thing Jessica had said for weeks.

'Oh, well, like the nurse said, the muscles and tendons will need to learn again. I kind of thought you'd leap up and be fine again,' he added sheepishly. 'Shows you what I know.'

'Me too.' She was feeling decidedly morose.

Tiffany would say, 'Clearly the universe thinks you need more rest.'

Stuff the bloody universe, I'm sick of all this, she would have replied.

Chapter Sixteen

The next day, Jessica woke and enjoyed the feeling of no hard cast between her and Steve. She still felt down about life, generally, but liked the subtle change. She snuggled into him and he responded.

Everything will be okay, she told herself later, as she watched Steve getting dressed, after they'd made love – it had felt so right. She thought about the bath they had shared after coming back from the hospital, totally decadent – eating the desserts they had brought home from the café and luxuriating in the warm bubbles – and what had happened when they'd dried each other off.

She waited for him to leave the room before getting up herself. She wasn't sure why. When she put her feet down and then stood up, she was reminded again of not being totally fine with her leg. She'd made the difficult trip to the loo during the night and almost collapsed when the healing leg hadn't felt strong enough to support her. Luckily, the sturdy bedside cupboard had caught her and, even luckier, Steve had slept through her distress. She'd sat on the loo and given into her tears of frustration and anguish before returning to bed. Her eyes still felt a little puffy.

Jessica got dressed and concentrated on carefully putting one foot in front of the other to make her way out to the kitchen. She couldn't continue with the shuffling, dragging gait she'd used yesterday if she didn't want to end up with a permanent limp. It was excruciating; both the pain in her protesting leg and the effort needed not to give in to the sick feeling in her stomach, caused, she imagined, by spasms shooting from her right foot. She plastered on a smile as she emerged in her track pants and running shoes.

'Wow, look at you; you've barely got a limp!' Steve exclaimed.

'Yeah, it's feeling good,' Jessica lied through clenched teeth. It was excruciating. 'I'm just going to go for a walk.'

'Want me to come with you in case it lets you down?'

'Thanks, but I'll be fine.' She wasn't fine and wasn't totally sure she wouldn't collapse somewhere along their driveway, but she had to stop being so damned dependent. And at least while she had the pain to concentrate on it took her mind off Prince and Beau, her stupidity and haste in giving up her dream, not to mention how badly she'd let her father down. And how much she missed him. She still felt sure that if he were here none of this would have happened. She wanted to be angry with him for leaving her, but every time she was, guilt consumed her. The best she could do was get her leg better – everything would flow from that.

Jessica set off down the road, being careful that her steps were even and normal. It was slow going and very painful, but no pain, no gain. Hell, she'd been a successful eventer; that took guts, courage, determination and the ability to focus and ride through the fear and, at times, pain. *I can do this*, she told herself. Though halfway down the driveway, she wasn't sure she could. She was sweating from the exertion – and from the shock and queasiness of dealing with a limb that still didn't totally feel part of her.

She wanted to stop and sit down – give up. But she kept going, putting one foot in front of the other. Just to the end and back, that was her goal for the day. Stuff this taking it easy idea; when did that ever get you anywhere?

The dogs had long since given up on her – she was going too slow – and had raced ahead, darting here and there as they followed various scents. If the horses were still here they would have kept her company, following the fence line. She missed them.

Jessica leant on a gate post and looked back to the house. It was miles away. Jesus, she was in agony. She was surprised to find herself starting to cry. She pulled herself together, hoicked her shoulders up, and prepared to put one foot in front of the other again to make her way back. She yearned to throw herself onto the plush couch. That would be her reward. She just had to get there. No, she *would* get there, no matter how long it took.

She was around halfway back when she looked up to see Steve's ute coming towards her. He stopped and wound down the window.

'Do you want a ride back? That's probably far enough for you on your first day,' he said.

'Thanks, but I'm fine.' Damned pride!

'Well, if you're sure?' he said, sounding doubtful. She mustn't have been quick enough to replace the wince on her features with a light, carefree smile. She noted the dogs had taken up Steve's offer and had leapt onto the back. He got out to chain them on securely and she took another grating, painful step forwards as if to prove her point, then raised her hand and put her head down to concentrate on each step on the uneven ground.

'Okay then,' he called, before getting back in and driving off.

★

Jessica allowed herself to lie back on the bed while no one was around to see just how much the short walk had taken out of her. She was clearly unfit – she'd been huffing and puffing after just a few metres. She was used to pushing herself physically, but the pain had been so bad it had actually taken her breath away with each step. When she put weight on the defective leg it was like a knife being driven through it. When the leg was raised and not bearing weight, the pain changed to an uncomfortable dragging, grating feeling that set her teeth on edge. And now she had a headache starting up. Her leg was supposed to have healed while in plaster, but it didn't feel at all mended. Jesus.

She hoped Steve would be away for hours so she'd be spared having the extra burden and exhaustion of putting on a happy face for him. It was all very trying. Hopefully tomorrow she'd be stronger. But what the hell would she do for the rest of today? At this rate she'd be collapsed on the couch when he came home.

After lunch she'd have another go at a walk. She'd take some ibuprofen to mask the pain. If only she still had some decent pain-killers … Jessica's mind strayed to how she could get some before telling herself off. Until recently, the easy way out had never been her gig. Hard work was what everything worthwhile took. No buts about it. The accident had changed her in more ways than she realised.

Jessica lay on the bed doing the exercises she'd been given. It was almost as painful as the weight-bearing walking, but in a different way. At least there was no sharp pain; this just felt weird and icky.

Had Steve said how long he'd be gone, or where he was going, for that matter? She couldn't remember. There was a time not so long ago when she would have enquired and he would have told her, would have asked her if she needed anything or if she wanted to go along. She pushed aside the feeling that they were slipping away from each other. Hadn't they proved last night – and again this morning – how committed to each other they were? No, she was just feeling lousy, generally, and that was affecting how she saw everything.

★

Over the following week Jessica detected no further improvement in her strength or stability. The annoying achy, grating feeling was there when she did exercises and the shooting, searing pain when she bore weight. She continued to force herself to work through it and thought she was probably due an Oscar for the acting job she was doing in front of Steve and Tiffany. Her mantras, if anyone caught her wincing, continued to be 'All good' and 'No pain, no gain'.

She ignored the worried glances between her husband and her best friend. She was doing the best she could; there was nothing else she could do. She still desperately hoped to become pregnant and feel useful again, and have her future laid out. It'd be a nice distraction from the emptiness of her days and something to look forward to.

The day her period arrived, Jessica retreated to bed. Steve brought her cups of tea and told her how worried about her he was; that she hadn't been herself since the accident. Jessica thought he probably really meant since the horses were sold, but they were both careful never to mention that particular elephant in the room. Jessica tried to reassure him she was fine; it was just her period and the hormones laying her low. He seemed to reluctantly accept that and left her to her wallowing.

As miserable as she was, it was good to be able to let down her guard and release some bottled-up emotions that were as exhausting as dragging around her damaged, plastered leg had been.

Steve was being so kind, she felt terrible for not being honest with him. But she didn't want him pitying her, didn't want him trying to fix things, which would probably mean ruining someone else's life by attempting to get the horses back. That was a done deal; she just had to get over it, which was proving more difficult than she ever would have thought. Where was her business brain when she needed it? If her father were here, he would give her a severe talking to – about everything. But he wasn't.

Jessica sank lower again at the thought. But she got up and carried on. She couldn't stay in bed any longer, else she might just never leave. She dismissed once more Steve's suggestion that she see a psychologist – didn't they only ever really just point out what you already knew or ummed and aahed and said, 'And how do you feel about that?' No, she'd pull herself together sometime, somehow. A new thought struck her and she felt light-headed: If she'd given up eventing sooner to start a family, would she be pregnant now? Had she left it too late? Had her stubbornness cost Steve his chance to be a father?

When Steve announced he was going to the first of a series of clearing sales and asked if she wanted to go along, she was surprised. She never went to clearing sales, mainly because she'd always been busy with the horses and whatever else she used to fill her days doing. She wouldn't actually mind going and seeing different people, having a change of scenery, but clearing sales were Steve's thing; it didn't feel right to cramp his style. She'd listened to years' worth of his stories of all the men standing around catching up and solving the problems of primary production and the world. It wouldn't be fair to disrupt that. Anyway, he was probably only asking out of politeness.

'Thanks, but I'm going to do the washing,' she said.

'Okay.'

Definitely out of politeness, she concluded, given his easy acceptance of her answer. No doubt he'd be pleased to escape her for a few hours. She had noticed he spent even more time driving around checking the stock than he used to. He said it was because of the recent shootings; he wanted to be extra vigilant and make sure there were no animals writhing in pain anywhere. But Jessica suspected her gloomy mood – as hard as she tried to appear otherwise – might be rubbing off on him.

Even Laurel and Hardy seemed to have given up on her and rarely ventured inside these days. She'd have liked to have believed it was because of the weather being so much warmer, but she was too far into her self-pity.

Jessica waved Steve off from the verandah and felt her heart sink. She wished she'd decided to go too. This sitting at home day after day, looking out at the empty horse paddocks, was excruciating. A couple of times it had entered her brain to suggest selling up and moving, but she quickly dismissed it. She loved the place, really, didn't she? And, anyway, Steve wouldn't even consider it without a damned good reason. *Just suck it up, Princess*, she told herself, and picked up her phone to call Tiffany. She knew she'd neglected her friend of late. She hadn't been feeling sociable and the less time she spent with Tiffany, the less she had to fight to keep from blurting out the truth. Tiffany had been busy with her new job and they'd spent a lot of time missing each other's calls and then catching up on the phone rather than face to face. She was probably at work today too. Jessica couldn't remember what days Tiffany was working; she'd been too wrapped up in herself for too long.

Tiffany had also been busy with dressage training schools. Thankfully Jessica wasn't expected to attend – she'd found the dressage championships too depressing. She'd thought it had been about not wanting to see people she knew, so going to watch Tiff and staying in the vehicle would be okay, but it had turned out that wasn't the only problem. Seeing horses performing full stop was a cruel reminder of her failings.

Now, when they did manage to speak, Tiffany kept mention of horses to a bare minimum, which suited Jessica just fine. She knew she was being selfish and cruel in not showing more interest in her friend and her pursuits, but just couldn't seem to pull herself out of the abyss. She was also worried about her façade cracking under too much scrutiny from Tiffany. Steve was different – men generally tended to be less observant – but she knew even he was seeing through her act, and while he looked at her oddly he didn't attempt to probe too deeply. Tiffany wouldn't be so easy to convince.

Jessica was disappointed to get her friend's voicemail. She left a message and headed out for her walk. Today she aimed to make the highway and back, no matter what. So, with water bottle in hand and teeth gritted, she focussed on carefully putting each foot in front of the other. She took care to place her heel down first, ignore the searing pain and uncomfortable stretching of ligaments and assorted soft tissue and lower the length of her foot, then with weight on the ball, raise herself up onto the toes, then pick the leg up and move it forwards and go through it all over again.

She'd worked hard – and painfully – to strengthen the side-to-side movement and lessen the risk of rolling her ankle on the uneven gravel surface beneath her. But still quite regularly she felt the grip of fear as she stumbled ever so slightly on a stone and held her breath, waiting to see if this was the moment she would end up on the ground, unable to get up.

Jessica knew she was being far too melodramatic and worrying far too much, but the thought of snapping the fragile bone again, or worse, the other ankle, kept her worried to the point of paranoia. Doctor Grant had said it would heal stronger than the undamaged one, but she didn't believe him. He'd been so young and, anyway, he couldn't feel what she could feel.

She'd much rather lock herself away in the house and avoid all risk, but a stronger part of her was a doer. Sitting around just wasn't in her makeup. And the last thing she wanted was to end up with a permanent limp because she hadn't followed the instructions of the experts. She didn't want a lifelong reminder of this accident and to keep having to explain to people why she limped.

Jessica hoped to both outrun her grief and disappointment in herself while healing. And to fill in her days that were now so empty. She often rubbed her stomach as she walked and silently pleaded, to no one in particular, *Please give me a baby to occupy me.* If she were pregnant she could busy herself with preparing a nursery and shopping for the little one. She knew it was silly and dangerous to put so much hope in something largely out of her hands, but it was all she had. She was a little wary, also, of wanting something too much and for the wrong reasons, but she chose to push that aside. She didn't notice a few tears had escaped and were running down her cold face, which held little feeling thanks to the brisk morning air. She paused, knelt down on the soft grassy verge and allowed herself the indulgence of a flood of tears of self-pity while no one was around to see.

After a few moments she wiped the tears away with her sleeve, took a deep breath, stood back up and carried on. Enough was enough. How she felt was her own doing and no one else's. She turned out from the driveway and onto the main road.

Horses in nearby paddocks looked up from the grazing and stared at her for a few moments before resuming. They were used to seeing her out walking and no longer trotted over to the fence for a pat. The few times she had gone over to the fence she'd spent the rest of her walk going over past dressage tests and show jumping and cross-country rounds in her mind, which would come back to her in her dreams that night. She missed the thrill, the pride of achievement, especially on a horse she and her father had bred or stumbled across for sale, cheap. It had been their thing. It was over now.

She just wished the memories would leave her alone too.

Chapter Seventeen

Jessica woke to the familiar, deep metallic rattle of the horse float approaching the house. She looked around the room, momentarily disoriented. The shadows were long outside and the sun had gone behind the house. She checked her watch. Four p.m. She'd been asleep for a full four hours! She was reminded she'd missed lunch by a painful gnawing in her stomach and sat up, stretching her leg out and rolling her ankle around. It was stiffer than ever. She should have iced it when she got back.

Instead of pulling the horse float into the large barn-style shed to unload his clearing sale spoils like he normally did, Steve pulled up outside. Curious, she edged herself higher, put her forearms across the back of the couch and watched out the window as he undid the bolts on the tailgate and slowly lowered it. The dogs were wriggling about on the back of the ute, clearly annoyed at still being restrained. Usually he got out and set them free to check out what scents had been left on their patch while they'd been away.

Jessica looked back to Steve and was stunned to see a wiry chestnut tail and the rump of a horse in the back of the float. From what little she could make out, it was a thoroughbred, a very thin one, by the looks of the poverty lines running down either side of its tail. It wasn't huge, probably only around fifteen-two hands, though it was often hard to tell with them standing in a float. Her mouth dropped open and her brain began ticking overtime. Why was her non-horsey husband unloading a horse from the float?

Perhaps he was doing Tiffany a favour and the horse was in transit, or something. Though, if that was the case, why wouldn't her best friend have shared the news? Jessica felt a stab of guilt. It was her fault she and Tiffany hadn't spoken much lately, especially about horses.

Jessica sucked in a breath when the creature appeared. Jesus, it was one of the skinniest, scrawniest pieces of horseflesh she'd ever seen: its hip bones stuck out prominently and its ribs were clearly visible. Despite the bright sunshine, not a hair on its coat glistened. The tail, she now noticed, was not only thin and raggedy, but matted – most likely with faeces.

It stood there with its head hung, barely even turning to take in its new surroundings. Jessica's heart lurched. Who could let a horse get into that condition? Someone should have called the RSPCA. Should she? She was surprised the horse could stand up, being so emaciated. Surely it didn't have any energy.

Steve encouraged it forwards as he headed the few metres across to the stable's day yards. She could see it could barely walk. He stopped and spoke to the horse, rubbed its face when it stumbled, tripping over its own feet. Jessica could almost hear his gentle, soothing tone as he looked deep into eyes that were most likely sunken into bony sockets. While he'd never had much to do with the horses, he was great with animals generally. It was the main reason their meat was so sought after – they had a reputation for their quiet, well-tended stock, all thanks to Steve's affinity with animals.

As mesmerised as Jessica was, she could sit there no longer – she had to know what was going on. She ignored the pain that shot down her leg and right through into the soles of her feet and stormed, as best she could, out of the house and across the turnaround area. She stopped far enough away from Steve and the horse so as not to spook it. God, it looked a lot smaller up close – probably only a shade over fifteen hands. And it seemed to be in a hell of a lot worse condition than she'd thought. Whoever had bought this horse and had Steve bring it home for a stopover during transit had clearly purchased it sight unseen. Bad move.

'What's this?' she demanded. She hadn't meant to sound so cold, so aggressive, but the shock at what she was seeing and the annoyance of not knowing what was going on had caught in her throat. The horse eyed her warily and shuffled sideways.

'Shh, you're scaring her,' Steve said. 'It's okay, girl,' he said, rubbing the horse's neck.

'Well?'

'It's a horse, Jessica,' Steve said wearily.

'I can see that, but who does it belong to?'

'Me, well, us,' Steve said, and offered her the slightly boyish, lopsided grin she'd found so endearing all those years ago. Right now it infuriated her. She didn't have the patience for the runaround. He knew he was doing the wrong thing bringing the horse here, otherwise he'd simply tell her what was going on, without the cheeky grin.

'Well, mine, then,' he said, standing straighter. 'Come on, girl,' he urged, tugging gently on the lead rope.

The horse obediently followed in its uneven, foot-dragging shuffle. Its head was down and it cut a forlorn figure. Jessica didn't think it would have the energy to object even if it wanted to. She felt herself softening slightly. She supposed they could spare some hay. And the stables weren't being used. But she was stuffed if she was going to be taking care of it. Not when she hadn't had a choice in the matter.

God, what's he thinking? In their six and a half years of marriage he'd never shown an interest in the horses beyond providing occasional assistance to her. Jessica found this shift in their roles quite disconcerting.

'But you don't know anything about horses,' she called.

'Well, I'll learn, then. If you won't help me,' Steve said. She felt a twinge of guilt; all the times Steve had cooked her dinner while she'd been busy getting ready for events, all the times he'd done shifts leading colicky horses around, or sat and kept her company while waiting for vets to turn up. Not to mention everything he'd done for Prince and Beau and her since she'd been laid up.

But this was different. She couldn't provide hands-on help; she'd get sucked into the vortex of horses again for sure. There was something about them. But she was done. She was at a different stage in her life — she was going to devote her life to being a great mother to someone.

'But why?'

'I couldn't leave her there, Jess, standing at the fence staring at me like that. You didn't see her, or talk to the old lady ...'

If it wasn't such a serious situation, Jessica would have laughed. Instead, she stared at him with wide, disbelieving eyes. She almost shook her head sadly at him. He'd fallen for 'the look', hook, line and sinker.

Her father had drummed it all into her early. Proper horse people learnt early on not to gaze too deeply into the eyes of a forlorn-looking horse: the pull to save them was just too great, and before you knew it, you'd taken home a dozen mouths and were buying feed by the semitrailer load. And you certainly never listened to the sob story of the owner. It sounded hard-hearted, but you couldn't save every lost soul. She couldn't believe Steve, the businessman, man of the land, a man who made a business of selling livestock for meat, for Christ's sake, had fallen for it. It was almost laughable. Almost, but not quite.

While he was kind to all animals, he was also pragmatic, being a farmer who raised stock to send off to slaughter. A huge part of his life was about not getting emotionally involved, keeping a professional distance and seeing the stock as a mass and not individuals where the long lashes could too easily suck you in.

Was she being too hard now? Probably. But if Steve had suddenly lost the plot and become a total sucker for a stray, which was what this seemed like, then she'd have to be the voice of reason. Someone had to be. And when it came to horses, she was the expert in the family. She'd been raised to only have the best stock on the premises. She and her father before her were serious horse people – there was no place for stock of dubious breeding or conformation. She knew it sounded snobby, but you had to draw a line somewhere. Otherwise you'd end up with paddocks filled with useless horses just waiting out their final days. Fine if you were the RSPCA or some other rescue organisation, but not fine for Collins Park.

'I suppose we could feed it up and sell it on,' Jessica said, thinking aloud. They might have a decent-looking thoroughbred, though a plain one, once the bones were covered. Its legs seemed long and straight enough from this distance.

'No,' Steve said, 'she's staying. I like her.'

'But what do you know about her?'

'What do I need to know other than that she needed saving?'

'But why you, why us?'

'I don't know, Jessica, but you could at least be supportive.'

'I am being supportive.'

Steve stared her down.

'Well, what if it's been doped and turns out to be a dangerous nutcase?' she persisted. There was probably a very good reason why the horse hadn't been sold through the normal channels. *Who sells a horse at a clearing sale with fencing equipment and farm machinery, anyway? Weird.* She was finally starting to come to terms with not having horses – the last thing she needed was to see one again out of the window every day. It was all too confronting.

'As if, Jessica. And anyway, dealing with anything with a brain is a gamble. We both know that only too well.'

'You're right. Sorry.' Still, she eyed the chestnut warily. *I guess you're staying then.*

'So just a brick of meadow hay, or should I give her something else as well?' Steve asked.

'No, just the hay. And leave her out of the stable and just in the day yards in case she freaks out.' It made sense – the day yards were more secure and Jessica didn't want her stables destroyed if the horse got a fright or went crazy when the drugs wore off and it was inside and not used to such confinement. The horse might never have been inside. Though it had clearly coped okay with being in the float.

Jessica did think the horse looked drugged from what she could see; its eyes were far from alert. But that could be resignation to being in a new place with an unknown fate or simply severe malnutrition.

'No, I'll open the stable door – she can have the run of both. It's going to be chilly tonight.'

Jessica fumed at being overridden about something to do with horses. She'd had a lifetime of experience. She almost pointed out that the horse was clearly quite used to being outside.

'Should I put a rug on her – there'd be one to fit, wouldn't there?'

'I think you should just leave it in peace and wait until we see what it's like before mucking around with it too much. It might never have had a rug on and you don't want to terrify it. Let it settle in first.' While she was appearing supportive – well, she hoped so – what she was really hoping was that by morning Steve would have come to his senses and had agreed to fatten the creature up and on-sell it.

Jessica watched while Steve gave the horse the same amount of hay she would have given it, filled the water tub up, and stood rubbing the chestnut's mud-caked neck for a few minutes. She refused to acknowledge the jealousy and annoyance that swept through her. But she did admit to feeling quite unsettled by the horse. Who could have let it get into such a state?

She thought of Prince and Beau and how she'd just cast them aside. To ease the guilt threatening to overwhelm her, she moved to where Laurel and Hardy were still on the ute, gave them each a pat, and unclipped their chains.

'Now, go quietly,' she warned them. They seemed to understand, because they silently hopped down and trotted closer to the yards to check out the newcomer. Jessica knew it was ridiculous, but she felt ganged up on, an outsider. Yet she didn't want to join Steve with the horse because she might just get drawn into its vortex too. Someone had to keep a level head. So, instead, she made her way slowly back to the house.

'Leave it in peace,' she called to Steve at the door.

*

Later, Jessica tried to tune out her annoyance at Steve overstepping the clearly defined roles in their marriage and concentrate on *CSI* on the TV. But Steve was like a jack-in-the-box, leaping up to go out and check on the horse every few minutes. After the third time in the first hour, Jessica snapped at him to sit still; she was trying to follow the clues of the show and wanted to watch in peace.

'And,' she added, softening at his crestfallen expression, 'how would you feel if every time you felt relaxed, someone you were afraid of poked their head around the corner, startling you?'

'I don't think she's afraid of me,' Steve said. 'How could she be when I'm the one who rescued her? She knows and understands.'

'Well, wary then,' she conceded. 'And for all we know it was drugged and could be a complete dangerous nutcase in the morning, when the drugs wear off.'

'Why would anyone go to the expense and trouble of drugging her? As if, Jess.'

So some patsy would take it off their hands, she wanted to say, but didn't. If Steve wasn't prepared to see the situation like it was, then she wouldn't be helping matters by pointing it out. He was also decidedly testy with her for her clear lack of support. But as much as she loved Steve and the soft side that showed itself occasionally – like the dogs being allowed inside – she thought he was being ridiculous. Not to mention straying way too far onto her turf.

They went to bed annoyed and without a kiss goodnight, and rolled to their respective edges of the bed with their backs to each other.

As she waited for sleep to claim her, Jessica seethed at the horse outside that was unsettling their lives after just two minutes.

Her eyes flew open as she realised she hadn't asked just how much Steve had paid for the beast. Far too much, no doubt. The money was as much his as hers, though – it was probably best not to get into that.

Chapter Eighteen

Jessica was lacing up her runners for a walk when Steve came in after checking on the horse. She was beginning to like the mornings again because she now had a routine in place, a way to kill a few hours from an otherwise dull day.

'Can you keep an eye on her water?' Steve said. 'She must have knocked it over. It's full again now, but can you check again later?'

'Oh. Okay.' That was a little odd; never had a horse managed to knock over one of the twenty-litre flexi plastic tubs. *Must have got quite a fright to bash into it that hard. Great, he has brought home a bloody nutcase*, she thought with a groan. *That's all we need.* She didn't like that she'd have to get up close and personal with the horse, but there was no other way to check its water. And as much as she wanted to avoid any involvement so she wouldn't be sucked into horse land again, she'd never be cruel or neglect an animal. Jessica knew she'd check its water supply twenty times a day if necessary, and regularly look out the window to check it hadn't somehow got itself caught in the fence, no matter how much she disliked the idea of the horse being out there. She let out a sigh of resignation.

'Right, well, I'm off. Wish me luck in finding a good boom sprayer at a great price,' Steve said cheerfully.

'Good luck,' she said. 'Have fun,' she added, trying to lighten the tense atmosphere. Things were civil and reasonably friendly, but not exactly lovey-dovey. Jessica wanted everything to be back to how it was before the accident.

No, she corrected, before her dad had died. She'd give anything to have his no-nonsense advice now. On what, though? He wouldn't have let her give up the horses and would have told her sternly to get her act together, to stop feeling sorry for herself and get back up on that bloody horse. Jessica smiled sadly.

If only the money hadn't been so tempting. And a split-second later she heard what she could have sworn was her father's voice in her head, saying the money was just an excuse. Oh well, it was too late now. Everything happened for a reason and the right reason, didn't Tiffany always say?

Distracted by thoughts of her father, she left the house with a lighter step, and it took her a hundred metres to realise the ease with which she was walking and the pace she was keeping up. Finally, some real progress! She pushed herself hard and even managed an ambling jog for a few metres on her way back.

As she showered, she revelled in feeling better than she had in months – not just physically, but mentally and emotionally too. Tomorrow she was going to start running. Properly. Soon she would be back in shape and her broken ankle a distant memory.

Sitting at the table eating her sandwich, her eyes were drawn to the stables – a place she'd consciously avoided looking at for weeks. Now she watched, stunned, as the horse put a hoof into the water tub and thumped it up and down, spraying water everywhere.

'What's your bloody problem?' Jessica said aloud. She went outside and yelled at her. 'Oi! Stop that!'

The horse ignored her and, as if in a moment of pure defiance, swapped feet. After a few moments it removed its hoof, stood back, lifted its head, and neighed loudly.

'Well if you think I'm filling it up, think again, missy,' Jessica growled. But of course she would; she'd never knowingly leave a horse without access to clean drinking water. She stomped across the gravel. The horse darted to the far side of the yard when it saw her approaching and stood eyeing her warily.

'No more fun for you, miss,' she said, dragging the tub under the rail and outside the yard. She positioned it where the horse could put its face in and drink, but wouldn't be able to get a hoof into it without some seriously fancy footwork, and filled it up with the hose.

She'd just got settled back in the house when something made her go to the window – just a feeling. The horse had its face in the tub and was swishing it back and forth, sending water flying everywhere.

'Jesus,' she exclaimed. 'Just what is your bloody problem?' She was not going to spend all day filling up the tub. It was a waste of water, not to mention annoying.

Perhaps if the horse went without for an hour or so, it might appreciate it enough to leave it alone next time. A part of her said horses didn't possess such cognitive skills. Another quieter voice, told her they always had the capacity to surprise.

Twenty minutes later she stole a quick glance outside and was relieved to see the creature standing quietly. Forlornly, if she was being honest. *Careful, you're being sucked in.* She probably should give the horse a brush, it was no doubt lonely. But as good as Jessica's ankle was feeling and even with the improvement in her strength and stability all round, she didn't think it wise to get in the yard with a horse she knew nothing about when Steve was away and wouldn't be back for hours. God, she really was turning soft; she'd never had such qualms before the accident.

In an effort to ignore the creature – and her guilt over ignoring it – and the pull to learn more about it, Jessica sat down to a marathon of *Law and Order* she'd recorded.

Some time later she heard a car pull up outside and pressed pause. She got up to check through the window. Tiffany. She looked at her watch. Three p.m. Shit, two hours had passed since she'd checked the horse's water. It seemed to take an age to lace up her shoes and when she got over to the yard, Tiffany had put the hose in the tub and was stroking the face of the chestnut over the fence.

'Who's your new friend?' Tiffany asked, when Jessica appeared beside her.

'Nothing to do with me,' she said. 'And that will be empty again soon,' she added, nodding at the tub Tiffany was filling. 'She seems to have a fascination with water.'

'Cute.'

'Yeah, real cute,' Jessica said, groaning and rolling her eyes.

'So what's her story?'

'No idea. Some stray Steve bought at a clearing sale yesterday.'

'Seriously?' Tiffany stared at Jessica disbelievingly.

'Yep. And now he's gone off for the day, so it's down to me. Typical.'

'Well, it's not like you don't know what you're doing. And I'm sure you're looking for a new hobby right about now. Probably all ...'

'Don't you dare say it's perfect timing, meant to be, or any of that crap. I'm done with horses, Tiffany.' In the silence the words

But are you? echoed in her head. 'And anyway, as if I'd take on something looking like that.'

'Don't you listen to her,' Tiffany said to the horse. 'It's not personal; she's getting over some horse stuff not to do with you.'

'It's all right for you, Tiffany, you ...'

'What?'

'Nothing.'

'Go on, say it. "It's all right for you, you only do dressage." That's what you were going to say, wasn't it?'

Jessica stayed silent, scraping at the dirt with the toe of her shoe.

'I might not have the guts to do cross-country, Jess, but I'm not the one who's standing there unable to touch a horse because of some pathetic all-or-nothing complex. Just face it, Jessica, only doing dressage is not being a failure. Giving up on horses altogether because you've lost your nerve to ride cross-country – that's a bloody failure!'

Jessica opened and closed her mouth. Where had her meek and mild friend gone?

'And for the record, if I thought this was the person you would become, I would never have helped you sell Prince and Beau!'

'We couldn't afford to keep them,' Jessica said quietly.

'And that's why I helped. But I'm now wondering if that was just an excuse. It was a difficult time. But it's over now. You need to stop feeling sorry for yourself and get your shit together before you lose everything!'

'What? Has Steve said something?' Jessica suddenly started to feel uncomfortably hot under her clothes.

Tiffany blushed slightly and looked down at her feet.

'What? What's he said?' Now it was Jessica's turn to blush.

As Tiffany went the few metres to turn off the tap, the horse darted to the far side of the yard. *Great*, Jessica thought, *even the damned horse is against me.* She scowled.

'And give this girl a break. And Steve. It's not their fault you've got a bloody screw loose!'

Jessica watched, stunned, as Tiffany stormed to her car, got in, slammed the door, and drove off with a spin of wheels.

She glared at the horse eyeing her warily and stomped back to the house.

*

Jessica sat in front of the laptop scrolling through the Facebook pages and websites with descriptions of missing horses and pausing to wonder at Tiffany's reaction. It was so out of character.

But for all she knew her friend was experiencing PMT and she'd just struck a nerve. And grief was a weird thing, too. She felt a shard of guilt tear through her, but pushed it aside. Tiffany did tend to blow a lot more hot and cold than Jessica did; no doubt one of the reasons Tiffany stuck to the more sedate sport of dressage. Jessica didn't like to be too judgemental, but she did believe that while dressage took nerve, it certainly didn't take the guts that riding cross-country and show jumping did. She sighed, thinking of her father. The sentiment could have come out of his very mouth.

Jeff Collins had always seen dressage as a necessary evil to eventing. Yes, he understood that the partnership formed through flatwork was essential, he just didn't see why anyone would be content going around and around an arena day after day, year after year. Not to mention how bored the horses must get. Jeff would have told Tiffany exactly what he thought out there; in fact had, on a number of occasions. They'd had some fine debates and Jessica knew it was only because of Tiffany's restraint and respect for elders that she hadn't told him to fuck off on more than one occasion. In the last months of Jeff's life he and Tiffany hadn't had many cross words, Jessica suddenly realised, trying to picture their last altercation. It was almost as if the universe had been protecting a sick man. The thought turned the blood in her veins cold, until she told herself she was being ridiculous and far too melodramatic. It didn't happen like that. Tiffany had been quiet around Jeff generally because of all the upheaval in her life. And, anyway, they'd hardly seen each other in the last months.

Jessica had learnt to keep her opinions to herself where her father couldn't or wouldn't. But now she realised she was very much a chip off the old block, although she hoped she was sanded a little smoother.

Jessica shook thoughts of Tiffany and her father aside and shut down the computer. It didn't matter that she didn't know the brand of the chestnut horse outside – or if it even had one – because there were no horses listed with similar markings.

'Damn it,' she cursed under her breath. She was really hoping to have had a legitimate reason to insist Steve get rid of the horse. She could see it was going to be more trouble than it was worth, which wasn't anything – certainly not the several hundred dollars Steve had most likely paid for it.

Another stab of guilt passed through Jessica. She sighed. She was being too harsh. All horses had their merits; they were God's creatures – one of her father's well-used comments. Not that they were remotely religious, but her father was brought up in that era where God was considered the creator of all, end of story. Yet he wasn't a softy when it came to questionable horse flesh. No, his kind comment was almost always tempered by a snide 'even if it's only as dog food' followed by a chuckle.

Yes, Jeff Collins had been a tough nut and that probably meant Jessica had a bit of a tough edge to her as well. She missed her father with an ache that ran right through her, the physical pain of which she'd never have believed. She hadn't felt like this after losing her mother.

Pull yourself together, Jessica. She literally did: she tightened her shoulders and sat up straighter.

Her father had also dominated her – she was only just starting to truly realise to what extent. Now she was in charge of her own life and on a new path: motherhood, fingers crossed. Horses were the past, her connection with the indomitable Jeff Collins, which had been frayed with his passing and severed with her fall. She ignored her father's voice in her head, telling her how pathetic she was to throw in the towel.

Well, I wouldn't have if you'd been here, she said back silently, the voice in her mind sounding not unlike a petulant teenager. If only Steve hadn't brought home the bloody horse that was making her think about all this again. She'd been getting along fine, not looking at the empty stables, avoiding the neighbouring horses in their paddocks on her walks.

Deep down she knew this horse was staying; no doubt as a cruel joke by the universe to taunt her or as a way for Steve to make some point or other – probably that he was the man of the house, and land, and had some say. And when Steve made up his mind on something, it was best to just leave it alone.

Jessica couldn't shake her remorse over Tiffany taking off while angry at her. She wondered what she should do about it. But then her mind strayed to the fact there was a horse out in the yards that she didn't want to be there despite feeling drawn to it.

So far she'd managed to refrain from going out there again, even though she watched from the window as, yet again, it managed to empty its water. Jessica was practically fuming with the thought of having to go and sort it out – bloody attention seeker – when Steve's ute passed by with the horse float attached.

Jessica frowned. *Let's hope there's not another bloody horse in there.*

She was out on the verandah when he emerged.

'You'll have to sort out that bloody horse – it keeps emptying its water and I'm not filling it up again!' She went back inside and shut the door loudly behind her.

A few minutes later, Steve poked his head into the lounge area where she sat.

'Do you need anything in town? I'm going to go and get a water feeder.'

Jessica shook her head, too stunned to say a word. Five years ago she'd started asking Steve to set up small water feeders in the stables and day yards so she didn't have to deal with hoses and tubs and buckets. Three years ago she'd given up dropping hints after he'd told her that they were too expensive for such a small inconvenience. 'If it's such a problem, get rid of the horses, the budget is tight,' he'd said on more than one occasion.

And now this bloody horse had been here two minutes and he was trotting off to town to spend money that was half hers – worse, money from the sale of *her* horses. Jesus! She knew if she said all this aloud it would sound very childish – hell, it did in her own mind. But she couldn't help how she felt. The situation was ludicrous.

★

Steve came in just after dark. Jessica had itched to eat dinner without him and leave his plate in the oven, but had refrained. Just.

As they ate, Steve chatted away and Jessica chewed silently. The steak that was as good as ever felt like cardboard in her mouth and was just as hard to swallow.

'I think she was lonely. Didn't touch the tub while I was there,' he said. 'Oh well, least she can't waste so much water now. I've told the dogs to stay over there and keep her company. Wonder what her fascination is and where it comes from?'

Just a naughty habit picked up by a bored horse. But Jessica stayed silent. She wondered when it would start chewing the pristine timber of her yards. If it did, Steve would be bloody well fixing it. She frowned; Steve always did the maintenance. Jessica could carefully place a horse at a jump – well, more often than not – but she barely knew one end of a screwdriver from the other. Otherwise, she might have had the proper feeder troughs in well before now.

'I'll let her out in a few days, once she's cleaned out and won't introduce any new weeds. I wonder if she likes cows or sheep,' he said thoughtfully, and got up to get another beer from the fridge.

Jessica knew she should keep her mouth shut, but just couldn't.

'And then what?'

'What do you mean?'

'You're just going to put it in with the sheep or cows depending on what it prefers?'

'Yeah, what's the problem?'

'And it's going to just live out its days grazing?'

'I don't see why not,' Steve said cheerfully, sat back down and resumed his meal.

'But …'

'Jessica,' Steve said, looking up at her after placing his knife and fork carefully on the sides of his plate. 'I wouldn't have had a problem with you keeping Prince and Beau, but you chose to get rid of them because of your ridiculous notion that they had to pay their way and were too valuable to be doing nothing.'

'They would have cost a fortune in upkeep.'

'We would have found it somewhere. Stop using that as an excuse.'

'But …'

'Jessica, I have never told you what to do with your life, your horses, but quite frankly, I'm getting a little tired of you moping about feeling sorry for yourself and beating yourself up – or whatever it is you're doing – over getting rid of Prince and Beau. That was your decision and no one else's. You either get them back or learn to live with it, but don't be taking it out on me!

'That horse out there needed saving. I don't know why it was me who had to do it, or why, but it was. And it feels bloody good. So don't you dare start making me feel bad because you've realised how badly you've fucked up. I won't have it. This is as much my land as it is yours and if I want a chestnut horse – or a donkey, for that matter – in a paddock, then I bloody well will, and there's not a damned thing you can do about it!

'And if you stopped being so damned self-righteous for a minute, you might just realise that a creature doesn't have to be a winner in some competition in order to bring meaning and joy to someone's life.' And with that, he thumped both clenched fists on the table, got up and strode to the bedroom. She heard the ensuite door closing loudly.

Jessica was left gaping – at his words, as well as at the forceful-ness of their delivery. Steve was the silent, brooding type, not an angry ranter. She felt unsettled and was shocked to find herself shaking slightly.

Chapter Nineteen

Steve's words continued to bother Jessica as she tried to focus on watching the evening's television.

Her husband sat silent and brooding on the other couch. Golly, this horse really had got under his skin. She gnawed at her lip as she wondered why: why this one, why now? Was it because of her, was she driving him away, into the solace of rescuing some worthy creature, fixing it, because he couldn't fix her? She was sure she'd been doing well at hiding her angst, her true feelings, but Steve had uncharacteristically snapped at her – more than snapped, actually bellowed – as had Tiffany.

Though it might not all be about her – wasn't that one of the latest sayings: 'It's not all about you'? Whatever was going on, she would have to work harder at pretending everything was normal. And she could see that meant humouring Steve with his new hobby. She would show an interest, guide him if necessary, but definitely keep a healthy emotional distance from the horse. It was Steve's project.

She wondered if he would take it so far as learning to ride. There wasn't much point having a horse if you couldn't ride it. Only horses showing promise and recovering from injury were allowed to loll about for any length of time in the paddock, not being ridden. Early on, she'd become used to horses coming and going at her father's whim. She'd shed many tears over them as a child and become hardened as a result. She'd thought that was a good thing. Now she wasn't so sure.

It wasn't a whole lot different to people keeping a pet cat or rabbit, or whatever – completely useless except for the apparent health benefits the medical fraternity were now lauding: reduced blood pressure and incidence of depression. Oh well, Steve had put up with her horses cluttering up the place and the money and hours she'd put into them, so she supposed she could be a bit more supportive. No, not just show support, but actually *be* supportive. She'd force herself to; she owed it to him, their marriage.

Actually, it might be quite nice to have a horse without any of the expectations and pressure caused by eventing. Jessica frowned. Did she really think that all those years of competition were down to fulfilling expectations? If so, whose? Hers? She frowned harder. No, she'd loved the exhilaration of competing, the thrill of taking a green horse and turning it into a champion. Hadn't she?

But now she thought about it, she didn't miss all the hours going around and around the arena, perfecting each pace, each dressage movement. That was hard work, and also incredibly boring at times. She felt a stab of guilt at wondering how the horses had coped with it. It had been necessary, but they wouldn't have understood that, though they had appeared to enjoy pleasing her. And she didn't miss being yelled at by her father or being made to repeat a jump over and over until she could barely stay upright in the saddle and the horse felt like jelly underneath her.

Shit, had she just been carried by his will, his dream, all those years? Had she been on a merry-go-round and thought it easier to stay on than try to get off while it was moving? It had well and truly stopped now. The thought made her feel weird, which was weird in itself – the merry-go-round had stopped when she'd sold the horses; when they'd left the property. It had slowed enough to let her off when her father died, but it hadn't stopped, and she hadn't got off, until her decision to sell Prince and Beau.

She noticed her heart rate was very slow. Rather than being jittery about this realisation – really, it wasn't all that new, but seemed to be coming at her from a different angle, and thus felt new – Jessica felt strangely free. There was some residual remorse when she thought about letting her father down, but if she let herself be annoyed with him for dying on her and being such a smothering, forceful figure in her life, she could push the stab of red-hot guilt aside.

A new realisation hit her like a bolt of lightning passing from the top of her head down to the soles of her feet: her courage to ride cross-country had more to do with fear of her father, more to do with letting him down and having him yell at her, than letting herself down. But that influence had served her well through twenty-odd years of competing. And they say if your heart's not in it, you don't achieve. Well, hadn't she proven that wrong? The realisations were tumbling from her mind like dominoes now. The secret to her success wasn't passion, it was fear. *I got more out of my father being proud of me than winning.*

Damn you! she cursed under her breath. She meant her father, but knew deep down she was referring to herself. He hadn't exactly tied her to the saddle and forced her to do anything. She'd willingly fed, rugged, groomed, learnt dressage tests by heart and walked cross-country course after cross-country course. Gone on with it all after she'd left home and got married. But if she had to be totally honest, she'd got as much gratification out of seeing a shining coat as she had tackling the nation's toughest cross-country courses.

She'd loved pony club – roaring around as a youngster without a care in the world – but somewhere it had all become so serious. No, Jessica realised, it had always been serious. She'd been as well groomed as her horses to fulfil Jeff Collins' lifelong ambitions that he'd never accomplished. While it hadn't been discussed in any detail, Jessica suspected a lack of finances was the reason – a topic rarely discussed in their family – given he had so often declared the trip to a competition a waste of money if she didn't do well enough.

She could see it all now as clearly as a movie showing in front of her. She'd always loved jumping and might have been a jumps jockey if her mother hadn't expressed her horror. Besides, Jessica had grown too tall and robust. She'd also never have found the will to starve herself.

She thought about Jasper – a horse she'd loved but who, in her father's opinion, hadn't measured up. She'd come home one day from school to find him replaced by Billy, a feisty grey straight off the racetrack. Apparently Jasper was for the fun rider and Billy for the serious rider. Thus the line was drawn in the sand and the hard work began. Jessica didn't have the time or energy to pine for Jasper and, in a matter of weeks, she was now ashamed to admit, he'd been largely forgotten.

But you couldn't be a twelve-year-old pony clubber forever. A time came to either give up or get serious, according to her father. And she'd been swept along in his wake. She loved horses and didn't think life was worth living without them. And her father had apparently just spent a fortune on Billy, so she couldn't exactly have gotten out of it even if she'd wanted to. The thought of letting her father down in any regard cut her to the core. So, as much as Billy didn't have a fun, quirky sense of humour like

Jasper did, they'd bonded and made a pretty successful team, quickly climbing the ranks of pony club eventing. Just like many Olympians had started out. That was the goal.

Now she thought again with a slight shock and then a strong wave of sadness that Olympic success had been Jeff Collins' goal not hers. If it had been hers, she wouldn't have dropped the ball as soon as he'd fallen off the perch. She'd have remained driven. And if it really had been her goal, she wouldn't have let her head full of doubts convince her she could never ride cross-country again and she wouldn't have sold the two horses. Instead, she'd have done everything to get back to where she'd been. Oh well, it was done now.

★

The following morning Steve stomped back into the house after feeding his new acquisition. They had barely spoken the previous evening and had exchanged curt greetings since. He set about making two mugs of coffee. He was silent, but frowning, shaking his head, running his hands through his hair as if something was really bothering him.

Oh, God, please, not another round.

After a few minutes, Jessica's curiosity overrode her fear of the consequences; she could stand it no longer. 'What's wrong?' she asked.

He leant back on the bench and surveyed her as if trying to decide if he should tell her something or not before saying, 'She's terrified of me. I don't know what I've done.'

'What's happened?'

'Well, nothing really. It's just, if I go to put my hand out to pat her she freaks out and leaps back. And then she stands eyeing me like I've hit her, or something. It's terrible. She was fine when I loaded her in the float – though the old lady was there, and some other woman – and that first night she seemed fine when I fed her, and yesterday morning.'

'She's going to need time to adjust to her new surroundings, to us.'

'But she was fine when she arrived.'

'Maybe she was so hungry she didn't have the energy. She is very thin.'

'She's probably dangerous. I don't know anything about her. What an idiot.' He sighed. 'You're right, a horse is not just a horse – it was a big mistake. I don't know anything about horses. What was I thinking? I've been feeling so helpless – I really wanted to do a good thing.'

'You did do a good thing.' Jessica felt like her heart was being wrenched out of her. He was really distressed. The only times she had ever seen him like this was when he had to put down injured stock or when he came home after a CFS callout for a motor vehicle accident.

'But look where it's got me.'

'She's been here two minutes. Let's give her a few more days. Perhaps she's had a bad history with men, or something.'

Steve appeared shocked. He eyed her warily. Clearly he was surprised at her being supportive when she'd been so against the horse in the first place.

'Okay. But could you see if she has the same reaction to you – um, test your anti-men theory?'

'Later, after I've been for a walk. Um, what's her name?'

'Faith. Thank goodness I'll be at CFS all day. I can't stand to look at her; it breaks my heart.'

Jessica's heart surged. That's what she'd fallen in love with: Steve's big, soft heart buried under his tough, blokey exterior. She would have loved to have got up and embraced him, but was too afraid of having read the situation wrong and of being rejected. They would come back from their estrangement. For the first time in weeks, she felt everything would be okay. But they needed to ease their way.

Aha! I'll start by cooking one of his favourite meals. She half-smiled at the thought and began planning her shopping list.

Her excitement about the surprise she was planning for Steve made Jessica hurry through her walk, and she cut it short. A weight seemed to have lifted at the prospect of a trip into town. She hadn't been out in the car on her own since getting her leg out of plaster; had been content to shut herself away. Not anymore. It was utterly silly, but if anyone had asked, she would have said she felt like a bird leaving the nest for the first time; eager to see what the world had to offer. She shook her head at the absurdity of it all.

With her handbag over her shoulder and her keys in hand, she made a detour to the stables and yards behind the car shed. Surely the horse couldn't be as bad as Steve was saying. Tiffany had given her face a rub. Sure, she had been a little wary, but hadn't walked away, which she quite easily could have. Jessica shook her head. She really had to start using the horse's name and stop thinking of her as a nonentity.

'Hello there, Faith. How are you this morning?' she said in her authoritative voice. The horse was standing with her head lowered and eyes closed. The sun shone on her face. *Well, at least she's looking relatively relaxed. That's a good sign.*

The horse's eyes flew open and bugged. She snorted and took a leap to the right, away from where Jessica was standing at the fence. Jessica got such a fright she took a step back herself and brought her hands to her chest, trying to calm her wildly beating heart. God, was it deaf? She had spoken to her, for Christ's sake, given plenty of warning. Maybe she *was* deaf. *Knowing my luck,* she thought. Just what the hell has Steve taken on?

'It's okay, I won't hurt you,' she said, soothingly. She should have brought some carrots as a peace offering. The horse eyed her sideways, nostrils flared. Jessica felt torn between getting started on her mission into town and sorting out the apparent misunderstanding with Faith, smoothing things over. It was usually best not to leave a problem unresolved, otherwise it tended to take longer to sort out later.

But if she was to lure Steve back, and hopefully conceive a child, she had to get into town and get dinner organised. The determined side of Jessica wrestled with staying, but her more practical side won. It might take a few minutes to have Faith eating out of her hand – literally – or it could take hours. Once she started, she didn't want to have to cut things short. One of the golden rules of dealing with horses – all livestock, for that matter – was to approach any task as if you had all the time in the world. Animals could always sense when you were in a hurry. That was when things went awry. So, damn it, as much as she didn't want the horse to feel she had won this particular battle, Jessica needed to leave, which she did, with a big sigh and a glare at the horse. Faith. What a silly name!

It seemed the same rule about time that applied to dealing with animals also applied to Woodside and its townsfolk. And it seemed everyone was in town that day. Parks were few and far between. Jessica finally managed to snare one in front of the newsagent.

Three people accosted her in the fifty or so metres to the supermarket and then down every aisle inside. She smiled, nodded and over and over answered, 'No, I haven't been away, I've just been busy.' She was somewhat astounded that the grapevine wasn't all over the fact she'd broken her ankle. Or perhaps they'd forgotten. She wasn't about to update those who didn't know and be caught for hours talking about their previous injuries. Those who did know asked how the recovery was going and offered every old wives' tale under the sun for reducing the swelling, building up the muscles and dealing with other unrelated ailments.

By the time Jessica was back in her vehicle, it was one o'clock and she was exhausted, frazzled and feeling claustrophobic. Before the accident, she could spend hours on the footpath happily chatting to all she knew; now she couldn't wait to get back to the tranquillity of the farm. Not to mention being very keen to get on with sorting out the horse.

She'd better pick up some horse pellets and a big bag of carrots at the feed store on her way out of town. The idea that she was also keen to prove it wasn't her Faith was afraid of crossed her mind briefly, but she scolded herself. It was not a popularity contest with Steve – he'd asked for her help and she would give it. Ulti-mately the horse was his.

She wondered if Tiffany would be on shift today, and if she was still annoyed. Jessica felt shameful, hoping her friend wouldn't be around. She was on a mission, and becoming more and more keen to get it under way. But she was out of luck: Tiffany rushed over to Jessica's car as she was getting out.

'I'm so sorry about yesterday,' she cried, enveloping Jessica in a tight hug.

'It's okay. And I'm sorry too. I really don't think dressage is any less serious a sport.' Well, she kind of did – it was far less danger-ous, for a start – but to each their own.

'I know, it's just different. So we're good?'

'I am if you are,' Jessica said, grinning broadly. Gosh, they'd got through that row easily. She wondered if it was resolved far too easily. Was there something going on with Tiffany? But Jessica knew if Tiff wanted to tell her she would have and she didn't have time for analysing her friend's mood today.

'You could have rung, you know. And, hey, you're actually out, driving, on your own,' Tiffany said, suddenly realising the magnitude of the situation. 'And here I was thinking we'd have to kidnap you to get you out sometime. So, how is it to be out in the daylight again?'

Jessica rolled her eyes at her friend. 'Very funny. I'm not a mole who's just come out of its hole for the first time after winter.'

'It seems like it.'

'Yeah, you're probably right.' Jessica did feel a bit as if she was out in the sun for the first time in ages, which was strange, given she'd been out walking in it for days now.

'So, what brings you into town anyway?'

'Exciting stuff. Groceries.'

'Oh, right,' Tiffany said, looking puzzled.

'I'm cooking a special dinner.'

'Ooh, what are we celebrating?'

'Nothing, really, just me coming out of my cocoon, I guess,' Jessica said with a shrug. She didn't want to admit she had Steve offside as well. 'But I do need a bag of carrots and some horse pellets.'

'Hmm, that's some dinner you're cooking your man.'

'Oh! Ha ha. No, they're for the horse. Steve's asked me to do some work with her – seems she doesn't like men – and I need some bribery treats.'

'Aha!'

'What's that meant to mean?'

'It all makes sense now.'

'What does, Sherlock?' Jessica frowned, genuinely puzzled.

'Your bright and sunny disposition.'

'Really?'

'Yep. It's horses that does that to you – you've got horse face.'

'Gee, thanks very much. Very flattering,' Jessica said, but she was grinning. Now she thought about it, the challenge of working with the horse had put a spring in her step – she couldn't deny it.

'And, please, surely this horse has a name.'

'Faith. And don't you dare say it's a sign!'

'Wouldn't dream of it,' Tiffany said, smirking. 'Come on then, we'd better get you your magic ingredients.' She led the way into the shop.

'Don't get too excited,' Jessica muttered to her friend's back. 'She's Steve's horse – nothing to do with me.'

'Yeah, whatever.'

Jessica opened her mouth to protest, but as she did, the owner of Millers' Fodder cried, 'Jessica Harrington, how the hell are you? Long time, no see. How's that ankle of yours?'

'Doing fine thanks, Barry,' Jessica said.

'A bag of horse carrots and one of pellets, thanks, James,' Tiffany said to the young lad lurking to the left of the counter as she went around behind to ring up the purchase. Jessica marvelled at how settled she seemed in her role, and she didn't miss the slightly smitten, flushed look of adoration that crossed James's face before he disappeared out the back into the warehouse. Jessica grinned to herself. Trust Tiffany to have the place running like clockwork and the staff falling for her.

'Good news, good news,' Barry said, still at his office door. Jessica turned to see him rubbing his hands together. 'We've missed your orders of late. Good to hear you're back in the game.'

'Oh,' Jessica said, 'I'm not, really. This is just …' She lifted and dropped her hands in a helpless gesture.

'Don't worry, you'll have the bug again real soon,' he said, tapping the side of his nose.

'Hmm,' was all she could come up with in reply. She thought of protesting, but the quote, 'The lady doth protest too much, methinks' ran through her head. And, anyway, if she'd learnt anything these last few months, she'd learnt that nothing was for certain. You didn't know what was around the corner or over the next jump. She realised she was actually really looking forward to working with Faith, to getting her eating out of her hand. And not to prove a point to anyone! Well, maybe, just a little.

She handed over her key card, put in her pin and then slid the receipt into her wallet as James appeared beside her with one of the steel trolleys.

'Well, I'd better get cracking. I've got groceries in the car,' she said. 'See ya.'

'Thanks for shopping at Millers' Fodder,' Tiffany said in a very business-like tone, which nearly caused Jessica to laugh.

'Hopefully we'll see you again soon,' Barry called from behind his desk, and gave a cheery wave.

'Take care,' Tiffany called. 'See you soon.'

★

Jessica unloaded the groceries and mentally calculated what time she had to be back in the house in order to have dinner ready for Steve when he got home. She was itching to get started with Faith, but was mindful that she now had less than three hours, which went against the all-the-time-in-the-world rule. But she'd promised Steve, so she had to go ahead. And, anyway, she was only going to get the horse to come up and eat from her hand. No horse could resist the lure of a carrot being held out or pellets being rattled in a bucket for that long. And Faith wasn't that bad if Tiffany had patted her. It probably was a fear of men.

'Yep, it'll be fine. Piece of cake.'

Jessica stacked the carrots from the big bag into the fridge in the shed, turned it on, and then put the bag of horse pellets in the decommissioned chest freezer. She opened the bag and scooped a few handfuls into a bucket, just enough for a nice enticing rattle and worthwhile treat, and filled her pockets with juicy carrots.

She stood at the chest-height timber railing, bucket in one hand, carrot in the other.

'Come on, Faith,' she called. 'Do you want a carrot? Or perhaps some pellets? Come and get them.' She rattled the bucket.

Faith stood back and eyed her warily. She tossed her head and licked her lips, but stayed put.

By the time the horse took her first tentative, shuffling, steps in Jessica's direction, the muscles in her arms had turned to jelly from holding the bucket up, even though it wasn't heavy. She'd grown unused to this kind of activity and was seizing up. She hadn't wanted to change arms and risk startling the creature when there were signs of progress. She also wanted to scratch an itch on her nose but, again, didn't feel she could move a muscle. She snuck a glance at her watch, just visible on her outstretched arm. Ten minutes had already passed.

Never before had she had a horse hold out this long. Pellets were failsafe. At least, she'd thought they were. The creature looked half starved; surely any edible substance was too hard to resist? The horse had pluck, Jessica had to give her that. But she wasn't going to give up. If she had to stand here until midnight, she would. She would get this damned horse eating out of her hand if it was the last thing she did. She gritted her teeth in determination. *Two can play at this game.*

She put the carrot back in her pocket, took a fistful of pellets, held her hand above the bucket and opened her fingers. The pellets dribbled into the vessel, a cacophony of thuds and rattles. Faith lifted her head with interest, but stayed where she was.

'Come on. They're yours if you want them. Come on, I know you do,' Jessica urged.

The horse took another step towards her. Twenty-five minutes had passed. This was excruciating; something so simple, so easy, yet one of the most difficult things Jessica had ever done. This bloody horse was testing her! She was not used to untrained horses that didn't know basic commands. She wondered if this one did and was deliberately challenging her. No, horses didn't think like that; humans were the ones who were capable of cruelty in a psychological way. The animal kingdom wasn't. This one was scared. End of story.

Regardless, she was running out of patience. She thought about giving up, walking away. Then she thought about how the horse had taken two small steps towards her of its own accord – that should be rewarded. But she wasn't going to just give her the bucket – that would be as good as giving in. She pulled the carrot from her pocket again and held it out.

She wondered how the creature had been put on a float in the first place. Perhaps it was just her Faith didn't like, didn't trust. *It's not all about you,* she told herself. Tiffany and Steve had patted Faith over the fence. No, Tiffany had, but Steve had led her from the float to the yard without incident – she'd seen it with her own eyes. Don't take it personally, she'd told Steve. *Don't* you *take it personally, either.*

'Oh, God, this is excruciating. Just take the bloody carrot,' she groaned through gritted teeth, 'and put us both out of our misery. I've got stuff to do.'

She leant her head on her arms. Her shoulders were tight and hurting. And now she was thinking of pain, her healing leg was beginning to smart too. She tried to ignore the nagging feeling that this was some cruel joke – that it was personal. She was being tested in the most basic way possible and she was failing. She felt like throwing the bucket as far as she could.

She looked at her watch. 'I'll give you ten more minutes.'

Jessica heard a shuffle and raised her head slowly and carefully to covertly survey the situation. Faith was a long neck stretch away from her. She stood boldly in front with her head raised, as if asking, 'Now what?' Jessica held out a carrot. The horse stretched further, leant in from her chest and wrapped her lips around the object to gently take it from her, and stepped back.

'Is that good?' Jessica asked as the horse munched on the sweet, juicy vegetable. She knew they were good because she'd had a nibble on the end of one while stacking them. The movement of the horse's lips while chewing made her look like she was smiling. Jessica stared at her eyes. Her heart lurched. There was a real sadness there; none of the bright cheekiness and arrogance Prince and Beau had had.

She knew it was probably a little over the top, but she had the feeling this horse really wanted to eat from her hand and reward her patience and perseverance, but was battling many layers of fear thanks to a lot of mistreatment. If she knew her history, perhaps that would help. She sighed. She'd tried looking the horse up. If there was anything to know, it would have appeared when she'd searched online. Her father would say she was being soft, that she should quit while she was behind. But she was beginning to see that she didn't agree with all her father's methods and philosophies.

A part of her knew that the risk and work would most likely far outweigh any reward. But it did feel good to have focus again and a challenge, though she could do with one that was easier on her patience. She would have loved to have just got in the yard and pushed more directly, but with such an unknown quantity, and considering her recent injury, it wasn't wise to expose herself to any danger while no one was home.

'Come on, now have some pellets and I'll leave you in peace,' she said, rattling the bucket. The horse pricked her ears and took one small but bold step forwards. Suddenly Faith was standing right in front of her. She held the bucket close to her – out of Faith's reach – and slowly put her hand out towards the horse's face. Faith took a leap aside, away from her hand. Damn it! She would have definitely tossed the bucket and walked away if it wouldn't have set her back further.

God damn it, she was Steve's bloody horse! Jessica didn't need to be doing this. But the itch of the need to win kept her standing there rattling the bucket gently and cooing soothingly at the horse.

It took another fifteen minutes, and she could barely believe it actually happened, but the horse was finally standing in front of her, eating pellets from her hands. It was a small step that had taken an hour to achieve. And she still hadn't actually touched the horse. But it was something.

As she stood there surveying the situation, she had the uneasy feeling that it was not she who was in control. Nor was it she who had won this small battle. She longed to rub Faith's face and lavish her with praise, but clearly that was for another day. Instead, she placed the bucket with the few remaining pellets on the ground just inside the fence as a reward, and walked away.

Thank Christ no one was planning to ride the damned creature. She shook her head slowly as she made her way back to the house. And how long would it take to get her to a stage where the farrier could visit? Faith would need her feet done soon.

She kicked off her boots and went into the kitchen to put the kettle on. Oh well, one step at a time.

Bloody Steve. She wasn't sure why she was annoyed with him, and she wasn't sure she now had the energy or inclination to woo him tonight. She wasn't really looking forward to confessing she hadn't got far with the horse. *I'm meant to be the horse person, for Christ's sake!*

With a jolt, she realised she was feeling competitive with Steve. Over a bloody horse, of all things! It did not bode well. Perhaps she should admit Faith was beyond her and that it would be best to pass her on. Fattened up, they'd get a decent amount at the abattoir. But the itch of determination niggled at Jessica painfully.

Admitting defeat wasn't really in her nature. Her father would turn in his grave if he knew she'd given up on a horse because it wouldn't come up to her. Even worse, that she couldn't *get* it to come to her. No, he'd have it cornered in the yard and, watching out for flying feet, would demand it do as it was told. Perhaps that was how they'd got Faith on the float in the first place the other day.

Yes, she probably could 'break' her, but she still had the odd feeling that taking a longer, slower route would get a better result. She almost snorted. You couldn't get much slower than today. And anyway, what result?

She was intrigued by this horse and was beginning to feel there was a lot more to Faith than met the eye. So the need to at least figure her out a little had been ignited. And she had to be able to be handled – what if she got injured and needed treatment?

And it was clear Steve wouldn't let Jessica off the hook easily – the horse had got under his skin too. What was it about this creature that had them both turning so soft? *Ridiculous*, she thought, sipping her tea.

★

'Something smells good,' Steve said, as he took his boots off at the door.

'Hey, how was your day?' Jessica called from the pan of sauce she was stirring at the stove.

'Exhausting. Ooh, is that what I think it is?'

'I don't know; what do you think it is?' Jessica said, grinning cheekily.

'Ooh, it is,' he said, peering into the slow cooker and seeing the lamb shanks. 'Goodie.' He wrapped his arms around Jessica's waist and kissed her on the neck. They both agreed the weather was never too warm for braised lamb shanks.

'Wine?' he asked, as he let her go.

'Yes, please.'

Jessica watched, smiling, as Steve made his way from the cupboard where the wine glasses were kept to the drawer where the corkscrew lived. Feeling that they were at least a little back in sync was nice. So far, so good for her evening.

'So, how was Faith?' Steve asked wearily, after a long slug of wine and a deep sigh.

'Okay.'

'Did you spend some time with her?'

'I did.'

'And ...?'

'Well, the good news is it's not just you she's afraid of.'

'Right, so that would mean the bad news is she's a write-off all round then,' he said, clearly dejected.

'No, I didn't say that,' Jessica said, shaking her head slowly.

A day ago that was exactly what she'd been hoping for – to be able to have a good reason for getting rid of the horse. But she'd obviously caught the bug she'd dreaded. Rather than feeling annoyed with herself, she felt better than she had since the accident; she liked the feeling of purpose, of determination coursing through her. It was good for her, she'd realised as she'd stared in the mirror earlier and noted the colour in her cheeks and the glint in her eye. Tiffany had been spot on with her observation.

'So things can't have gone that badly then?' Steve said.

'Well, it took an hour for her to take a carrot and a few pellets from my hand – and I was on the other side of the fence. So it wasn't exactly a piece of cake.'

'Oh.'

A thought occurred to her. 'Is she actually broken in? Do you know?'

'Yes. Well, I was told she is.'

'I wonder if she's ever been ridden.'

'It doesn't really matter, does it? If she's just going to be a pet.'

'Hmm, I guess not.' This whole idea of having useless horses in paddocks still grated on Jessica.

'How's the leg doing?'

'Great,' she said, and realised with slight surprise that it was the first time she'd told the truth about it in ages. In fact, now she thought about it, there was just a gently nagging ache to remind her of her injury. Otherwise, she wouldn't know it'd ever been fractured. Perhaps it might be safe to get in with Faith tomorrow after all and be a little pushier with her. Maybe then she'd see some progress.

This thought was still on her mind when they went to bed and made love. It was what she'd worked towards all day but, as she lay entwined with Steve – lovely Steve – all she could think about was how she'd tackle Faith the next day.

Later, when she was still awake and so deep in thought about the horse, she became very annoyed with herself – she was starting to get obsessed. Again. Already. Jesus, she'd missed having horses. She felt a stab of guilt at realising she didn't miss Prince and Beau specifically. That was a bit heartless, and far too much like her father.

She thought perhaps she could retrain horses banished to the scrap pile. And then she thought, *Yeah, right, because you got so far today.* The voice sounded so like her father's. Had he been prone to putting her ideas down?

Yes, she realised. She almost sat up, but stopped herself. Steve was asleep beside her and she didn't want to wake him.

Lying there, she felt committed to getting Faith back on track, to the point she could be ridden. The horse hadn't looked nasty, just frightened; there had been no mean spirit on show. Perhaps she might become a horse suitable for mustering the sheep and cattle. God, when had she last done that on horseback? They used the ute or quad bike. She'd tried with Prince and Beau but, really, they'd been too highly strung. They'd been okay, but it had been hard work – and certainly not fun – keeping them under control. They hadn't been the sort of horses you could hold the reins by the buckle and lope about without a care in the world.

Jessica was surprised to find tears spring into her eyes. Where had they come from? Pregnancy brought about unexpected waves of emotion, didn't it? But of course she couldn't possibly be pregnant unless it had happened an hour or so ago. And there probably wouldn't be any signs for weeks anyway. *Silly!* She crossed her fingers that tonight would prove successful and returned her thoughts to Faith. Tomorrow she'd get a really good idea of what she was dealing with.

As she was falling asleep, Jessica wondered if she should get a friend for Faith. She'd never liked horses on their own – they were pack animals. Right on the edge of sleep, she almost laughed at herself. *Listen to you: yesterday you didn't want any, now you're thinking of getting more.*

Chapter Twenty

Jessica woke up early and immediately felt restless. Steve was still asleep beside her. She wouldn't have minded another shot at making a baby, but she had plans and she wanted to hop to. Carefully and quietly, she got out of bed and pulled yesterday's clothes on.

Cup of tea, breakfast with Steve – if he got up soon – feed Faith and, while she's eating, get in and clean the mounds of horse poo from the yard. Normally Jessica kept her yards immaculate, cleaning them twice a day, but she'd wanted to leave the horse alone to settle. Three days was long enough and Jessica wasn't going to put up with an unkempt yard any longer. She really hoped she'd be able to catch Faith once she had eaten her hay and her full belly made her more relaxed. Then she could tie her up and get the mud from her coat and tangles from her mane and tail. She really hoped the horse wouldn't turn out to be a biter or kicker – Jessica knew she'd have to keep her wits about her.

She downed one cup of tea waiting impatiently for Steve for breakfast, drumming her fingers on the table. She could go ahead without him and had done so most mornings of their marriage, but since the accident and their subsequent slight estrangement, she'd felt the need to make an extra effort to connect. Sure, he could come over and lean on the fence and talk to her while she scooped poop, but it wasn't the same as sitting down for breakfast together.

Part of Jessica was keen to harness her enthusiasm, another part was concerned her enthusiasm might wane if she didn't get cracking. She was excited at the prospect of progress, no matter how small the step — excitement the likes of which she hadn't felt for years. She pushed her fear of making no progress with Faith from her mind. Sure, she'd had plenty of great achievements with horses over the years, but it now dawned on her that not since Jasper had she had goals this low. The last fifteen years had been about taking horses to the next level of competition, never actually getting them to first base.

The thought of getting Faith from her current wary state to being ridden and maybe even mustering filled Jessica with the same heady feeling of pride and accomplishment that completing her first high level cross-country round clear had and making the state team should have.

She thought she now had a better understanding of why Tiffany took on the horses she did. God, she really had been a fool, only wanting the best horseflesh. She snorted. Her father's influence, and he'd been the dominant force. She couldn't have pushed a different view even if she'd realised she had one. She felt a little sad and guilty for being a traitor to his memory and thinking ill of the dead. But everything had changed — she'd changed — the day of the accident. Just not in the way she expected.

When Steve did finally appear, fully dressed but tousled, Jessica was feeling decidedly edgy and keen to get her day with Faith underway, despite telling herself over and over that a half-hour, or even an hour or two, would not make one iota of difference in the scheme of things.

'You're early,' he said, coming over to the table and leaning down to kiss her. 'And look at you, you're glowing.'

'Am I?' Jessica asked frowning before getting up to put bread in the toaster.

'You are. Something you're not telling me?' he said, wrapping his arms around her waist.

'Darling, even if I am, I doubt you'd notice anything yet. It was only last night,' Jessica said. There was always a chance, but it wouldn't show up in a pregnancy test so soon. She'd wait before checking – negative results were not just disappointing, they were heart-wrenching. It was probably best not to know.

'So what's on the agenda for you today?' he asked.

Jessica shrugged. 'Going to spend some time with Faith. I don't think it's a good idea to have a horse we can't handle, in case she has an accident and needs a vet or something.'

'You say it like it's a chore. But look at you – the glint's back in your eye and you're definitely glowing. You're excited. Come on, just admit it.'

She hated to admit she'd been wrong. Worse, that Steve had been right. She sighed.

'You're right. I am actually. I haven't felt this fired up for years.'

'Are you even giving up your walk for her? Wow.'

It made sense: this was much more her thing. If she was brutally honest, pounding dirt tracks and pavements kilometre after kilometre really wasn't her idea of fun. It had been fine while she had to walk for rehabilitation and as a distraction while she tried to outrun her issues, but it didn't feel natural to her. She realised with a start that that was just what she had been doing – running away.

God, she'd got things so terribly wrong. But when she analysed it, standing there, waiting for the toaster to pop up, she wouldn't actually change a thing. She wasn't sure she'd ever be able to admit it out loud, but she liked that there was no pressure, nothing to strive for. How Faith reacted to Jessica's efforts was beyond her control. She couldn't make the horse be comfortable with her – that was up to Faith. Goodness only knew what the horse had been through and how deep the fear and damage ran. Jessica could only offer kindness and understanding, and take things one slow step at a time. It might take weeks, possibly months, before she could get a saddle on her, let alone climb aboard.

And Jessica found she really didn't mind. It was weird, and again probably wasn't something she'd admit to out loud, but she felt in Faith's case – well, her relationship with Faith – that it was all about the journey, not the destination. It dawned on her that she felt the same way about falling pregnant. Yes, it was something she badly wanted, something she knew Steve wanted so much too, but it was out of their hands. If they were supposed to have a baby, they would – she'd just make sure they took every opportunity to plant the seed. She could almost hear her father yelling at her that that kind of thinking was a lot of poppycock. That she'd gone soft. Maybe she had gone soft, but she didn't care.

'Are you okay?' Steve asked, jolting Jessica back to the present.

'Just thinking about Dad. He'd have had a fit if he'd seen Faith.'

'Hmm.'

'So what are you up to today?'

'Another clearing sale. It seems to be the season for them. Sadly, a sign of more farmers going to the wall,' he said. 'They must be pretty desperate for money to have sales when people are harvesting crops.'

Jessica wanted to tell him not to bring home any more sad, sorry horses, but realised she wouldn't mind if he did return with another lost soul. If Faith didn't seem so content alone, she might have even encouraged it. But Steve had said the horse had been alone when purchased, and she certainly hadn't spent hours whinnying and crying out for company. The only noise she'd made was nickering to the dogs when they went near.

'Don't worry, I'll restrain myself from buying another horse,' Steve said, grinning. 'I seriously don't know what came over me.' He shook his head. 'How many horses have I seen and not felt the need to rescue? I tell you, there's something about her. I couldn't resist her and now you can't. She's got magical powers or something.'

'Possessed, more like, the way she's been behaving,' Jessica said with a laugh. 'But, seriously, I wish we knew more about her. If I knew what her problems stemmed from it'd be easier to figure her out.'

'I've told you all I know, which is practically nothing. She was standing looking sad in the paddock, an old lady – the owner, I suppose – all but begged me to take her, and I just couldn't leave her there. Even though she clearly hates me,' he added with a sigh.

I'm glad you couldn't leave her there, Jessica thought, but she wasn't prepared to lay all her cards on the table just yet.

'You're not planning on riding her, are you?' Steve said. 'Only I don't think it's a good idea if no one's here – especially since your leg and everything.'

'I agree. And, no; she's a long way off that yet. I'm just hoping she'll let me in the yard to clean it without freaking out. And then maybe I'll be able to give her a brush, or at least a pat.'

'Well, as long as you're careful. And keep your mobile in your pocket – just in case.'

'Don't worry. I won't take any risks. But I don't think she's nasty or dangerous – just scared.'

'Yes, but she can still lash out.'

'I know. I promise I'll be careful.' Jessica wanted to point out that she'd been dealing with horses her whole life and knew a thing or two more about them and their behaviour than he did, but wasn't about to put their progress in jeopardy. Anyway, she had to admit this was pretty new territory for her, too.

★

'Good morning, miss, ready for your breakfast?' Jessica called as she walked towards Faith carrying a biscuit of hay. The horse nickered and tossed her head. It was nice to be appreciated, Jessica thought, feeling a slight sense of triumph. This was the first time the horse had shown any positive feeling towards humans at all. She chose to take it as a good sign and refused to admit that the dogs beside her or the hay in her arms might actually be the intended targets of the affection.

She put the hay in the tub from outside the yard. Faith walked over and stood beside the hay with her head up, clearly not wanting to eat while being observed so closely. Jessica held her ground.

'It's okay. Eat. I'm not going to hurt you.' She figured the horse still had to be pretty hungry, so would give in and eat before long. She'd stand there as long as was necessary, but saw this as an important first step in their bonding – building trust. Once the horse was comfortable enough with her presence to eat she could get in and clean the yard.

With her arms folded across the top rail, Jessica waited. It took just a few minutes for the horse to lower her head gingerly and begin munching, keeping her gaze fixed on Jessica. When Jessica backed away to go and get the pooper scooper basket and scraper, Faith lifted her head to watch before resuming eating.

Jessica leant over the fence to put the implements inside the far corner of the yard, took a deep breath, and then entered through the small gate. Faith shifted position to keep Jessica in view.

'It's okay, girl, just going to get rid of the poo,' Jessica cooed, and got on with the job.

So far, so good, she thought as she looked at the half of the yard she'd cleaned. Some horses did their business in one spot. Faith clearly didn't – there were clumps deposited all over the place. Jessica wondered if she should try her luck and get close to the horse for the last few mounds or wait until she'd finished her hay and moved away. But the horse didn't seem at all uneasy with her moving about the yard with pooper scooper in hand, so she gave it a go. She approached until she was around a metre and a half away from the horse. She leant down and reached out.

Suddenly there was a snort and the sound of scrambling hooves and Faith bolted past Jessica to the other side of the yard, hard up against the railing.

'Come on, silly thing, it's just me. You're fine,' Jessica said. She was a little annoyed at herself for pushing too far and a little annoyed at Faith for not trusting her. *Not having* faith *in her*, she thought ironically, as she finished collecting the mounds while Faith was out of the way. She dumped them in the trailer nearby. She'd give the horse the time and space to finish her hay in peace and come back later. She needed a cup of tea anyway, after the fright she'd got. Her heart was pounding.

Halfway to the house she paused and turned to see Faith back at her feed bin, apparently relaxed again. The dogs lay in the sun nearby.

When Jessica returned to Faith's yard with her box of grooming equipment and halter with lead rope attached, the horse was standing with her back to the house. Her ears were twitching and taking in every noise and movement around her.

'Take two,' Jessica muttered. Halter in hand, she re-entered the yard and approached Faith.

The horse lifted her head and took a step backwards.

'Come on, girl, it's okay. I'm just going to give you a nice brush.' Jessica didn't want to tempt fate by not tying up the horse to keep track of where the front and back ends – the dangerous bits – were at all times while she groomed her. Horses could move incredibly quickly when they wanted to.

She walked directly up to Faith, who seemed so taken aback by her boldness that she stood, mesmerised, as Jessica slipped the halter over her nose and carefully eased the strap around behind her ears before doing it up firmly. In seconds she was tugging on the rope and urging the horse forwards, and the horse was following.

Good, the bold approach seems to work, she thought, as she tied Faith up to the rail. The horse dropped her head in what could have been submission, or could have been a simple inspection of her feed bin for any last remnants. Jessica ran her hands along the horse's body, patting her all over firmly. Not once did Faith flinch, but Jessica did as she touched the visible ribs and hip bones.

Taking a deep breath, Jessica ran her hand down the horse's scarred, uneven near foreleg – what a bloody mess – then leant into her shoulder and gave the hoof a gentle tug. Faith responded by lifting her foot obediently. As she inspected the underside of the hoof, she felt hot breath on her back through her T-shirt. *Fingers crossed you're not about to bite me.*

She put the foot down and moved around to the next leg – again, clear signs of having once been torn to shreds, most likely by a fence. She made a mental note to tell Steve that Faith looked like she might be prone to getting caught in fences and that they could only put her in paddocks equipped with electric fencing to be sure she wouldn't injure herself.

She managed to successfully inspect each hoof, noting they really did need some attention by a farrier. 'Good girl,' she said, back at the horse's head and rubbing her face. The horse seemed to enjoy it and closed her eyes a couple of times before opening them quickly again. She stared into Faith's eyes. They were kind eyes, but still with an edge of fear, unease. 'That's the formalities over.'

Jessica liked looking directly into horses' eyes and marvelling at the three-dimensional mountain ranges that she saw there. Faith had a very vivid set, and lovely long eyelashes. She was actually not bad looking once you stopped noticing the ribs and hips; there was a good shape to her face and apart from the scarring, she generally had nice straight legs.

'Okay, time for a brush. Let's get that horrible mud off you and see if we can make you shine.' Jessica was enjoying being motherly.

She bent down to retrieve the stiffest of the brushes from the kit on the other side of the rail. But as she stood up, brush in hand, there was another snort and flurry of hooves. This time, because she was tied up and unable to back away easily, Faith reared.

It all happened in a split second, but to Jessica it felt like minutes were passing as she watched the horse haul back on the rope until it snapped and she was free to bound to the far side of the yard.

Jessica brought a hand to her racing heart. Jesus! She hadn't had anything like that happen for years. But she quickly brought herself back – it was Faith who needed to be calmed down. The horse was wedged in the corner of the yard and quivering all over. Within seconds she was dark with sweat. *Jesus. You poor thing. What has happened to you?*

'It's okay, girl, I'm sorry. I don't know what I did, but I'm sorry.' Jessica was almost in tears, she felt so badly for the terrified horse. This was more than just simple fear.

Jessica stood a metre or so away, wondering what to do. The horse had her back to her – almost within striking distance. Jessica couldn't get to her head to comfort her and calm her down without putting herself in the firing line. No one was home if she got injured, and she'd promised Steve she'd be careful.

But Faith was terrified. She needed comforting, to be brought back from this fear. And if Jessica walked away now, she knew she might never have the confidence to face the horse again – and Faith wouldn't have any respect for her. She'd be letting them both down. Lots of people mistakenly thought horses performed out of fear, but Jessica knew they did what they did for their humans out of love and respect – and trust. It was the only way. How else could a fifty- or sixty-something kilo person get half a tonne of horseflesh to do anything it was reluctant to do? They couldn't.

No, if she didn't step up, boldly go up to Faith now, their relationship, what little they had, was as good as over. And, anyway, Jessica had seen a glimmer of trust shine through while the horse had been eating. This was just a minor setback. She felt for her mobile tucked into her jeans pocket.

'Come on, girl, we can get through this,' she said, as she stretched a hand out and stepped towards the horse. Faith was tense; a tightly wound spring ready to uncoil. Jessica only hoped she wouldn't uncoil in her direction.

'What's the problem?' she said, putting a hand on her rump. It was hard to tell, but she thought the horse might have relaxed ever so slightly. It didn't matter. What mattered was that Jessica was now beside the horse and had got there without receiving a double-barrelled kick to her chest.

Her racing heart started to return to normal. She tugged on the short piece of frayed rope gently, letting the horse know what was expected. She was surprised when Faith obeyed and followed meekly back to the rail where the rest of the rope hung limply.

Jessica stood there stroking the horse, thinking. Did she have a problem with being tied up or was the problem with Jessica? She nibbled on her bottom lip. No, Faith had stood fine, tied up for a few moments.

Until I bent down and picked up the brush.

Jessica wanted to tie the horse up again and do things properly, but didn't want to walk away and signal the end of things by going to get another lead rope from the shed. Perhaps the horse would stand there. Jessica bent down to pick up the brush that had been dropped.

As she stood up, Faith snorted and leapt back again, but this time only one large step. Better. Progress. But the horse was eyeing the object in Jessica's hand. Jessica's heart lurched and a lump lodged in her throat. 'Oh my God. Have you been beaten? You poor thing,' she said gently.

She held on to the brush, grabbed the short lead rope and led Faith forwards to the rail. The horse obeyed.

'It's just a brush. See,' she said, holding the object under the horse's flared nostrils. Faith was quivering all over. Slowly, Jessica put the brush up to the horse's neck and ran it down to her chest. She did it again and again until Faith seemed to relax.

'See, nothing to worry about. I won't hurt you.' Jessica made a mental note not to bend down and pick anything up in front of Faith. No doubt someone had picked up a whip or something, and given her a belting. Jessica's heart ached. The horse seemed to have a sweet nature, but sweet nature or not, how could anyone do such a thing to a horse? If you got angry and frustrated with them – and she had, plenty of times – you walked away until you'd calmed down.

It took an hour, but Jessica managed to rid the horse's coat of mud and untangle her mane. Her tail could wait until they were more comfortable with each other. The horse was still tense, but no longer appeared afraid; the shaking had stopped and she seemed content to stand there in the sun having attention lavished on her. It was a good sign. Her coat was still starry and dull – it wouldn't get a decent shine until the better nutrition had worked its way through her system and she'd been wormed. *That'll be fun*, Jessica thought wryly, imagining trying to get one of the paste syringes between Faith's lips.

Finally she went to get some pellets as a reward. She hoped that when she got back the horse would still be okay and not reverted to where they'd started. Returning to the yard, Jessica got a big buzz of satisfaction from watching Faith's ears twitch back and forth as she munched the pellets, her head buried in the bucket, trusting that Jessica wouldn't hurt her while she was so vulnerable.

Chapter Twenty-one

While Jessica waited for Dave the farrier to turn up, she brushed Faith, who really seemed to enjoy the attention. A week had passed and the horse was now quite at ease with Jessica, though Jessica was very careful not to make any sudden moves and to keep one hand on a part of the horse if she was reaching down for something.

Faith seemed to particularly enjoy having her head and forelock brushed and her ears rubbed. She stood with her head lowered at the perfect height for Jessica to oblige her, eyes closed and long lashes fluttering. At one point Jessica thought the horse might have sighed in contentment, but the stench that wafted past her a moment later told her differently.

When Dave's vehicle pulled up, Faith was groomed and relaxed. Jessica just hoped she would stay that way; even the best behaved horses could take exception to having their feet tended to, or the person doing the work. At least a good feel in the horse's mouth had revealed no sharp teeth that needed filing – another string to Dave's bow. Things still needed to be taken one small step at a time. Though in her experience, Dave tended to be quite well received by the horses. He was big, strong and calm, with a no-nonsense air about him. She'd never seen him get annoyed with a horse yet, even those who leant on him and those who fidgeted. And no matter how tight his schedule was, he always approached each patient as if he had all the time in the world and would be there until the job was done. It didn't take long for cantankerous horses to give in to him, and the battles were only ever on their first meeting. On his next visit they were usually putty in his hands.

'G'day, Jess,' Dave said, shaking her hand as they met behind the stables where he'd parked. 'How's things?'

'Pretty good. Leg's almost back to normal,' she added, to clear any elephants from the room.

'Yeah, I was sorry to hear about that. And that you'd moved the boys on.'

'Hmm. Didn't want them rotting in the paddock. And I won't do cross-country again. It really put the wind up me.'

'Yeah, we don't bounce as well as we used to, and when you've got farms to run and responsibilities, you really start thinking things through, huh? I totally understand.'

'Thanks.' Jessica smiled warmly at him. She hadn't realised how much she'd feared this encounter, this conversation – this example of everything and nothing being the same. She felt her shoulders relaxing and tension she didn't know she was holding onto seeping away.

'So how's the little one doing?' Jessica asked, remembering he had a small child.

'Great. Growing like a mushroom. We got her first pony the other day.'

'Wow.'

'Yeah, let the fun and games begin,' Dave said with a roll of his eyes and a hearty laugh. 'I have to admit to a stab of jealousy at seeing her kick the pony up and canter to the end of the paddock without a care in the world. She's only five for goodness' sake! Oh, to be that fearless again.'

'Ain't that the truth?'

'So I have to say, I was very surprised to get your phone call. I thought you'd completely gone out of horses.'

'I have. I had.' It was Jessica's turn to roll her eyes. 'Today's patient is someone Steve picked up at a clearing sale. Some poor, lost, skinny soul he couldn't leave there.'

'I didn't have Steve pegged as such a softy.'

'No, it's quite out of character. But this one got to him. Actually, I'm starting to see why – she's quite sweet. Though I suspect she's had a tough time somewhere along the way.'

'She? Gosh, Jessica Harrington, you are full of surprises today, aren't you?'

Jessica chuckled. Dave was right, she and her father had never had mares for competition – they preferred geldings for their more even temperaments. Though, again, that might have just been Jeff Collins' preference.

They stepped around the yards, giving a wide berth so Faith had plenty of time to see them and was less likely to get a fright.

'Here she is. Faith, this is farrier Dave. Dave, meet Faith.'

'Well, hello there,' he said, placing his bag of equipment on the ground a little way from the yard. 'Gosh, you're in a bit of a state, aren't you?'

Something in his tone made Jessica turn and look at him quizzically. 'Do you know her?'

'Yes, we've met before, haven't we, girl? And you're right on both counts, Jess. She's a sweetie *and* she's had a hard time along the way. Where did you say Steve found her?'

'A clearing sale. I can't remember the owner's name. Some old lady who practically begged him to take the horse.'

'Hmm, she would have,' Dave said thoughtfully. He was now at the fence rubbing Faith's head. Jessica noted Faith was instantly totally at ease with him.

'So what's the story?' she asked.

'Do you remember hearing about a girl, Talia Jackson, who was killed over at the Two Wells Pony Club one-day event two years ago when her horse shied and she came off?'

Jessica nodded. She hadn't been at the event – she'd been interstate competing – but news of the tragedy went through the horse community like wildfire. Apparently Talia Jackson had been thrown from her horse when it had been spooked on its first ever cross-country run. She'd been cannoned into a tree and had broken her neck. She'd died upon impact. And now a few more details were coming back to Jessica – namely that Talia was being raised by her grandmother at the time, after losing both her parents in a car crash. There was no way Jessica would recognise the horse's name, because she would have competed under a different, official, name – Faith would be her stable name.

'God, is this Talia's horse?'

Dave nodded. She felt some of her blood drain away – partly out of sadness for Talia, for her grandmother and for Faith, but also from a sense of relief. She was so thankful she hadn't ridden the horse yet – and she doubted she would now.

Dave must have noticed her odd expression, because he said, 'Jess, she's fine. It was a freak accident. She got a fright, Talia came off. Just one of those things.'

'Yeah. I know.' He was right, but still, she'd put plans to ride the horse aside now. Anyway, Faith was Steve's rescue project, his pet. She did feel a sense of disappointment, though. She had to admit she'd been looking forward to having a nice quiet horse to potter about the farm on. She looked at Faith sadly. Her entire opinion had changed. She felt like her whole world had shifted on its axis again. The horse wasn't the same creature as she'd been five minutes before.

'Seriously, Jess, she's a lovely horse. Don't give up on her. God, I wish I hadn't said anything.'

'It's okay. I'm fine,' Jessica said. But that wasn't totally true.

'Well, girl, let's see how your feet are. Bring her out here,' Dave said.

As Dave worked his way through tidying up each of Faith's feet, Jessica stood making small talk. In her mind she went through how things had changed and eventually had to accept that nothing had changed, not really. Faith was still Steve's horse and he'd made it clear she was staying, no matter what. All that was different now was that she wouldn't be saddling her up and going for a ride.

The thought sent another wave of disappointment through her and her heart sank. The horse was sweet, standing there with her head against Jessica's chest. Looking at her, Jessica couldn't imagine her capable of killing her rider. She really did seem to have the sweetest nature. Even the dogs around her feet didn't bother her. But all animals were unpredictable.

'Good as new,' Dave finally said, putting his rasp in his bag and undoing his leather apron. 'Good girl,' he said, rubbing Faith's face. He packed up his gear and they headed back to his ute. 'I feel terrible that you see her differently now. If you want me to come over and hop on and prove she's safe, just give me a shout.'

'Thanks,' she said, noncommittally. 'As I said, she's Steve's, really.'

'Well, the offer's there. She really is a darling, and it really was a freak accident,' he said, as he handed over a receipt in exchange for Jessica's cheque. He got into his ute and started the engine. Jessica waved him off and then took a handful of horse pellets over as a treat for Faith.

As the horse stood munching, Jessica frowned. She too wished Dave hadn't told her about Faith's past. It changed everything. She knew it shouldn't, and six months ago she'd have been up for the challenge of putting Faith to the test, but now she wasn't prepared to take the risks she once had, thanks to her recent accident. Her hand flew to her belly. She might even have a baby growing inside of her to think of. She glanced at Faith one more time and wondered if the horse realised that she'd killed her previous rider.

'God, listen to you,' she said aloud, 'now you're the one going all soft.'

On her way back to the house, Jessica felt a great sense of sadness for Talia's grandmother. The poor woman had had to part with possibly the last solid connection to her granddaughter; perhaps her only remaining family. She'd ask Steve for the woman's name and see if she could find her and assure her the horse was being well cared for. Was she in a nursing home? If so there couldn't be too many in the area. Yes, that's what she'd do. Jessica felt a little better.

Back in the house she thought about cancelling the vet's visit, but decided against it. It was probably too short notice and anyway, even if the horse wasn't going to be ridden, she needed to know she was healthy and not in any pain. She felt she owed it to Talia's grandmother to take extra-good care of Faith.

Perhaps all this soppiness and maternal feeling meant she was pregnant. But a little voice inside reminded her she wouldn't be so quickly affected, even if she was.

★

Jessica was enjoying a cup of tea after lunch when she was surprised and pleased to see Tiffany's car pull up outside. She was still feeling discombobulated after learning the news about Faith and getting restless to learn more from Steve, so she was pleased to have the distraction of company.

'Hey, what brings you by?' she said, greeting Tiffany at the door with a big hug.

'Just missing you now I'm working full time and wanted to see how things are going. It's my lunch hour, so I haven't got long. How's Faith?'

'Well, *that* you need to sit down for,' Jessica said. 'Cup of tea?'

'Yep. Sounds good,' Tiffany said, following Jessica inside and taking her usual seat at the table. 'So?'

'Dave the farrier was here earlier.'

'And how did it go?'

'Great. No problems.'

'That's good. So, what is it I have to be sitting down for?'

'Cake?' Jessica asked, standing with the freezer door open. 'I've got lemon and poppy seed muffins, chocolate cupcakes, carrot cake or plain cupcakes with jam and cream.'

'I've had a sandwich, but I'll never say no to your cake. Whatever you're having.'

'Carrot cake it is then,' Jessica said, taking two individually wrapped pieces of iced cake out. Tiffany watched while Jessica silently unwrapped the cake, put them on plates and popped them in the microwave to thaw.

'Jess? The suspense is killing me,' Tiffany finally said with a laugh as Jessica stood in front of the humming appliance, watching the turntable go around.

'Two secs. I don't want to ruin them.'

'Yum,' Tiffany said, when they each finally had a cup of tea and a plate of cake. 'So, what's going on?'

'It turns out Faith is the horse that girl fell from and died at Two Wells the other year,' Jessica said.

'Oh. Right,' Tiffany said, looking down and digging her fork into the cake. 'Wow,' she said through her first mouthful, 'great cake.'

Jessica stared at her friend. 'Did you hear me? I said Faith is ...'

'I heard you.'

'And you don't care?'

'It was a freak accident, Jess. The horse got spooked, shied, and she was thrown off and hit a tree, and died,' she said with a shrug, and dug her fork back into her cake.

'Oh my God. You knew?'

'Not really. I thought I recognised her the day I saw her, but it was only that night I remembered where I knew her from.'

'And you didn't say anything?'

'Like what?'

'Like, warning me not to ride her.'

'Why, Jess? There's nothing wrong with her.'

'How do you know?'

'Okay. I don't. But I do know everyone said it was a freak accident and the coroner said the Pony Club Association was freed of any blame. Jessica, all horses are an unknown quantity, a risk. I can't believe you're being so hard on her. Once upon a time this news would have been like a red rag to a bull for you – you'd have been itching to saddle her up and prove she's safe. Sorry, I really didn't think it was worth mentioning and, yes, probably because I didn't want you to be put off. I hoped you'd give her a go and let her prove herself. How many times have you said, "It's the combination of horse and rider that matters, not just the horse and not just the rider"?'

'I guess I just got a shock. I was actually thinking of saddling her up sometime. Maybe using her for mustering, checking the stock.'

'That's great. You should.'

'Hmm.'

'So, Dave told you?'

'Yeah. And I feel differently about her now. I know I shouldn't, but I do.'

'It wasn't her fault. And she's the same horse she was before you found out.'

Jessica knew she was being overly sensitive and pathetic, but she just couldn't shake the feeling that she'd taken two steps back. Oh well, perhaps it was good she'd had this wake-up call. It had happened for a reason – why wasn't Tiffany saying *that*?

'If you want me to hop on her, I'd have no qualms.'

Jessica started to seethe. If anyone was going to ride the damned horse, it was her! She was being gutless. First Dave – which wasn't so bad; he was well known for working with green and difficult horses – but now Tiffany was offering, and she didn't have a gutsy bone in her body! Gah!

No, stop it; don't be so ungracious. Tiffany is your friend. She's just trying to help.

Steve's noisy arrival prevented Jessica from responding to Tiffany's offer, and she was secretly pleased.

'Hi,' he called, tossing his hat and boots noisily on the floor and coming over. 'Hmm, cake. Yum.' He kissed both girls on the cheek and went over to the kettle. 'Another cuppa?'

'Yes, thanks,' Tiffany said brightly.

'Steve?' Jessica said.

'Yup?' he answered from where he was peering into the freezer, trying to choose a piece of cake.

'Did you know Faith's rider was killed?'

'Um, someone might have mentioned it at the sale.'

Out of the corner of her eye Jessica noticed Tiffany blush slightly and look down at her mug. Suddenly she had a vision of the possible description of Faith's lot at the clearing sale: 'Lot 68. Chestnut mare, 15.1 hands, white star, seven years of age, killed her last rider. Buyer beware.' She might have shared it and had a laugh if she wasn't so annoyed with Tiffany and Steve for their deception.

'Why didn't you say something?'

'And have you insist on getting rid of her? What does it matter? You're not going to ride her anyway. You said so yourself – she's nice to handle. And, anyway,' he went on, getting louder and clearly gathering steam, 'how many times have you said a horse needs to be given the benefit of the doubt – that it's the partnership that matters? But I suppose that was only fine when it was you justifying something you've brought home. Well, this place is half mine, so I get equal say.'

Tiffany was shifting awkwardly on her chair.

'Okay, fine, you've both made your points,' Jessica said, wanting to stop the argument in its tracks and tired of hearing her words parroted back to her. They were right – she had said those things plenty of times. She was still miffed they hadn't told her, but even more so that they thought she was so badly damaged that she had to be protected. Was she? She obviously wasn't the actress she thought she was. And, yes, she had become pathetic. But hopefully her caution would be warranted and she'd have a baby to think of.

She'd go back to plan A: Faith was Steve's pet and once their self-imposed quarantine period was over, they'd turn her out and she'd just become another four-legged creature wandering around a paddock.

Again Jessica was surprised by the depth of disappointment that engulfed her. She really had fucked up selling Prince and Beau. Though to keep them would have been a waste of their talent. And they weren't the sort of horses to be content pottering about with her aboard, she reminded herself. No, tomorrow she'd resume her fitness campaign and put horses out of her mind. Well, after the vet had been.

Chapter Twenty-two

The following morning Jessica went out to greet the occupant of the silver four-wheel drive. She had really hoped Steve would have been here to meet the vet and hold Faith for the inspection, but he wasn't. He was off on the tractor, spraying some weeds. And with spraying, timing was everything – it had to get done when the weather was calm and before the wind came up. He couldn't have hung around to do this, and it wouldn't have made sense to ask him when she was right here doing nothing. She wondered for a moment if it was a ploy on his part to make her deal with Faith and, in time, change her mind. But Jessica told herself she was being paranoid. She was ready for the horse to be turned out with the livestock, and to have no more contact – essentially to forget all about her. Her history was all too unsettling. On the one hand the horse was nice to handle, calm. But on the other, Jessica couldn't be putting herself at risk.

While part of Jessica was disappointed after having got her hopes up about Faith and having started scratching that itch, she also felt a little vindicated in her original decision to get rid of the horses. She certainly didn't seem to have the same guts and determination she'd had while her dad was urging her on. It was probably best her ambition had died with him. It made sense. She was free to move on with her life; devote herself to her family.

She refused to listen to the voice in her head saying over and over that Talia's death was a freak accident and it wasn't Faith's fault that her rider had fallen. And, also, the voice continued, how many falls had Jessica had over the years when she'd leapt back into the saddle unscathed?

'Hi, I'm Toby,' the tall, blond lad said, holding out his hand. Jessica was pleased he didn't know her and was spared discussion of her accident, her leg and the sale of her horses. He must be a visiting locum or recent recruit to the practice she'd always used.

'Jessica,' she said, offering her own. 'Thanks for coming out.'

'No problem. I'll just get my bag.'

Jessica hovered as he retrieved a large black bag from the back of the vehicle and then led the way to the stables.

'So, it's a new horse you've got?' Toby said, making small talk as they went. 'They said it was a simple vet check.'

'Yes,' she said. 'But I think she'll be more of a pet. My husband picked her up at a clearing sale.'

'Pretty amazing setup for having horses as pets,' Toby said, casting his wide eyes around the stables.

'I used to be an eventer,' she said with a wave of her hand.

'Ah, that explains it. Not any more then?'

'No, lost my nerve.' The words seemed to come out of their own accord. She was shocked to hear them. Oh well, there, she'd said it. As much as she hated to admit it, it was the truth. She had to accept that.

'Fair enough. So, any particular area or problem you want me to look at?'

'No. She's very underweight – we're working on that – but other than that she seems fine. I just wanted to be sure. There are quite a few scars on her legs … I'll just get her out.'

He put his bag down, opened it up and began searching for something.

'Well, hello there!' he said, clearly recognising the horse that was now standing in front of him. 'You're a long way from home.'

'You know her?' *God, who doesn't know the damned horse?* Perhaps he was at the event the day of Talia's accident.

'Yes,' he said, rubbing Faith's face. 'She was an RSPCA rescue case.'

Great, it just gets better and better.

'I'm from down south – do my share of pro bono work for them.'

'Oh. So what's her story?'

'These scars,' he said, pointing to her front legs, 'are a result of some fool hobbling her incorrectly and without the right equipment. They used rope. And she was left to die, by all accounts.'

'Oh no, that's terrible.'

'Yes. Someone driving past the paddock every day reported noticing that she hadn't moved in four days and wasn't near a trough, and didn't seem to have access to any other source of water.'

'God. Poor thing,' Jessica said, stroking Faith's neck. 'I knew something must have happened – but I just assumed she'd been caught in a fence. It's such a common accident with horses.'

'Well, I'd put money on there being a lot more to her story, but we only treat them. The how and why is up to the inspectors. But she'd definitely had a rough time of it somewhere along the line – she was initially terrified of being handled. Not in the sense of kicking or biting, but she'd stand there quivering. Heartbreaking to think what must have happened to have her in such a state.'

'Hmm,' Jessica said. She thought back to Faith's reaction to her bending down and picking up the brush and shuddered.

'She was really good to handle, given her injuries – her legs were practically down to the bone. Must have been excruciating for her. But she seemed to understand we were there to help. I patched her up and then showed one of the volunteers what to do and left them to it. Next time I was back there I heard the volunteer had taken her home to treat her and then went on to adopt her. So what's her name?'

'Faith.'

'Very apt, considering the faith she had in us trying to help her and the faith the volunteer had to take her on. So, you said she came from a clearing sale? It's sad to think it didn't work out with the girl who took her on. Now, what was her name? I think it started with a T,' he said, biting on his lip in concentration.

'Talia?' Jessica offered.

'Yes, that's it.'

'She died. Apparently Faith shied and she fell during their first cross-country round at a pony club one-day event.'

'Shit, how awful. Great that she got her to the point of competing – quite amazing given the state she was in when I saw her.'

They lapsed into silence while Toby concentrated on giving the horse a thorough going-over.

Finally he said, 'Right, just take her for a quick trot up and back.'

It was in Jessica's mind to tell him she hadn't led the horse further than a few strides and certainly not at a trot, but she simply followed his instruction. And it turned out Faith had been taught to lead properly: she was responsive to voice commands and didn't even need a tug on the rope.

'Great,' Toby said, when Jessica halted in front of him again. 'She looks good to me. Perfect for pottering around the farm, or whatever you want to do with her.' He rubbed the horse's mane. Faith stood with her head lowered, lapping up the attention. *She really is a sweetie,* Jessica thought. *Damn lucky for Steve.* It could easily have gone the other way.

'Well, nice meeting you. And good luck with her,' Toby said a few minutes later as Jessica swapped a cheque for a receipt. It hadn't exactly been money well spent, but at least she'd done the right thing by the horse and they could turn Faith out without any qualms.

Back in the house, Jessica couldn't stop thinking about her. The poor horse. How could anyone have been so cruel – to any creature, but especially one that didn't seem to have an unkind bone in her body? Her thoughts were brought back to riding the mare. Would she be so kind and willing with a rider on her back? Was the accident with Talia really a result of the horse simply getting a fright?

Jessica was still standing at the window staring at Faith in the corner of her yard, who was in turn staring out into the distance, when Steve came in ten minutes later.

'So did she get the all clear?'

'Sorry?'

'The vet. I saw him leave. How was Faith?'

'Oh. Yes. All good.'

'So when are you going to get on her?'

'I don't think I am.'

'Why not? Surely you're not put off by the story of her previous owner. If she was dangerous, wouldn't she have shown some sign of it before now? And don't tell me you're not itching to see what she's really made of,' he said with a smirk, his eyes twinkling as he came over and wrapped his arms around her waist.

'I'm done with horses. I told you that.'

'So why are you standing here at the window watching her with those cogs so obviously turning in that pretty little head of yours?'

Jessica stayed silent. It was frightening, sometimes, how well he could read her.

'Since when have you shied away – pardon the pun – from putting a horse through its paces?' he persisted.

'Since I broke my ankle. Remember that small matter of me being laid up for six weeks?' she snapped, louder than she'd meant to. She'd meant to keep it at a light banter, but she was unsettled by the conflict between her head and her heart.

'That was a totally different situation. And, anyway, how many years have you ridden – often on cantankerous beasts – without incident? Faith looks like a pussy cat compared to most of the others you've had.'

He was right. And she did want to satisfy her curiosity. But she didn't like him pushing her like this – clearly so desperate to fix her. As if there was something wrong with her, which there certainly wasn't! No, if she was going to ride the horse it would be when she was ready and on her own terms. Not that she knew what they were or if there would ever be any such terms.

'I think it's time we let her out. Just into one of the smaller horse paddocks. And just during the day. She must be bored cooped up in the yard like that. What do you think?' Steve asked, making an effort to change tack.

'Okay.'

Jessica seethed. Horses were her domain. She should be the one calling the shots on them. But she had to concede that she had forfeited that position by not embracing Faith the moment she arrived. She'd made it clear she was Steve's horse. The only way she would re-establish the natural order here was to make

Faith hers: start riding her; do something useful with her. But she wasn't prepared to do that just to make a point.

God, it was worrying that she was feeling so insecure and competitive with her own husband. They were meant to be a team, for God's sake. The question now was what she was going to do about it. Things had to return as close as they could to the way they'd been, especially if they were going to raise a baby together.

It was all too much. This thinking was doing her head in.

'I'll go and let her out and then go for a walk,' she said. 'I'll catch you later.'

'But it's almost lunchtime.'

'Eat, then, if you're hungry – don't wait for me.'

Steve's crestfallen expression pierced her heart, but she turned and walked away.

Jessica's brain buzzed with nothing coherent, just a general sense of unease and confusion. She frowned as she laced up her runners, called the dogs and walked across to the stables.

Standing at the fence in front of Faith, she felt a wave of sadness sweep through her. The poor horse. And now she was neglecting her too, by shunning her. As irrational as it sounded in her head, she couldn't shake the feeling that the horse was lonely and it was her fault. While Faith didn't neigh, she did look pleased to have company whenever someone approached her yard – her ears pricked up and she tossed her head as if in greeting. And Jessica didn't think it was all about the prospect of being fed. Even though the horse no longer showed fear, she still didn't dive straight into her feed bin. She really seemed to prefer human company over eating.

Faith was evidently what people referred to as a people horse – horses who loved their human owners and wanted to spend as much time with them as possible. It was usually the result of being kept alone, or having been bottle fed as foals and forming an attachment to humans that way. Jessica wouldn't mind betting that if there were more than one horse, Faith would still look to a human for company. She just had that look about her – as impossible as it was to prove. She'd never had a people horse, and had never been fond of the idea of them; from what she'd heard, they tended to be too disrespectful and pushy on the ground.

Before she knew it, Jessica had in her hand the lead rope she'd left hanging on the gate, the gate open, and the end of the rope clipped onto Faith's halter.

'Would you like to come for a walk with me and stretch your legs?' Jessica asked, leading her out. 'A change of scenery would be nice, wouldn't it?'

Jessica half expected the horse to become skittish outside the confined space, but she didn't; she walked alongside Jessica with her ears pricked, taking it all in, but her head was lowered, indicating she was perfectly at ease.

Jessica smiled as she thought about what Steve would be seeing from the window: Jessica, Faith and the two dogs all walking companionably down the road. As silly as she was being, she thought Faith was smiling. She could have sworn the corner of Faith's mouth closest to her was ever so slightly turned upwards. She patted the horse's neck, and she turned towards Jessica and gave a gentle nudge. She gave the horse's ears a ruffle.

'You're a good girl.'

What a lovely creature. And definitely a people horse. Jessica was surprised to find this thought didn't bother her in the slightest.

As they turned out of the driveway onto the public road and the wind blew their scents to the animals across in neighbouring paddocks, horses, sheep, goats and alpacas lifted their heads from their grazing and came over to the fence to inspect the interlopers. Jessica chuckled to herself. It was like the opposite of the parting of the sea. She felt like Doctor Dolittle, strolling along with her menagerie, though it wasn't as if she was being followed by a line of chooks or ducks. She was simply a woman leading a horse and being kept company by two brown kelpies. Nothing to write home about. Still, she couldn't shake the great feeling of contentment that had settled upon her. The sun was shining, there was a gentle breeze, it wasn't too hot, and she was leading a sweet, kind horse, who was ambling beside her with a smile on her face.

She led Faith over to a patch of lush, green grass and stopped. A horse, a few goats, a couple of sheep and three alpacas were nearby, and had resumed their grazing. Faith didn't seem at all interested in making friends with anyone other than Jessica and Laurel and Hardy.

'Go on, enjoy the grass,' she urged. But Faith just stood there beside her obediently and patiently, waiting for them to continue. Jessica bent down and pulled out a clump and offered it to the horse, who took it and then the hint.

After grazing the edge of the road for a few minutes, Faith was happy to be turned around and for them to make their way home with the sun on their backs.

Chapter Twenty-three

Jessica stretched out like a starfish across the bed, enjoying the feel of space and the warm patches on Steve's side – he'd left earlier for a CFS working bee. She luxuriated in the thought of a lie-in. Then she'd go for a walk and take Faith with her for another graze of the roadside grass; she'd seemed to enjoy that once she'd figured out what was expected.

And then what? Perhaps she might put the horse on the lunge and see what happened. Maybe she'd even be brave enough to hop on. Just a sit to make sure Faith was okay about it. With that thought she drifted back into sleep.

Jessica woke sometime later with a start. She was sticky with sweat. God, she'd had a bad dream. What was it about? Not the water jump one again, was it? No, thankfully she hadn't had that one for a while now. Not since … when? Jessica lay with her eyes closed frowning, trying to remember. It didn't matter. What was the cause of her being so dishevelled?

Snippets started coming slowly back to her: An old lady was standing at a fence, crying. Off in the distance was a chestnut horse. The horse was saddled but riderless, its reins hanging. Oh God, she'd dreamt of Talia, of her grandmother, of Faith.

Great, just when she'd managed to banish her own nightmare, she'd conjured up someone else's! She opened her eyes and was surprised at just how much light was in the room. It must be after nine o'clock. Since when did she ever stay in bed that late unless she was unwell? She took an inventory of how she was feeling and was almost disappointed to find no nausea threatening. When was she going to be blessed with a baby?

She threw the covers back and got out of bed. She was still sticky underneath her pyjamas and longed for a shower, but that would be wasteful. She'd wait until after she'd worked up a good sweat on her walk and from cleaning out the yards. She dragged clothes on, downed a cup of tea and two pieces of toast, laced up her runners, and headed out. Faith looked up as she approached, and nickered. Jessica smiled. She loved the unconditional love animals offered. The dogs, who had been snoozing in the sun, got up and frolicked around her, bantering between themselves and clamouring for her attention.

'Good morning, everyone,' she called. She felt brighter and cheerier than she had in months. She must have needed the extra sleep, though why, she wasn't sure. *Stop analysing it and ruining the moment. You're feeling good, end of story.*

Looking at Faith standing beside her empty feed bin, Jessica was overwhelmed by the feeling she just had to know more about the horse. And now. Today she would not take her out, but would saddle her up and lunge her on the arena. See just what training she'd had.

Bubbling with energy and excitement, she went into her tack room, selected a saddle that looked like it would be the best fit and a bridle that might shorten up enough for the face that was considerably smaller than any of those of the horses Jessica had had for many years. She looked down at her attire – track pants and sneakers – and deliberated going back to the house and changing. And risk losing the momentum? No way. Compromising, she slipped on her short stable boots and wrapped leather chaps around her calves and did them up. She stuck a helmet on and did it up before carrying everything out. She'd worn a helmet to lunge ever since a young horse had kicked up its heels on the lunge and nearly connected with her head years ago. It was hot, uncomfortable, and it made her head sweat, but it was worth it to be safe – especially when no one was around to call if anything went wrong. And, anyway, after a few minutes concentrating on other things, the discomfort of wearing a helmet always melted away.

'What do you think about being saddled up?' Jessica asked Faith, as she draped everything over the rail of the yard. She wondered how long it had been since the horse had been saddled. Perhaps she hadn't even been ridden since the day Talia had died. Would it bring back fearful memories for her?

Even with those concerns, Jessica found herself genuinely excited about embarking on a small quest to figure something out about this unknown quantity standing in front of her. Staring at Faith staring back at her with curious patience, she thought this might even be more rewarding than any run in a high-level eventing competition or being selected for the state or national team. God, she'd missed this.

Calm down, she heard her inner voice say, *you're only saddling her up and testing her on the lunge*. For all she knew the horse might have a flashback and freak out like she had when Jessica had bent down that first day.

She led Faith out onto the arena, which she preferred to use for lunging rather than her dedicated round yard; it kept the horses more interested and stopped them getting so bored. The horse was in a nice low frame and calm but alert, and seemed no different from before she'd been saddled. She'd accepted the bit just fine and hadn't used any dirty tricks, like moving so Jessica couldn't get the girth done up or puffing her stomach out to prevent it being done up tight enough to fully secure the saddle. Jessica felt cautiously optimistic.

'Who's a good girl?' Jessica cooed, rubbing Faith's face. The dogs had retreated to their old spot beside the arena, taking up their usual positions of heads on paws, bored expressions on their faces. Jessica smiled. It was almost like old times.

Except it wasn't, was it? Her father wasn't there in his deck chair beside them, ready to shout orders and criticism and offer the occasional gruff word of praise.

A wave of sadness surged through her and she swallowed tightly as Faith nudged her gently as if to say, 'It's okay', or perhaps, 'Well, come on, let's get this show on the road.' The horse's touch almost sent the gathering tears tumbling down Jessica's face. After all Faith had been through, here she was, still kind and calm and urging her on. Jessica Collins-now-Harrington, who had dealt with big, difficult horses and huge jumps for many years and who had a history of disliking mares and horses without impeccable breeding, was being urged on by this little misfit. *Get a grip, Jessica, you're being melodramatic and overly emotional.*

'Okay, come on, Faith, let's see what we've got. And walk on,' she commanded, very gently slapping the loops of the lunge rein against her leg. She fed out the excess through her gloved hands as Faith started walking away from her. 'Good girl. Walk on. That's it.' A slight sense of relief tinged with excitement rippled through her. The horse knew what to do. And she wasn't frightened.

'And trot,' she called. 'Trot on.' Again the horse responded beautifully. She actually had reasonable movement. Once the ribs stopped showing, Faith would probably look a half-decent piece of horseflesh.

As the horse completed her fourth circle, Jessica wondered if she dared ask for a canter. But really, what was there to lose?

'And canter,' she called crisply. Again the horse responded instantly. Jessica's heart filled, but with what, she couldn't quite determine. She scrutinised the stride. Not bad. Actually, really quite good. She was smooth and balanced, and quite long and loping for her small size. Jessica found herself making a bet with the ether that Faith would be very comfortable to ride.

But this might be her better side. As she well knew, horses, like humans, had a favoured side. To their better side they were always smoother, more balanced, found it easier to bend and flex. She'd have to see. She brought the horse slowly back down through the paces to halt and was especially impressed to see her stop on the outer track and not turn and walk in towards her – a mark of a horse who was well trained and obedient, and who had obviously done plenty of work on the lunge.

Jessica wasn't a huge fan of having a horse go 'round and around at the end of a rope, but it was useful to warm them up, get any excess energy out of the way and check for any lameness or ailments. She preferred to long-line them, which, like driving horses, involved two long reins. It meant she could turn and change direction without stopping them to unclip and change the rein to the other side.

But Jessica wasn't about to run two reins down the sides of Faith in case she'd never experienced that before, especially while she was alone. If the horse got a fright and freaked out and kicked her in the head or bolted and dragged her, she'd be in real trouble. This was a pleasing start. Best be satisfied with this and not push things too hard or too fast.

'Who's a good girl?' she said, rubbing Faith's forelock. 'Okay, how about the other way?' She unclipped the rein and went around to clip it onto the other side of the lunge cavesson underneath the bridle. She gave the horse a final pat on the shoulder.

'Okay, off you go. And walk on,' she commanded. Again the horse obediently moved away from her and started on a large circle. 'Walk on. Good girl.' She really did have a lovely stride. 'And trot on.'

Jessica marvelled at how the horse seemed equally happy and smooth and balanced going this way. She smiled at her calm, long frame. Yep, when she was well covered and her coat was healthy and shone, Faith wouldn't be a bad looker at all.

Jessica became mesmerised by her rolling gait as she watched her canter. And then she felt the ember of excitement that had been bubbling within her ignite into a fire. She was going to hop on the horse – right now. See if she really was as comfortable as she looked.

Shaking off the niggle of fear and trepidation – mainly about being home alone – she called Faith to a halt, rolled up the lunge rein, unclipped it and dropped it on the ground. Excitement fluttered in her belly. She tried to keep it down – she didn't want it to turn into full-blown nervousness and transfer to Faith and upset her.

She double-checked the girth and stirrup length, gathered up the reins and put her foot into the stirrup. Normally she used a mounting block so she couldn't drag the saddle painfully on the horse's withers, but Faith was so much smaller than anything she'd recently ridden she figured it would be fine. Hell, if she was fitter and about five years younger she'd probably have been able to vault onto her bareback!

Jessica sprang off the ground and leant her weight on the saddle a moment to test how Faith was going to react. Just an ear-flick of acknowledgement in her direction. She swung her leg over slowly and carefully, and lowered herself gently into the saddle. The horse shifted her weight to account for Jessica, but stood calmly and to attention. Careful to keep her wits about her, Jessica rubbed the horse's mane reassuringly.

'Good girl,' she murmured, and stroked the horse on the shoulder. 'Who's a good girl?' She tightened her reins after a few moments sitting quietly, applied a little leg pressure and said, 'Walk on, Faith.' The horse responded.

Jessica made her way around the outer edge of the arena, concentrating on feeling the horse's stride beneath her. Just as she'd looked on the lunge, she felt smooth, even and light. After one full lap she gathered up the reins tighter to indicate something was going to happen and that the horse needed to pay attention, then applied more leg pressure, and said, 'And trot. Good girl, trot on.'

Jessica was instantly surprised and impressed at how even Faith's trot was – even better than she'd looked from the ground. As she made her way around the arena, Jessica found Faith's stride was equally comfortable to sit-trot to as it was to rise to.

Gosh, what a lovely little horse, she thought, looking along the neck that was lowered nicely in front of her. She longed to really gather her up into a shortened frame and then, after that, ask for a longer, medium trot – really put the horse through her paces. It was just so exciting. But she curbed her enthusiasm; pushing for too much too soon could end in a boilover and huge setback. She didn't think it would happen in this case – Faith seemed far too at ease and willing – but horses were horses and she'd been well indoctrinated by her father to always expect the unexpected and not become complacent.

Horses had brains and anything could go wrong in a split second. As well she knew. She shook the thought aside. She wasn't going to allow any negative memories to seep in and ruin this.

Dare she try for a canter? Yes, just a few strides. She gathered Faith up and applied her legs correctly. 'And, canter.' Again the horse responded beautifully. Canter could often be a little tricky but there wasn't even the extra leap that so often happened with a new combination before they figured out how much pressure was needed and what response was expected.

Jessica wanted to let out a cheer, feeling like she was a little girl all over again, saying, 'Look, Dad, no hands,' for the first time. But she didn't want to scare Faith. And, anyway, there was no one around to hear or see. She felt a wave of disappointment, but pushed it aside. She was a grown woman with years' worth of similar horse experiences, for goodness' sake.

As with her other paces, Faith's canter was beautiful and easy to sit to, just like a nice comfortable rocking chair. After a lap of the arena, Jessica brought Faith back to trot, then walk, and then halt. She didn't want to push her luck. Another golden rule with horses was to always aim to end a work session on a good note. Anyway, the poor horse was starting to darken with the first signs of sweat. She probably hadn't been ridden at all in the two years since that accident.

Jessica got off and made a big fuss of the horse, who lowered her head and buried her face in Jessica's chest in what Jessica took to be affection. Although she might just be tired and relieved her rider had dismounted.

'What a gorgeous girl you are. Thank you,' Jessica said. She was surprised to find tears filling her eyes, and a few escaping down her cheeks. Her heart swelled and her chest began to tighten.

'Would you like a hose off?' she asked. 'I think you would, since you seem to like water so much, cheeky thing.' She put an arm over Faith's neck.

As she turned to walk back to the stable yard, she started slightly at seeing Tiffany standing in the shade by the corner of the building, almost out of sight. The dogs were beside her.

'Hi,' she called.

Tiffany responded by clapping her hands and then saying quietly, 'Bravo! Woo hoo! Well done, you!'

'Did you see?' Jessica called excitedly. 'She's gorgeous!'

'I did. And, yes, she is,' Tiffany said, making her way over to Jessica. 'You looked great together.'

'She was awesome,' Jessica said, grinning like a kid at Christmas.

Tiffany beamed back. 'I'm so pleased for you.' She hugged her friend briefly before reaching out and patting Faith, who offered a friendly nudge in return. 'What a sweetie.'

'And did you see her move? I would never have believed it.'

'Is she easy to sit to? Looks like it; though you always look effortless in the saddle.'

'Beautiful,' Jessica said with a sigh. 'I'm just going to hose her off since she seems to like water.'

'Okay. I'd offer to help, but ...' Tiffany said, indicating her uniform with both hands.

'No worries. Just a quick hose off then I'll be with you. Are you on your way to or from work?'

'Both. I had an early start to supervise a delivery. I'm on an early, extra-long lunch break. Sorry, but I need some company and a fortifying cuppa after having Betty Green in for an hour, quizzing me over pellet composition.'

'Oh God, you poor thing,' Jessica said, rolling her eyes sympathetically. Betty Green was well known in horse circles as being all talk and no action. She'd been on the dressage circuit for ever, but had never progressed beyond the basic levels. But by the way she spoke, the money she spent on gear, horseflesh, etc, she gave the impression she was on the Olympic team.

She apparently came from an 'old money' family – not horsey old money – and was desperate to fit in, but didn't seem to grasp that doing well in horse sports required some talent and a lot of hard work, and not simply tossing wads of money around. Jessica and Tiffany often chuckled that she'd be better off donating a stack of cash to the Olympic team and have it as a tax deduction rather than waste it on lessons with the Olympic riders. Though at least she helped keep money flowing in the industry.

They giggled as Faith turned her nose up playfully and then grabbed the end of the hose in her teeth.

'My Brandy hates being washed. This one's a real water baby,' Tiffany said in awe.

'Yeah,' Jessica said. 'See the new mini water feeders over there? That's because she definitely seems to have somewhat of an obsession – wouldn't leave the tub alone. Wasteful child, aren't you?' she said. When Faith released the end of the hose, Jessica put her finger over it and squirted her. She tilted her face into the spray and let out a snort.

'Righto, enough is enough, let's see how you enjoy the sand,' Jessica said, reaching over and turning the tap off.

The girls stood shoulder to shoulder, their arms crossed on the top of the railing of what had once been Jessica's round yard, but was now a dedicated sand pit for horses to frolic in. The sun beat a beautiful drum on their backs.

'I wonder if she knows what she's meant to do,' Jessica said, as they watched Faith slowly checking out the new space, having shaken the excess water from her coat.

'It seems so,' Tiffany said when Faith, having dug up a patch of sand to make it softer, began turning around and then bending all her legs, preparing to roll.

'Clever girl,' they said in unison as the horse gave a big harrumph and lowered herself to the ground with a flop.

Faith rolled over one way, paused to rub her back, and then continued onto her other side, covering her wet coat in sand. She rubbed her face against the ground and they laughed at how well she'd managed to plaster herself so fully.

'She's clearly done this before,' Tiffany said.

'Hmm. She looks happy enough,' Jessica said, after Faith stretched out on her side in the sun. Jessica smiled and made a mental note to not panic if she came out one day to find Faith lying in the paddock like this. When most horses lay on the ground, it was with their legs tucked up underneath them. Faith clearly preferred a pose that made her appear dead. It was a great sign she was so relaxed and trusting that she was prepared to lie in such a vulnerable position.

'Come on, let's leave her be,' Jessica said. She packed everything away in the stable before they made their way back to the house.

'So how's the ankle feeling after your first ride?' Tiffany asked as she settled at the kitchen table and Jessica set about putting the kettle on.

'Great. Wouldn't even know there was anything wrong with it,' Jessica said, her voice coloured by the hint of surprise she was feeling. She hadn't actually given it any thought while riding, and hadn't noticed if it felt any different. Now she was focussed on it, though, the joint was aching. She decided it was a good ache; riding used different muscles and tendons to walking and running. In fact, she felt a little tight all over. But, again, it was the lovely feeling of tired muscles that told her she'd exerted herself. It felt good. But, crikey, she was unfit!

'It's incredible that she's so trusting and relaxed, considering what she must have been put through at the hands of humans,' Jessica mused a few minutes later as they sat clutching their mugs.

'Hmm. She's a smart horse,' Tiffany said. 'Has clearly figured out what side of her bread is buttered. But seriously, this unconditional love and capacity to forgive that's part of most animals' makeup is just so amazing. I'd want to kill someone.'

'I do,' Jessica said forcefully. 'I'd love to track down the bastard who treated her badly.'

'Hopefully the RSPCA did and whoever it was got prosecuted.'

'Even if they did, the sentences are never enough.'

'Don't go there. And don't go looking online for court transcripts. Just don't think about it at all. Knowing exactly what happened to her and who did it will only upset you. Just be thankful that you've given her a good home.'

'Well, Steve did,' Jessica corrected.

'It doesn't matter who did, Jess. She's here, and she's loved.'

'I feel awful for thinking so badly of her when she arrived.'

'Well, you've been in a pretty bad place. And it's not your fault you were raised to be a horse snob.'

'Yeah, I was, wasn't I?' *On both counts.*

'Yes, but I still love you.'

'Thanks. I'm really starting to see how messed up I am, thanks to Dad.'

'God, Jess, that's a bit harsh on him – and you. It was what it was. And look where it got you. You were picked for the state team, for Christ's sake – that's one hell of an achievement. It was one of your big goals.'

'You know what?' Jessica said, looking up at her friend.

'What?'

'My ride today was one of the most rewarding and satisfying of my life.' She was slightly shocked at the forcefulness of her words, but she meant every one of them. She'd thought she'd enjoyed eventing, but perhaps that had been for all the wrong reasons.

'Wow,' Tiffany said. She raised her eyebrows and looked at her friend with a quizzical expression. 'Faith really has got under your skin.'

'I'm serious. I know I was on her for only about two minutes, but I felt a connection with her I haven't felt since I was a kid. It's always been me who's been the boss, demanded respect, performance. Of course I've had great partnerships over the years … God, listen to me. I'm not making sense. But I feel like something big has happened to me. At a soul level.'

Tiffany laughed. 'Jess, you're starting to sound all earthy like me.'

'It's just the weirdest feeling, like I've learnt something major, but I'm not sure what it is yet. Would you listen to me? I need something stronger than a cup of tea – or perhaps it's time to call the men in white coats,' Jessica said with a laugh, waving an arm dismissively.

Instead of laughing or teasing her, Tiffany nodded knowingly. And at that moment, Jessica felt awful for all the times she'd been dismissive of her friend's comments about the universe providing. Granted, she'd rarely actually expressed her scepticism aloud, although she'd thought it often enough.

Now she had the strangest feeling that Faith had been sent to her at the right time, and for the right reason. And no matter how

many times she told herself it was bunkum and merely a coincidence, she couldn't shake it.

Tiffany said there was no such thing as coincidence – everything
was part of the grand plan of the universe. Jessica was beginning
to see that. She was sad, though, to think that Faith had had to be
treated badly in order to eventually find her way here. And that
Jessica had to lose her father in order to be ready to see it all. She
almost burst into tears at the thought, but managed to swallow
them down in time. God, she'd become emotional lately.

'So, enough about me, how's everything with you?'

'All good. Busy. But good busy – manageable. Is Steve off at
the CFS working bee?'

'Yeah. Yet another one. The usual scramble to get everything
as ready as they can.'

'I wouldn't be surprised if they have to head over to New
South Wales to help. A few of the guys were talking about it at
work.'

'Oh.' Jessica had seen on the news that the fires were out of
control and that some homes had been lost and many more were
being threatened, but Steve hadn't mentioned they were considering sending a contingent. Not that that was surprising: there was
always a chance the CFS would go and help interstate colleagues;
they were essentially always on call. He'd only bother telling her
when they were actually called upon to pack their bags – often
with just a few hours' notice. He always kept a spare set of clothes
and toiletries in his ute. Just in case. She didn't like him being away
during their fire season, but it was just the way it was sometimes.

She'd stopped worrying about him when he was away. She
was always concerned, but had accepted long ago, in this regard
at least, that what would be would be and she'd deal with any

consequences when and if they arose. Jessica regularly consoled herself with the knowledge that at least if he was injured – or heaven forbid, worse – it would have happened while he was doing something he believed in and was worthwhile.

'I hope they get it under control soon,' she said.

'Mmm. Even if they do, they're probably still going to need reinforcements to give them a break for a few days.'

Half an hour later, Tiffany left for her next shift and Jessica went over to check on Faith. The horse pricked up her ears at seeing her new mistress, nickered, and was standing at the rail when she arrived at the yard. Jessica patted the horse, who gave her a kiss back. She giggled as the whiskers on the horse's chin tickled her face. Faith responded by raising her top lip and showing Jessica her teeth, making it look like she was laughing too.

'You're a funny thing, aren't you?' Jessica said, rubbing the horse's face. Her voice was jovial, but her heart was heavy, reflecting her thoughtful mood. She couldn't shake the feeling something major had happened, had changed within her, like her whole being had shifted a little off-centre. There really was something very special about Faith. Well, that's how she felt, standing there in front of the mare. It was as if the horse was sharing her thoughts, the innermost thoughts she kept locked up in her soul.

God, what is wrong with me? I'm sounding like a mad woman – in my own head! She shook her head to try to clear it and went into the yard with the lead rope in hand.

'A quick brush and then would you like a couple of hours in the paddock before your dinner?' she asked. 'I think you would.' After the morning's session and her greeting from Faith now, she was confident she wouldn't have any trouble bringing the horse in again. If not, she could feed her in the paddock. Except she didn't want to leave the horse unattended for too long in case she decided to play in the trough.

As she brushed off the sand clinging to Faith's coat, the thought that perhaps the horse was the spirit of her recently departed father came to her. That would explain their strangely deep connection, wouldn't it?

Shit, where had that come from? She wasn't even religious, didn't believe in spirits, reincarnation and such. Anyway, Jeff Collins would be represented by a gruff, cantankerous beast, not one as gentle as Faith. As hard as it was to admit – not least because of society's norms dictating that one shouldn't speak ill of the dead – she reluctantly admitted, if only to herself, that her father had been a bully. Yet whatever he'd been and whatever he'd done, she was sure he'd meant well. He'd just been a tough-love sort of guy. And she'd coped fine. It was only now, since he'd gone, that she was turning to custard and becoming a pathetic, overly emotional softy – and somehow that change had coincided with the arrival of Faith.

Nothing wrong with being a softy, Tiffany would say, and no doubt Steve would agree, if she'd confided her fears. But it was a new feeling for her; she'd prided herself on being tough, and it was all rather unsettling.

Jessica felt a rush of emotion as she set Faith free in the paddock. The horse looked around her and then trotted off, leaving Jessica with a sense of disappointment. As outrageous as she knew it was, she had expected Faith to stand there and not want to leave Jessica's side. But she'd behaved like any other horse who had been cooped up for days would.

Jessica turned away and walked slowly and heavily back to the house, wondering how she could suddenly be feeling so down after being on such a high. No answer came to her.

Nor had it an hour later, after a lunch of a ham, cheese and tomato sandwich, when she was still sitting at the table, watching Faith through the window, wandering about the paddock. The horse looked content and happy. That was the main thing, Jessica told herself, as she turned away from the window and focussed on preparing a lasagne for dinner.

Chapter Twenty-four

Having made the lasagne and tossed a simple garden salad, Jessica was starting to wonder where Steve was. He hadn't texted or phoned to say he'd be out for dinner.

Despite telling herself the guys often got caught up for hours and lost track of time, she had become quite concerned when she finally heard a vehicle on the driveway.

Her excitement returned – she couldn't wait to fling her arms around him, then tell him all about her day with the horse and thank him for bringing Faith into their lives. She put down her tea towel and practically skipped to meet him. She stopped short at the edge of the verandah before bounding down the steps. She frowned. The ute that had pulled up was the same colour as Steve's, but was a slightly different shape and a different make. And Steve was getting out of the passenger's side.

Brad Atkins, one of the CFS guys, got out of the driver's seat. Something had happened. She took in how slowly and awkwardly Steve was moving and her worry increased. Shit.

'What's happened?' she asked, looking from Steve to Brad and back again. 'Are you okay?'

'I'm fine, just had a bit of a bingle,' Steve said, trying to wave his arm dismissively, but wincing instead.

'He got T-boned at the Balhannah crossroad,' Brad said.

Jessica was shocked into silence. She stood aside as they went into the house.

'I'm fine, just a bit bruised – damned seatbelt and airbags. Got one hell of a fright, though. Ute's probably a write-off.'

'Jesus,' she finally managed to say. 'Shit.' She followed them inside. He didn't look totally fine. She was stunned, and felt like her axis had shifted again.

'Do you want a beer, mate?' Steve asked, as he settled gingerly onto the couch.

'Nah, I'm right. Thanks, though.'

'How about a cup of tea or coffee? And you're welcome to stay for an early dinner – I've got a lasagne ready to go into the oven,' Jessica said. She hovered, wanting to demand all the details, but was wary of coming across as a hysterical wife.

'Thanks. Just a tea would be great. White with one.'

'Coming right up. Darling?'

'Tea, thanks – apparently with lots of sugar; that's what the nurse at the hospital said.'

'So when did it happen?' Jessica asked after she'd brought over three mugs of tea – each with a decent dose of sugar – and had sat down beside Steve. She'd calmed significantly during the time she'd taken to make the beverages. It wasn't like he was so badly injured that he was still in hospital; he was right there beside her. She should be grateful it wasn't so much worse. Far too regularly Steve was called out to road fatalities with the brigade. And at least he hadn't been macho about it and refused to go to hospital to be checked out.

'Couple of hours ago. There was a bit of a wait at the hospital. I was following right behind,' Brad said. 'I called the ambulance – didn't want to take any chances. It was quite an impact.'

Jessica's eyes filled with tears. She swiped at them, embarrassed. Steve must have noticed, because he gripped her hand and squeezed it.

'I'm fine,' he said. 'Seriously. Just a bit sore.'

Out the corner of her eye she saw Brad, on the couch opposite, shift uncomfortably. She remembered she'd heard he'd split up with his wife the year before. Such shows of affection must be hard for him to watch.

Steve and Brad talked about what an idiot the guy was for not stopping, how the impact had pushed Steve's ute across the other side of the road and over the embankment, and how the other driver had insisted he hadn't seen the give way sign he'd gone through. It was up to the police to sort out now.

As Jessica sat and listened, she marvelled at how quickly things could change. Luckily, Steve was only bruised, but first she had been injured, and now he was. What else did the year have in store for her – she wasn't sure how much more she could take. She said a silent prayer for only good things from now on, then felt a little guilty for being glad that this meant Steve wouldn't be able to go to New South Wales if they were called up in the next few days.

'Well, I'd better get going,' Brad said after draining his cup in record time. He stood up.

'Thanks so much for bringing Steve home – and for everything,' Jessica said, also rising.

'Yeah, thanks, mate,' Steve said.

'No worries. Don't get up,' Brad said, gesturing for them both to stay where they were. But Jessica ignored him and followed him out – it would be rude not to, when she was perfectly able.

She waved him off, her brow creased with worry. How bad was Steve, really? It was often so hard to tell with men, macho men like Steve, she thought, as she made her way back inside.

'Seriously, Jess, I'm fine,' he said, noticing her worried expression. 'I swear. It's the bloody seatbelt and airbags that have done the damage ...'

'Well, thank God you had them.'

'... And I'm feeling much better after that cuppa. I'm sure I'll be one hundred per cent after your lasagne. And another cup of tea?' he asked, looking a little cheeky.

'Of course. Anything else?'

'No, I'll wait for dinner if we're eating early.' Jessica nodded and got back up. He was actually looking better than when Brad had first brought him in. He had more colour and didn't seem to be wincing quite so much when he moved or spoke.

'So, I see Faith's out in the paddock.'

'Yes. It's been quite an exciting day here, too – though in a completely different, better, way to yours,' she said, refilling their mugs. She peered out the window. All was well; the horse had her head down, grazing.

'Oh? Do tell.'

Jessica told him every little detail of what she'd done and how she'd felt.

'Seriously, Steve, thank you for bringing her home,' she said when she'd finished her account. She wanted to throw her arms around him and weep, but restrained herself.

'God, she's really got to you, too,' Steve said in awe.

Jessica nodded. 'As ridiculous as it sounds, I feel like she'd changed my life, that she was sent to do that, and right when I needed her.'

'It's not ridiculous at all,' Steve said, quietly and kindly. He carefully drew his wife to him and held her, stroking her hair.

'I felt the same way when I met her. Honestly, Jess, and don't take this the wrong way, but I was so desperate to help you by getting another horse. You'd been so down since the accident and everything – I probably would have brought her home even if the old lady hadn't spoken to me. I know you've tried to hide it, but you're not nearly as good a liar or actress as you think you are,' he said, smiling warmly at her. 'I'm just so pleased to have you back, though I have to say, you are a little different. Not surprising, given what you've been through.'

'I only broke my ankle,' she said, despite knowing exactly what he meant, and that he was right. She had changed, she was different to the person she'd been just a few months ago. She just wasn't entirely sure how.

'Well, let's just call her a gift to both of us and leave it at that, then,' Jessica said, desperate to fill the silence when Steve didn't answer.

Steve nodded. 'Good idea.'

'I'm really looking forward to seeing how she goes on a trail ride. Tiff and I are going to go to the forest in a few weeks when she's got a day off.'

'That's great. I'd crack the champagne to celebrate your progress with her, but it's the last thing I feel like,' Steve said, apologetically.

'Can I get you anything? Paracetamol, ibuprofen?'

Steve checked his watch. 'In an hour. Until then I'll have a bit of a rest here,' he said.

'I'll leave you in peace and go and settle Faith for the night,' she said, taking their cups over to the sink.

Jessica was careful to close the door quietly behind her as she left the house. The dogs looked up from their slumber on the deck and slowly got to their feet. The whole mood of the property seemed to have changed – it was far from the high of earlier. And, damn it, her leg was now throbbing.

Faith was grazing at the far side of the paddock, doing what horses in paddocks did, but Jessica felt a rush of loneliness. She swallowed it down. She was, no doubt, still reacting to Steve's dramatic arrival home and her new worry about him and his injuries. It wasn't actually a whole lot different to riding a great cross-country round, only to find someone else had ridden it faster, or only to lose a couple of rails in the show jumping. She really should be used to these highs and lows; she'd spent the majority of her life on that seesaw – hell, she'd thrived on it!

If the last few months had taught her anything, it was that she could do calm and even. In fact, she'd come to prefer it. And the events of this morning had been so different: she'd achieved on her own terms and without all the drama her father used to create.

Jessica felt a stab of alarm. Faith looked like any other horse grazing in a paddock. What if she wasn't special? What if their success this morning had all been an illusion; what if she'd made more out of it because she *wanted* Faith to be special? Jessica sighed. No, she had *needed* it. She'd needed Faith as much as Faith had needed her, them.

Really, none of it mattered. She loved the plain little horse and whether she had exceptional powers or not – how ridiculous to even think she did, anyway! – Faith was special to Jessica. And they obviously had something to offer each other.

Jessica went over to the fence, cupped her hands around her mouth and called, 'Faith! Faith!'

The horse didn't even lift her head – she hadn't heard. The breeze was too strong, and in the wrong direction. Jessica cupped her hands again, pursed her lips, and whistled as loudly as she could – she couldn't do the louder version using two fingers. She watched as, this time, Faith lifted her head, turned, and stared in Jessica's direction. Jessica waved an arm, beckoning the horse with her hand, before whistling again. Suddenly the horse was cantering over and Jessica's heart was in her throat.

'Good girl, what a good, good girl,' she said, praising the horse and rubbing her face while she devoured the carrots offered as a reward. She clipped the lead rope onto the halter, opened the steel mesh gate, then led her through and over to the stables. She felt decidedly lighter than mere moments before – just as she'd felt earlier in the day in the horse's presence.

Walking back to the house after feeding and settling Faith in for the night, Jessica felt content again. The horse really was such a joy to be around. At the door, she called the dogs to follow her inside. They'd given her so much comfort when she'd been injured, perhaps they might do the same for Steve.

When it was time for dinner, Steve insisted he was fine to get up and sit at the table to eat, and Jessica was relieved to see his appetite was unaffected. And that his colour was gradually returning to normal.

They went to bed earlier than usual and held each other carefully. Jessica had been shocked to see the deep purple strip of bruising crossing Steve's chest, and the large but less obvious patches down his right side. He assured her they probably weren't as painful as they looked, but she suspected he was trying to spare her additional worry.

'And, anyway,' he'd said, 'what's a bit of bruising when it could have been so much worse – like death or ending up in a dribbling, vegetative state thanks to a head injury?' He spoke so matter-of-factly that neither of them could find any words for a few moments, so they just held each other that little bit tighter. The embrace told them they understood the magnitude of the bullet they'd dodged.

They didn't make love. Jessica didn't broach the subject or make a move, and, anyway, she didn't think they could be any more intimate than they were right then. They were back, thanks to Faith and some random guy who'd had a moment of inattention while behind the wheel.

★

Jessica woke with a start to find Steve muttering and thrashing about beside her. In the pale glow of the nightlight she'd plugged into the power point – she knew how disorienting it could be to wake under the influence of painkillers – she could see his features twisted in anguish. She put her hand on his shoulder where there was no bruising and gently squeezed.

'Steve,' she said in barely more than a whisper, 'wake up, you're having a nightmare.'

His eyes opened and he looked at her blankly, confused for a moment before he seemed to focus and clarity seeped in. She kissed him on the lips.

'You had a nightmare. Are you okay?' She realised he was sweating at the same moment he seemed to. He pushed the covers off.

'I'll get a towel,' Jessica said, getting out of bed. She soaked and wrung out a facewasher in the ensuite and handed it and a hand towel to him from the side of the bed before getting back in. She bunched her pillows up and leant against them, slightly upright.

'Jesus,' he said, wiping his forehead and face.

'Are you okay? Do you remember what it was about?'

'The accident. I keep seeing the car coming at me, knowing it's going to hit but not being able to do anything about it. Then Brad, the ambulance, everything; over and over. God, it's horrible, Jess.

I've never been so scared in all my life. And I think dreaming it's even worse than the real thing.'

Jessica's heart lurched. She rubbed his arm. She was surprised at how grateful she felt towards him for sharing this with her; for admitting his vulnerability. And then she felt a wave of guilt for not having been able to do the same after her accident. How could she have been so selfish? It felt so good to have him share his pain with her. This was what marriage should really be about; sharing each other's pain, sharing the burden, healing it. Not going it alone, locking yourself away in a prison of despair.

She blinked. She'd been lost in her thoughts, aware he'd been speaking, but unsure of his exact words. Now they came to her as if an untuned radio had been moved onto a station.

'I can't believe the force of the airbags. That was pretty scary in itself,' he was saying. 'And then I smelt smoke. I'm frantically trying to get the seatbelt undone and you know when you're in a panic or a rush and your hands don't work?'

Jessica nodded.

'Seriously, Jess, I thought I was going to die. Burn to death. It sounds so silly, melodramatic, especially now I know the smell was the airbags and not actual fire. But ...'

Jessica noticed there were tears in his eyes. 'Oh, Steve,' she said, reaching over and wrapping her arms around his neck and gently drawing his face to her chest. Steve sobbed openly while she stroked his hair. It felt so good to hold him and comfort him. How could she have denied him – them – this? Having him tell her the details and how he'd felt was probably healing her as much as him.

It dawned on her that this was the purpose of the group therapy sessions she'd heard about. She hadn't been raised to share her innermost feelings, especially fear; to do so was to show yourself as being weak, lacking in moral fibre, not in control. But here with Steve, instead of thinking these things of him, she thought he was being incredibly brave baring his soul like this. And she truly respected him for it. She'd had things so badly wrong for so long.

Gradually Steve's sobs subsided and his breathing quietened. She stroked his hair a little longer until she was sure he was asleep. Then she kissed him on the forehead and carefully eased herself away and back to her side of the bed, though she kept a hand on his arm so he might be reassured by her presence and sleep soundly.

Jessica lay in the pale light fighting sleep. She didn't care how tired she would be the next day; she wanted to be there to wake Steve the moment he showed any sign of distress. She saw it as her job. She figured it was the least she could do for him.

Chapter Twenty-five

'God,' Steve said, the following morning when he woke, 'I feel like I've been hit by a truck.'

'Well, you as good as have been. Anywhere in particular that's sore – do you need to go to the hospital?' Jessica was lying beside him, having snuck out earlier to feed hay to Faith in her pyjamas and robe, her feet encased in rubber boots. Amazingly, she'd managed to hop back into bed without waking him. It was now quite late for them – almost eight. The dogs had been out and come back in as well and had resumed their positions at the foot of the bed.

'No, I just hurt all over. I'm stiff,' he said, sitting up gingerly and then testing different movements.

Jessica cringed at the anguish on his face. 'Well, maybe you should just stay in bed for the day. I'll even bring you breakfast.'

'Thanks, but I'd better keep moving, else I might seize up altogether.'

'Well, I'll do bacon and eggs – hopefully the protein will help.'

'That would be great,' he said, smiling through his veil of pain. 'Lordy,' he said with a gasp, as he got out of bed and tried to reach down for the T-shirt and track pants he'd left on the floor.

'I'll get them,' Jessica said, bounding to his aid. 'Don't overdo it.'

She helped him get dressed, watched by the dogs. She insisted on putting his socks and Ugg slippers on for him. As she squatted down in front of him, she thought fondly that this would be what having a child would be like.

'Do you want one – or maybe two – of Dad's walking sticks?' she asked as Steve slowly got to his feet and started shuffling out to the kitchen.

'I should be right, thanks. Come on, you guys,' he said to the dogs, who got up and followed slowly.

'So, tell me you're just going to take it easy today,' Jessica said, as they devoured their big breakfasts.

'I don't think I have much choice.'

'Is there anything you need me to do? Do you want me to go into town and get some papers and magazines, or more painkillers?'

'Thanks, but I'll be fine. It looks like it's going to be a nice day. This morning I think I'd like to sit in the sun and watch you ride – if you're planning on riding, that is.'

'Oh.' Jessica couldn't remember the last time Steve had shown any interest in watching her ride. They'd been together so long the novelty had worn off years ago. Just like she'd stopped walking around the golf course with him or going to watch tennis. 'I hadn't really thought about it. I could give her a quick workout on the arena to check for any kinks and then head out for a stroll.'

'Sounds perfect. Then we could head over to Balhannah or Hahndorf for lunch.'

'You don't think that would be overdoing it?'

'Sitting in the car, sitting in a café, then sitting in a car again? I think I'll be right.'

'Okay. Sounds good.' Jessica shuddered at remembering their last two recent lunch dates: the day Prince and Beau had left and the day she'd come out of plaster. At least Steve seemed a more amenable patient than she'd been.

She buzzed with excitement and pride as she saddled Faith and then led her onto the arena to mount. Steve was wrapped in a checked woollen rug and ensconced in a deck chair beside the arena. As Jessica glanced at him, she realised he looked just as her father had those last few weeks. Her throat caught at the memory.

'We've got an audience today, Faith.'

She put the horse through all her paces – taking care to spend equal time going in each direction and giving her a decent workout. The whole time she marvelled at her little dream horse, who hadn't put a foot wrong. She was definitely a very good find.

At one point Jessica even began to wonder how Faith would do in a dressage test. She certainly had the movement and the temperament to do quite well in the lower levels. Then Jessica reminded herself that she was over making horses go around and around an arena for hours, not to mention being pretty over it herself. And she'd never even consider appearing in public without putting all the work in and doing the best job possible. No matter how much she'd changed, she didn't think she'd be comfortable with anything less than the best. She never put a young or green horse in a competition without it being at a level far better than it needed on the day. She – and by default her father – had a reputation to uphold.

Finally, Jessica brought Faith to a halt and hopped off. She was greeted with applause from Steve.

'Bravo. Bravo. You look great together,' he called.

Jessica grinned back. She never got tired of receiving approval –
from anyone.

'Aren't you going to take her out for a stroll?'

'No, I think she's had enough for one day. Haven't you?' she
said to the horse while she rubbed her face. In fact, she'd worked
Faith far harder and for far longer than she'd intended. Old habits
die hard, she supposed. She'd better start feeding the horse small
supplementary mixes if she was going to carry on like this.

Was she? Sure, why not, while they were both enjoying it?
And Faith certainly liked the company and attention.

'I'm going to head back to the house. It's actually a little cold
when the sun disappears,' Steve said, getting up and gathering his
blanket to him.

'Okay. I won't be long.'

*

They fell into a nice, comfortable routine for the next few days:
Jessica riding Faith while Steve watched, trips into town together
for groceries, and afternoons catching up on farm bookwork and
TV shows from the PVR.

Jessica was pleased to see how quickly Faith was regaining her
condition. Her coat was now lovely and glossy, mainly thanks
to some supplementary feeding. Her ribs no longer showed, and
she was developing a good top line and sound muscle definition.
Looking at her now, Jessica wasn't sure anyone would describe her
as a plain Jane. But perhaps that was more about what she'd found
inside the horse than her outer appearance. Every time Jessica cast
her eyes down her legs, though, she was reminded that it had not
always been like this for the horse, and how lucky they'd been to
find her.

The only thing that niggled at her was the horse's penchant for playing in the troughs. She was fine for a few hours left alone in the paddock, but any longer and they'd look out the lounge-room window to see at least one leg in a trough and water flying about everywhere. While they were concerned about damage to the equipment, they were more concerned about Faith injuring herself and not having enough water. If they were out for the day and it was hot, it would be disastrous. Summer was fast approaching.

They decided that they'd put her down in the paddock with a dam. She'd proven she would come when called, so the longer walk down there and back would be the only inconvenience for Jessica; a small price to pay to keep Faith and their troughs safe. And when Steve was fully fit again, he'd change the large troughs in the small horse paddocks to feeders like in the yards.

They turned Faith out into the large paddock and walked back and sat on the verandah to see how long it took the horse to wander down and find the dam, and what she would do when she did. If in a few hours she hadn't discovered her water source, or for some reason didn't recognise it – quite understandable for a horse who had never encountered dams before – Jessica would go down and show her and leave a bucket of water out just in case.

As they watched, Faith walked up the raised earth bank of the dam. She looked regal standing there on the high side, like a general surveying her domain. The horse then made her way around the top to the low side where there was a gentler slope down to the water line.

'I think she's figured it out,' Steve said.

'Yup, certainly has,' Jessica said, as just moments later they watched Faith stride down into the water so far that it lapped her belly. They laughed when she began to paw it with first one foot and then the other.

'We should take her to the beach; she'd love it,' Steve said.

'Mmm. She really is a funny thing. So quirky.'

After a few moments of splashing, Faith stopped, but remained where she was.

'I hope she doesn't fall asleep, topple over and drown,' Jessica said. She'd never encountered a horse who so clearly loved water before. There were plenty who enjoyed having their faces sprayed and would grab the end of the hose and play while being washed, but this was something else entirely different. 'I wonder why she likes water so much.'

'Maybe she's lived at the beach before or somewhere where there's a creek. It doesn't matter. She's here now, she's happy, and our troughs are safe. I don't think we should dwell on her past. Let's just focus on enjoying her – and the future,' Steve said sagely.

Chapter Twenty-six

Monday morning, Steve headed out early. He'd returned to CFS duties five days after his accident and though Jessica was concerned it was a bit too soon – he didn't seem to have full movement, and there was still a lot of bruising, various shades of red and purple, with tinges of mustard yellow around the edges – she was satisfied that he knew his body. Anyway, he was a big boy, and a relatively sensible one. She had been wondering – a few times aloud – how much longer this year's fire season clean-up would take. It was meant to be finished before the season officially started, but they were running over a week late. They'd been held up because half their team – mostly the youngest and strongest – were away helping New South Wales. Thankfully they'd got all their back-burning done and were now just finishing off gutters and doing final checks around the place. Hopefully they wouldn't be out in the elements when the forecast wet weather and thunderstorms hit. Though, the bureau tended to be more often wrong than right. Nevertheless, it was probably a good thing she would be stuck at home – since Steve was using her four-wheel-drive wagon – and able to keep a good eye on the dogs, and the stock, and bring Faith in if fire looked likely.

They woke early Tuesday morning to the sound of rain. A quick peep out the bedroom window with the binoculars at the strategically placed rain gauge told them it had probably been gently raining for most of the night. They lay in bed for a few minutes in silence listening to it before Jessica sighed and said, 'How good does that sound?'

'I never get tired to hearing rain on an iron roof,' Steve replied.

He got up when his CFS pager sounded in the other room. They frowned at each other. It was unlikely to be a fire in this weather – more likely a vehicle accident. They hadn't heard any storm activity where lightning could be a factor, though it could have been elsewhere. Jessica reluctantly got up and went out to the kitchen while she waited for him to find out what was going on.

'Blocked storm water drains at the school,' Steve said, before she had a chance to ask. They both visibly relaxed. 'I'll get something to eat on the way,' he said, turning back to the bedroom to get dressed. 'I'd better get cracking.'

'Okay.' Jessica hovered until he left.

She felt terrible when she looked out the window and saw Faith standing with her tail into the rain and her head hung, clearly drenched. The last few nights Jessica had taken some feed down to the horse and left her out. Now she nibbled on her lip, wondering if she should bring her in. She told herself she was being ridiculous – horses lived outdoors just fine. And Faith certainly did. Though for a horse who'd taken two dips in the dam every day since being introduced to it, she certainly didn't seem to be enjoying the weather.

Jessica turned away from the window, telling herself the horse wasn't cold and shivering, she only looked miserable because of the way she was standing. One glance at the weather station told her to stop worrying – it was nineteen degrees outside, for goodness' sake. Jessica set about having breakfast and wondering how to spend a wet day inside. She wasn't a fan of riding in the rain – it meant too much gear to clean and dry off afterwards.

It was while she was sitting with her second cup of coffee after her toast and peanut butter drizzled with honey that Jessica heard the first roll and clap of thunder. She started slightly and went to the window. Faith held her head high and was up on her toes.

Jessica grabbed a coat at the door 'Right,' she said to the dogs, 'you guys stay here.' But she hardly needed to – they barely looked up from the couch they were sharing.

Jessica raced down to the paddock and pulled the lead rope from the gate. Faith was already in front of her. A few strikes of lightning lit up the dark sky in the distance.

'Come on, girl, let's get you in.' She looked across at the newly weaned lambs in the left paddock, huddled against the trees, and the cattle in the far paddock on the other side of the creek. They were moving about, unmistakeably rattled. Hopefully they would settle soon. The ewes were up the back of the property behind the house and out of sight – most likely sheltering against the row of pine trees on the boundary. Faith led the way, keen to get to the safely of her stable. Jessica had to jog to keep up.

She had locked Faith in the stable and was halfway back to the house when a blinding display of lightning illuminated the sky above her, followed by deafening roll of thunder. The rain pelted down the moment she got inside the house.

'Golly, it's rough out there,' she told the dogs, who raised their heads and flapped their tails before settling back down to snooze. All around the house the sky was a deep purple. The storm really seemed to have set in – this was more than just a few passing showers.

Jessica made a cup of tea and tried to relax. Faith was safely tucked away undercover. The lambs were in sight in the next paddock from the house and had plenty of shelter thanks to the blue gum woodland they'd planted along the fences and in the corners a few years ago. The ewes would be okay; they'd been through storms before. She checked her concern. They were animals and were used to being out in inclement weather. But she had every right to be concerned; the stock were their livelihood. She looked beyond where the lambs were, down the gully to the creek. The cattle would be fine. She had to stop watching them all; she was worrying too much. And it wasn't as if she could do anything about them being in the rain – cold was really the major threat to stock, and it certainly wasn't cold.

She wished Steve was home, just for peace of mind. She didn't think anything would happen – they'd been through plenty of spring and summer thunderstorms before – but she did feel uneasy. She wasn't sure exactly why. *Get a grip.* She looked at the dogs, a great barometer of trouble. They were relaxed, snoozing on the couch. Occasionally their ears flicked like antenna picking something up, probably the tension coming from her. She had to calm down.

'All is well,' she told herself firmly, and settled on the empty couch and turned on the TV. She just caught South Australia's weather forecast: risk of severe thunderstorms. *No shit, Sherlock.* She wrapped her hands tighter around her mug. The rain started coming in under the wide verandah and belting the window. The wind had picked up.

Suddenly the dogs were up off the couch and had disappeared into the bedroom and under the bed.

'Great, that's all I need. Bloody wimps,' she called after them. 'Call yourselves tough farm dogs.' She forced a laugh, desperate to keep the rising hysteria at bay.

She hoped Faith wasn't too frightened as the storm continued to rage. The noise in the stable with its iron roof and walls with no insulation would be deafening – it was pretty loud here in the house. Jessica was sure she could now hear small hail. She looked out at the lawn. Sure enough, there was a fine carpet of white. God, she hoped the lambs were okay, poor little things. Should she try to move them? Perhaps put them in the shearing shed up behind the house? The barn with the horse float in it would be closer. She stood, uncertain, gnawing at the inside of her cheek.

There was no way she could move them anywhere on her own. They weren't yet used to being handled that much and would most likely just scatter in fear. No, they were safer where they were.

Jessica wanted to phone Steve and double-check, but no doubt he was frantically busy. He'd probably have left the phone in the car where it would stay dry if he was unblocking drains, anyway.

As she scanned the property, she noticed the cattle on the other side of the creek in the bottom paddock were looking even more unsettled.

'What's their problem?' Normally they'd be standing still with their backs into the wind and driving rain. She frowned, squinted and tried to focus. They were too far away to see if there was a fox or something stirring them up. She grabbed the binoculars from the sideboard and turned the knobs to bring the animals into focus.

Her eyes bugged and her heart slowed as she took in the scene laid out before her. The creek was flowing quickly; it had filled and strayed beyond its banks. The flat was half under water and the cattle were on the low side – on an island, thanks to the fences. The area of safe, dry land on the narrow strip against the fence looked very small. The water was coming from further up, from neighbouring properties, making the creek rise much more quickly than it otherwise would have. There was no way of knowing how much more was on its way.

Jessica put the binoculars down and churned through the options in her mind, trying to keep herself calm and logical, and not let the heavy thudding in her chest deafen her. She didn't have a four-wheel drive. The quad bike might drown. The tractor? It could terrify the cattle, who were already on edge. They'd never before seen a tractor coming towards them. The last thing she needed was for them to take fright and bust through the boundary fence and out onto the road. At stampede pace, they would be on the highway in just a few minutes.

She looked down at the dogs, who had materialised beside her. Could the three of them do it? No way, she needed to appear daunting; she'd never manage to drive cattle across a creek on foot with two dogs. And it was too deep. If they did make it across, there was a chance the cattle could turn and trample her.

Out of the corner of her eye she noticed movement at the bank and pulled the binoculars up to her eyes just in time to see a large gum fall, the ground beneath it eroded. The bank was collapsing. Shit. How long until the cattle were swept away as well? She had to get them to safer ground.

Could she do it on Faith?

'Right. Let's see what you're made of, Faith,' Jessica said. At the door, her fingers shook as she struggled into her long rubber boots, tucked in her track pants, and then dragged a waterproof jacket from the rack. Her heart was racing. The dogs looked apprehensive. She didn't know what to do about them. Surely they wouldn't knowingly put themselves in danger? She didn't want to risk them drowning in the creek and they had to cross it to get to the cattle. She needed them; had to at least give them a go. The culvert under the road might still be intact. Perhaps they would be able to go around.

Faith looked surprised to see Jessica at the stable gate laden with tack and wearing her helmet. The wind howled and the rain banged on the iron. The dogs were quick to seek shelter inside.

'Sorry, Faith, but I need you. The cattle and little calves need us. Good girl. We can do it,' she said, trying to convince herself as much as the horse. She fought to breathe against her racing heart, having to take the occasional gulping breath.

Faith didn't seem too bothered about the prospect of being ridden out into the atrocious weather – apparently she trusted that Jessica knew what she was doing. She turned her back to the wind while Jessica shut the stable door and checked her gear. She took a deep breath. Not only was she setting out in this dreadful weather, but she was doing it on a horse she knew very little about. And she had no way of knowing how Faith would react to seeing cattle up close. But she couldn't stay in the house and put their livelihood at risk by not trying to move them.

'Good girl,' she soothed, as she led the horse towards the gate just behind the house that opened into the paddock. Halfway across, Jessica suddenly realised the gate could be padlocked. Their policy was to keep boundary gates locked, with the exception of the area immediately around the house, to prevent stock thefts. They kept a set of keys in each of their vehicles for when they needed to move stock. Where the hell was the set from Steve's ute? She hadn't seen him put it anywhere, and he certainly hadn't mentioned it. It was most likely still in the glove box in the wrecker's yard.

Jessica paused. Should she go inside and look? No, she'd keep her fingers crossed the gate was unlocked. Now she thought about it, she vaguely remembered Steve saying he hadn't locked it after going out late to check the ewes after more gun shots were heard the other week. If she found it locked, it would probably be quicker to get the bolt cutters from the shed and cut the chain.

She pressed on, Faith and the dogs keeping step obediently beside her.

'So far, so good,' she said, unchaining the steel gate and leading Faith through after the dogs. She closed it behind them and moved on to open the double gates into the next paddock – a larger area with plenty of shelter. Also, it was a way of showing the dogs where they were to drive the cattle – if she got them that far.

Finally she checked her girth, put her foot in the stirrup, and rose from the ground. Faith was tense and jumped slightly at a fresh crack and shards of lightning zigzagging across the sky followed by a rumble of thunder. It was so close it seemed almost right over the top of them. Jessica's heart leapt into her throat, but she had managed to swing her leg over and was safely in the saddle. She was pleased she'd remembered to add a neck strap to hold onto – she was holding onto it tightly so she couldn't inadvertently pull Faith in the mouth.

'It's okay, girl. We're okay,' she said. The dogs had their tails between their legs and were sticking close; they were very reluctant participants, but too loyal and well trained to leave.

'Right, so we're going to go down to the creek to get the cattle and the calves, and bring them up here where it's safe,' Jessica said. She set off at a trot. She was in a hurry, but was too scared to canter in case Faith bolted. That she had once before was in the back of Jessica's mind. And she wouldn't blame any horse taking off in fright in this weather. She just hoped Faith wouldn't.

Every rise in the saddle caused Jessica's heart to leap into her chest. Her legs were like jelly. She tried to breathe through it and stay calm, not wanting her fear to affect Faith, but she was anything but calm. Faith skipped sideways, trying to put her tail into the wind, but was reluctantly obedient each time Jessica asked her to straighten up with a nudge of her legs.

'Good girl,' she cooed, rubbing a hand on her shoulder. 'Good dogs,' she called to Laurel and Hardy below, though she doubted they could hear her in the wind howling around them; she could barely hear herself think.

At the gate into the creek paddock, she got off and pulled it wide open. The cattle, now less than a hundred metres away, stopped their stirring and turned to look at her. They were standing on the long, narrow island and Jessica thought they looked appreciative of her arrival. They were a formidable sight, all lined up, staring at her, Faith and the dogs, protecting their young.

A few stamped their feet, which wasn't nearly as menacing as it could have been, given a splash rather than a thump ensued. The dogs whined as if to say, 'Please don't make us go near them.' Faith snorted. Jessica gave the slightest sigh of relief. At least Faith didn't seem afraid of the cattle. If anything, she thought, as she gathered her reins to get back on, Faith was looking like she was challenging them. That was a good sign.

'Okay, guys, we need to get around behind them and then bring them through this gate,' Jessica said, as much to herself as the four-legged trio.

As she made her way along the fence, she wondered why the cattle hadn't crossed the creek of their own volition. They were on the low side; there was much more space along here. Jessica tried to push aside thoughts that she would have to cross the creek to get to them that kept creeping in accompanied with images of *that* day. *Stay focussed.* She had to concentrate. She couldn't lose it now.

'Good girl, Faith.'

She'd been looking for the best place to cross, but the end of the paddock was now less than fifty metres away – she was running out of options. The creek was flowing fast and quite a bit of the bank on either side had been eroded, especially on the few bends, which were now considerably more pronounced than they'd been yesterday. She hoped she'd be able to stay on stable ground. Faith picked her way slowly. While Jessica wanted to, needed to, move faster – she could see the cattle were almost knee-deep in water – she couldn't risk Faith tripping. Anyway, she could barely feel her legs though her wet pants, certainly not enough to make the horse do anything. She could only trust Faith to make her way safely. The horse seemed to know what was going on.

As did the dogs, who were bounding ahead. They knew that something was happening with the stock, because the gates had been left wide open and they were now making their way around the cattle ready to drive them back towards the openings. They were in work mode, heads and tails lowered, concentrating, and seemingly oblivious of the weather raging around them. Jessica observed vigilantly – she didn't want them to get ahead of them- selves in their exuberance and plunge into the creek to be swept away to their deaths.

She stopped Faith at the fence line where the creek disappeared under the secondary road just beyond their property. In front of her and to her right on the other side of the creek two capped fences turned the boundary fences into jumps. She shuddered, thinking of how she'd jumped them hundreds of times, as had members of the local hunt club, which she and Steve allowed to ride through their land in order to complete the run their property split. Now she could no more imagine jumping one of them than she could flying.

'Right, Laurel, Hardy, go right round,' she called loudly into the wind. 'On to the other side.' She raised her arm and waved towards the road and crossed her fingers. She hadn't given a correct command – there wasn't one for what she was asking them to do. She held her breath as the dogs raced off, over the fence and back over the fence on the other side. They stopped and looked at her for direction.

'Good dogs. Now, go way back,' she yelled, and waved towards the cattle. This command they knew, and off they bounded, barking, towards the tail end of the line of cattle and calves.

Jessica looked down at the creek. Jesus. She felt the blood stop in her veins. She had to cross it. But how was she going to make herself ask Faith to go into it?

She had a flashback of herself on Prince at the water jump. She felt sweat begin to bead under her coat. Her heart raced. But she was frozen to the spot.

She looked back to where the dogs were, just ten metres or so away. Perhaps they could do it and she wouldn't be needed. She wouldn't have to face her fear. But the dogs were at the cattle, and all the beasts were doing was snorting and trying to stamp their feet in anger. Laurel and Hardy had given up barking and trying to nip their heels to get them moving, and were standing motionless, looking back at her helplessly.

'Oh, God,' Jessica said. She looked back down to the water churning below her. How deep was it? She tried to picture how high the bank was when it was dry and compare it to Faith's height. She swallowed hard. There was no choice. She gathered up her reins and gave Faith a half-hearted squeeze with her legs. A part of her hoped the horse might refuse to budge, but another knew that the cattle and the dogs were relying on her.

She was thrown back in the saddle as Faith lurched forwards and dropped down into the water. Jessica held on tight to the neck strap. She felt the surging water swirling against her legs. It was up to Faith's belly. Jessica held her breath. She desperately wanted to close her eyes, but even they seemed frozen open, staring straight ahead.

Before she could have another thought, Faith had made two leaping strides, and was clambering up the unstable muddy bank.

Back on level ground, tears stung in Jessica's eyes as a wave of intense emotion hit her. 'Oh, Faith, you good, good girl,' she croaked, and patted the horse on the neck.

But her quest was nowhere near over. Jessica pulled herself together with a gulp, gathered her reins again and gritted her teeth.

'Right, come on everyone, let's move these guys.'

She trotted Faith as boldly forwards as she could in the soft, squelching ground, feeling anything but brave. The dogs seemed to relish the larger reinforcements and rushed forwards with renewed enthusiasm. They barked and nipped at the heels of the cattle, which had started shuffling away from the approaching contingent.

Now the herd was moving, Jessica settled in the saddle enough to consider that Faith must have done more than just encounter stock before. But her thoughts were brief: another crack of lightning and roll of thunder caused her racing heart to leap and remind her again of what they were doing and why.

Where the cattle had been was boggy, and a few times Jessica was thrown forwards as Faith sank into the mud. She continued to give the horse her head, letting her pick her own way. How she went about this was crucial. As long as they drove the cattle up to the fence and across the creek by the gate, they couldn't go wrong. There was really nowhere else to go, anyway. And, as much as she wanted to, she couldn't rush them and risk the young calves falling down and being left behind by panicked mothers.

She hoped the calves could get across the creek. It was looking very deep, and just getting worse. The water even seemed to be flowing faster than just moments before. She tried to control her rising panic. She had to get the cattle across and herself, Faith and the dogs out of here, else they could all be swept away. She fought the urge to push the cattle harder but, like Faith, they needed to pick their own way to stay safe.

It seemed to be taking forever. In an effort to try to keep her composure, she began silently chanting: 'Slow and steady wins the race.' She kept it up, despite hearing and seeing chunks of the banks giving way behind and around her.

The first of the cattle were now standing alongside the fence facing the creek. They couldn't go any further without crossing and they began bellowing their protest.

'You have to,' Jessica cried, feeling the frustration and emotion starting to spill over. Her chest ached and a lump was lodged in her throat. 'Push them up,' she called to Laurel and Hardy. They went in, nipped a heel each and darted back out of the way of flying hooves. They couldn't push any harder than that and they weren't about to put themselves at risk of being kicked. Now what?

'Come on. Gee up!' she shouted, hoping Faith would understand it was the cattle and not her that the direction was aimed at. All she needed was one brave beast to take the plunge – literally – and show the way. The rate they were going, the bank would give way and do it for them.

She continued to sit on Faith in the drenching rain, waiting, feeling helpless. The dogs were hoarse from barking. With sheep, they would have leapt up onto their backs, raced forwards and barked in the ears of the leaders to get them going, and then darted back before hopping down onto the ground again to nip at the heels of those at the back. It didn't work like that with cattle, they were too big and menacing. And these were worse because they were trying to protect their young.

Jessica looked across at the fence spanning the creek to her left. So far it had held, thanks to Steve's ingenious invention of a series of floats and springs so the span could rise and fall with the water level without being swept away. Then she looked around for a long, narrow branch. Perhaps if she could poke some of the cattle in the backside, she could create movement. But the ground was so wet and churned up from all the hooves, all she could see was mud.

This felt like it was taking hours, but it was probably less than thirty minutes since she'd left the safety of the house yard.

Then she felt Faith lurch beneath her, and watched, stunned as the horse stretched her neck out and nudged the closest cow. This in turn sent the unstable cow's head into the beast in front of her. Suddenly the first three plunged into the water. *Shit*, Jessica thought, as two calves followed, only their necks and heads visible.

'Come on, get up!' she yelled. 'Good girl, Faith. Push.' She urged the horse forwards with her legs. And Faith pushed. Jessica's heart leapt into her mouth again and she choked on an intense rush of emotion. Slowly the cattle and calves crossed and streamed out into the next paddock at a rambling trot and then a canter, as they realised they were free and the ground was firm.

Jessica found herself staring at two muddy banks with filthy, bubbling white water racing between them. The cattle were all heading up the hill towards the house. Tears began to stream down her face. She had done it! They had done it!

'Good dogs. Good Faith,' she said, rubbing the horse on the shoulder.

A rumble of thunder brought her attention back. While she might have got the cattle to safety, she, Faith and the dogs were still stuck on the wrong side of the creek. She'd momentarily forgotten the wind and rain in her excitement. She wiped the tears away and looked down at where the cattle had crossed.

It was a quagmire. She couldn't see anything and didn't want to risk Faith sinking up to her belly in mud and getting stuck. The dogs would certainly be swept away if they tried to cross. She didn't want to leave them unattended, couldn't – it was too dangerous. They would want to follow their charges right to the end: the double gates into the next paddock; that was what they were trained to do.

'Laurel and Hardy, stay! Leave them now. Good dogs,' she said, and turned Faith so she could scan the bank from where they'd come. She shuddered at the thought of going back through the creek, could barely believe she'd done it earlier. But she had, thanks to Faith. What an incredible, courageous little horse.

Having looked the length of the creek, her gaze snagged on the capped fence and the road beyond. So far the culvert seemed to have held with just a bit of erosion in the gutter. She had to concede, though, that she was really too far away to be sure. Dare she tackle a jump on Faith? Could she, on any horse – ever again? Her chest thudded with a fresh surge of fear and adrenaline.

She looked from the creek to the jump and back again. She had to make a choice – she couldn't stay here. The gate out onto the road was locked; the jump was probably the safer option if it was dry enough underfoot. The cattle hadn't been that far up, so hopefully the ground would still be okay.

Another chunk of bank fell away nearby, startling Faith. She backed up. The far side began disintegrating too. The creek now took up more than two thirds of the paddock, Jessica realised. Even if she found somewhere to cross, by the time she got there she might be cut off from the gate the cattle had just gone through.

She gathered Faith up and gave her a gentle nudge with her legs. At least she knew the horse could jump.

'Come on, girl, we can do it,' she said, more for her own benefit. 'Come on, dogs.' They trotted with difficulty, squelching in the sodden ground. The dogs had to leap and bound to keep up. They must be exhausted.

Jessica brought Faith back to a walk for the last few strides to the capped fence. She checked the ground. It was raised and much dryer where they'd added a few loads of gravel and sand after it had been worn away by the hunters over the years. She pulled Faith up.

'Laurel, Hardy, go home!' she commanded, waving her arm towards the house. The dogs looked at her, seemingly dubious, unwilling to leave. 'Go on. Go home now!' she yelled. She felt dreadful as they took off over the fence, turned left, and ran up the road to the driveway with their tails between their legs, but she couldn't risk them getting under Faith's feet. This was scary enough as it was, and getting worse the more she thought about it. Jessica was quivering all over with fear.

She turned Faith away from the jump, put her in a trot, gathered her up, applied her legs, turned at the edge of the firm ground, and pushed her into a canter. Jessica could barely count her four strides into the jump in her mind, thanks to her heart racing so hard and pounding so loudly against her ribs and in her ears. *Oh God*, she thought. *Three, two, one ...* Again, she wanted to shut her eyes, but didn't. She sat hard into the saddle ...

Faith rose underneath her, taking off perfectly, tucking her legs in, and sailing through the air. They landed safely on the other side. Jessica gently turned her towards the house.

Oh my God, we did it! Wow, that felt good. A new rush of adrenaline fuelled her. She checked Faith, who seemed to have had her own injection of adrenaline. She was up on her toes, her head was raised, her ears pricked, now seemingly completely unaware of the atrocious weather still raging around them.

The horse didn't seem to care that she couldn't turn her back to the wind. Jessica was a little surprised at suddenly feeling the cold seeping through her track pants. And, God, she could barely feel her fingers. Time to get home and clean and dry.

Chapter Twenty-seven

Back at the stables, Jessica scraped the excess water from Faith's coat and towelled her off. It wasn't really necessary – the stable was quite warm despite the weather raging outside. Faith would be safe from catching a chill.

But Jessica couldn't bring herself to leave. She would be forever grateful to the little horse. What she felt for the horse now was so much stronger even than the overwhelming feelings she'd had for her the day she'd first ridden her. Every time she thought about what they'd just been through, tears streamed down her face.

'And to think I called you plain,' she said, shaking her head slowly. She still felt terrible about that, so part of the reason she was fussing over Faith so much now was to atone for her harsh early judgement. Faith hung her head and her eyelashes fluttered as she struggled to keep her eyes open. 'Okay, girl, I'll leave you be,' Jessica finally said, taking the hint. She gave the horse's neck one last rub, kissing her on the forehead. 'You're a good girl. Thank you,' she said, for probably the twentieth time. The words seemed so inadequate, given what the horse had done for her – for them. Perhaps, given Steve had rescued her from goodness only knew what fate, they were even.

No – they'd never be even. If it hadn't been for Faith taking the initiative at the edge of the creek, Jessica knew she couldn't have made her. She'd been frozen on the spot. She liked to think she might have found the courage to cross the creek, but knew she was kidding herself.

And then the horse had bravely pushed the cattle. Had managed to do what the dogs and Jessica hadn't been able to. Jessica shook her head in wonder, and for the umpteenth time since the horse had arrived on the property thought, *Yep, there's something really special about you.*

'Sleep tight. I'll check on you later,' she said, and turned away. 'Come on, dogs.'

Laurel and Hardy rose from the corner where they were curled up. They were clearly plum tuckered out, as her father would have said. It had been quite an ordeal.

'Don't think you're getting towelled off or blow-dried,' she told them as they trudged across the sodden gravel to the house. Suddenly she was exhausted and struggling to lift her feet. She couldn't decide what she wanted more – a steaming hot shower or to collapse on the couch. She sighed. She couldn't sit on the leather while she was this wet and muddy, and by the time she got an extra throw rug out of the linen press, she may as well just have had a shower. She shivered involuntarily. The dampness in her clothes was finally catching up with her and making her cold. It had been fine while she'd been moving and had had the warmth rising up from Faith. She sneezed. 'Great, that's all we need.'

Inside, she looked at the dogs, who stood looking forlorn, obviously realising they'd better not leap onto the leather lounges in their state either.

'Oh, all right,' Jessica muttered. Her shower would have to wait a few more minutes. Anyway, it wouldn't take long to towel them off. And she'd lay a few towels on the couch, just to be sure.

When she was done drying the dogs and covering the couch, she said, 'Okay, you guys, up you hop.' They did, and then looked mighty content. Jessica sighed deeply with her own sense of contentment at imagining the hot needles that would soon be hammering on her cold flesh. Finally the wind seemed to have died down and the thunder and lightning had moved on. But rain still drummed on the roof. God, what a day.

Jessica could barely get her buttons undone, her hands were so cold and stiff. If she thought she had the strength, she might have considered just ripping the flannel work shirt open and worrying about the lost buttons later. But she was sapped and all her muscles were beginning to ache and seize up. She was having trouble finding the energy even to remain standing. At last her clothes dropped to the ground with a wet plop and she reached in to turn on the shower.

She stepped into the warm water and immediately felt the tension running off her, along with the cold. Ah, it was blissful.

Suddenly there was a new rush of tears. Oh, for God's sake, it was getting ridiculous; she was just standing under the shower. She focussed on soaping herself all over and then washing and rinsing her hair, taking a lot longer than usual, very reluctant to leave this warm cocoon.

When she could no longer justify standing there, she turned the taps off with a sigh. She stood for a few moments in the steam, trying to summon the energy to reach for the towel, and knowing what an effort drying herself off would take. If only she'd brought her bathrobe in she could just wrap herself in that and be done.

You're sounding like an old woman.

I feel like an old woman, she silently replied with a weary laugh. She reached around and dragged her towel from the towel rail. It weighed a tonne, but she pushed on and a few minutes later she was sitting on the bed wrapped in her robe.

But now she couldn't face getting a clean set of clothes out. Just a few minutes' rest, then she'd get up and put some clothes on.

She was still sitting there in her robe when she heard heavy, rushed footsteps on the verandah and the door opening and closing, and then more footsteps inside.

'Jess?' Steve called.

'In here.'

Steve appeared in the doorway. 'God, what's happened? Where are the cattle? Are you okay?' He rubbed his hands over his face.

Jessica nodded, though she wasn't sure she was okay. She felt stunned, numb, kind of like something major had happened, but she wasn't totally sure what.

Steve knelt in front of her. He gripped her knees firmly.

'I came home to move the cattle away from the creek. But they're not there.'

'I moved them,' Jessica said, finally finding some strength to lift her head and open her mouth.

'What? How?' He was looking around, as if the answers were in the room somewhere.

'Faith. The dogs. They're up behind the house.' She raised her arm to vaguely indicate the direction. It was heavy. 'Oh, God, Steve.' She brought her hands to her face as she was swamped with emotion and a fresh flood of tears.

Steve leapt onto the bed and held her tight as her racking sobs caused her to shake all over.

It took a few minutes for the bout to subside enough for her to speak again.

'Faith was amazing. She's so special. You've no idea. She ...' Again Jessica's words were swallowed by tears. She struggled to breathe.

Steve rubbed her back. 'I know. I know,' he said quietly.

Jessica wanted to say, *No, you don't know,* but found herself unable to speak once more.

Finally there were no more tears to cry and she extricated herself from Steve's embrace before wiping the sleeve of the robe across her face.

'God, look at me. I can't stop crying.'

'Well, you've clearly had a shock. As long as you're sure you're okay.'

Jessica nodded again. 'It's happy tears, really. I think,' she said, with a tight laugh, trying to gather herself. 'But you should have seen Faith.' She shook her head with wonder, though she didn't go on.

'Let's get you dressed,' Steve said, getting up and pulling Jessica's underwear drawer open.

She didn't object when he knelt before her and put on her socks, nor did she when he helped her out of her robe and held her knickers open for her to step into. They had no secrets; they knew every wrinkle, every scar. Again she was reminded that this was what marriage was about, this intimacy and openness.

Eventually he kissed her on the forehead and led her, fully dressed, out into the lounge.

'Thank you for taking good care of my girl, you guys,' he said, going over and giving Laurel and Hardy a pat each.

Jessica smiled. God, she loved Steve. And Laurel and Hardy. And Faith. She was so lucky to have her little family, her little menagerie. She forced back yet another wave of emotion.

She wrapped her hands around the mug of tea Steve brought her and closed her eyes as the sweet liquid swirled around her mouth blissfully, then slowly made its way through her. 'Ah, that is good,' she said.

'So, tell me what happened,' Steve said, sitting beside her.

As she retold the story, she became emotional again and again, and had to wait for each new rush of tears before carrying on. *God, what is wrong with me? It's over. I'm fine. We're all fine.*

'I don't know what's wrong with me,' she said, feeling exasperated at her lack of self-control. But she really couldn't help it: suddenly her chest would tighten and a rush of tears would spring forth.

'You've had a big day. You saved our livelihood and countless lives, Jess, of course you're emotional. Not to mention conquering your fear by crossing the creek *and* jumping the capped fence.'

Jessica nodded. Her face was beginning to burn from the salty tears that had run down it.

*

Jessica couldn't shake the restlessness. It was as if the adrenaline was still mildly affecting her. Well, it had been a pretty exciting morning, so it was probably quite understandable that she'd still be a little hyped up, she thought as she silently chewed her cheese and tomato sandwich.

Beside her at the table, Steve was chattering away about the morning's activity, sand-bagging the school and preventing the flooding of the IT and science labs. He continued to be apologetic for not being there when she had needed him. Jessica felt bad that he felt bad.

If Steve had been there, he would have used the four-wheel drive to move the cattle, if they could have got it across the creek. There was no guarantee that would have worked, though, given the depth of the water and the fact the calves were not used to being rounded up and could have become flighty. Perhaps they would have had to use Faith anyway. And as Steve didn't ride, then it would have still been up to Jessica. Steve had given the table a light thump when he realised that, as if trying to drive the point home and absolve his guilt.

Jessica had nodded and mumbled her agreement. He was used to debriefing after CFS callouts – that was probably what he was doing now. All she'd really wanted was the moral support. But if Steve needed to talk it through, then there wasn't any point making him feel worse by reminding him. It would have been different if he'd been in the pub kicking back with his mates – not that he ever really was – but he'd been off working hard for the community they loved so much.

'Right, I'm going to go and do a quick check of the stock while you have a bit of a rest,' he said as he put their empty plates in the sink.

'Could you pop by Faith on the way? Perhaps take her a couple of carrots.'

'Good idea. I need to say thanks, anyway,' he said, going to the fridge.

'Not those, the horse carrots. In the fridge in the shed.'

'Ah, right, I knew that,' he said with a laugh. 'Right, see you soon.' He kissed her on the forehead. 'I'll take the dogs in case I need any stragglers moved. Come on, you guys.'

'Okay. See you. Be careful. And take your mobile – just in case.'

'Yep, got it,' he said, patting his shirt pocket.

Jessica lay down on the couch, pulled the throw rug over her and turned the TV on. She flicked though all the channels and back again. Nothing grabbed her fancy. She went through the list of recorded shows on their PVR. Some she wouldn't have minded watching, but they were mostly shows they had agreed to only watch together. She went back to the TV channels and finally chose a movie that had started twenty minutes before. Maybe she'd catch up with the story.

But as hard as she stared, she couldn't concentrate. Her brain was whirling – processing what, she wasn't quite sure. She was still restless. Her muscles ached and she felt pretty washed out, probably still a little shocked from the morning's events.

She turned the sound low, shuffled down the couch and shut her eyes. She doubted she'd go to sleep, but felt a bit of a rest might help. And maybe her brain would decide what it was trying to process and tell her, or at least quieten down. She hoped if she did nod off she wouldn't be back to having nightmares of plunging into water while on the back of a horse.

★

Jessica woke feeling a little disoriented. Wow, she had fallen asleep after all. And judging by her level of grogginess, she had slept for quite a while. Had she dreamt? She felt calm, so no nightmares. Good. But she had dreamt, she realised, as fragments began coming back to her. She squeezed her eyes shut to try to concentrate and sharpen the images.

A horse doing a cross-country round. Had it been her riding? She wasn't sure. The horse going around had been chestnut, like Faith. No, wait, it *had* been Faith. With her aboard? She frowned. Maybe. Maybe not. Probably not; she hadn't been feeling the ride, she had been watching it.

Talia.

And then it slowly dawned on her: Talia's grandmother should know how special Faith was – well, she probably already knew that, but she felt an overwhelming urge to tell the old lady the courage Faith had shown and how much she was loved, how much she'd helped Jessica recover. Her heart swelled. That's what her restlessness was telling her, of that she was now sure. Knowing how much Faith meant to Jessica and Steve would bring the old lady peace.

Jessica frowned. The horse had killed the woman's granddaughter – for all Jessica knew, the only family she had. Would bringing her news of Faith hurt her more? But she had practically begged Steve to take the horse when she so easily could have had one of the doggers pick her up.

Talia's grandmother definitely cared. She would want to know. That was what Jessica's heart was telling her, and she had to ignore the twinges of doubt in her head.

But it was time for the head to take over. What was the woman's name? Jessica tried to remember if Steve had said. But it didn't matter, she realised, feeling excitement surge. It would be written on the cheque stub and on the receipt from the clearing sale. She leapt up and went into the office. It took just a few moments to locate the details. Thank goodness for them both being organised neatniks.

Mrs E Rowntree. Damn, what was her first name? And where was she living? Her address was not listed, not that Jessica had been expecting it to be – the sale had been run through the local Landmark office. And there was no way they would tell her the residential address of one of their clients.

She tapped a pen on her lip, trying to conjure up what Steve had told her that day. She hadn't really been listening very carefully. She felt ashamed of her attitude all over again. She did think he had said the old lady was only there for the day and that the farm house was empty. So perhaps she lived in a retirement village.

Jessica took her laptop back to the lounge. She knew of at least one retirement village in Woodside. And each of the neighbouring towns had at least one.

'Fingers crossed she hasn't left the district,' Jessica muttered as she opened the Yellow Pages website and typed in her search. It took just a second for one hundred and fifty results to come up. *This will take forever!* Upon closer inspection, she saw many of them were for suburbs much closer to the city – up to an hour's drive away. So much for putting in the postcode she wanted and selecting the option for local businesses. Oh well, there was nothing for it but to pick out the local ones and start phoning. Jessica grabbed the phone off the coffee table and began dialling.

She paused at the last digit. How should she approach this? Probably like phoning a hotel guest, she supposed. They wouldn't give details out; she'd have to pretend she thought Mrs Rowntree was definitely a patient. Were they patients? No, they were probably referred to as residents. If only she had Mrs Rowntree's first name.

And she'd probably have to tell a few white lies when she found her if they asked if she was family. Oh dear. Or was that only in hospital emergency, or in hospital emergency on TV and movies? Regardless, she'd worry about that then, when she found Mrs E Rowntree.

She prodded the last number and held her breath.

It took whoever it was so long to answer that when a breathless voice came on the other end, Jessica was taken a little by surprise. She'd been just about to hang up and try again later.

'Er, hello, could I please speak to Mrs Rowntree?' she said. She suspected her eagerness meant she came across a little brusque. She'd have to temper that next time.

'I'm sorry, there's no one of that name here.'

'Oh, right, thanks very much. I must have the wrong place.'

As she hung up, Jessica wondered if that meant Mrs Rowntree had never lived there or if she'd perhaps left. She should have asked some more questions, so she knew for sure. Her eyes prickled at the thought that someone probably only left a retirement home on a gurney. God, she hoped she wouldn't be too late. But Faith had only been with them a few weeks and the old lady had obviously been well enough to be at the clearing sale.

As the second call was answered, Jessica decided to change her spiel.

'Hello,' she said, after the person at the other end had said the name of the facility and her name. 'I'm looking for a Mrs E Rowntree.' She almost added that she was an old family friend, but stopped herself at the last moment. The thought that not knowing someone's first name was a bit of a giveaway to not being a very close friend – or, more likely, not even knowing the person at all. It then struck her that professional people, like lawyers and doctors, probably rang these sorts of places all the time. They would be more formal. Yes, she could well be one of those, she thought, feeling a little buoyed.

The woman took a moment. Jessica could hear the tapping of fingers on a keyboard in the background.

'No, sorry, no one of that name here – and hasn't been in the last five years.'

'Okay, thanks very much.'

Jessica felt a little deflated. She'd imagined she'd have had Mrs E Rowntree's whereabouts after one call and would be planning when to go and visit by now. She hoped she wouldn't have to call every place in the search results. She decided to change tack and begin at the bottom of the list.

Steve came in halfway through her seventh call. She'd almost given up on six – had nearly accepted that this was not meant to be – but had countered it with the thought that seven was supposed to be a lucky number. Though, 'seventh time lucky' really didn't have quite the same ring to it that 'third time lucky' did.

She held her hand up to silence Steve as he appeared in front of her. She was stunned by what she was hearing.

'I'm sorry, she died a few weeks ago.'

'Oh. When, exactly?'

Jessica felt the blood drain from her face and her mouth drop open when she was told the date: the eighth of November. The same date as on the cheque stub and paperwork for the clearing sale – the same day Steve had brought Faith home.

'Thank you,' she croaked, and hung up. She held onto the phone in her lap and stared at it. Tears began to fill her eyes and then drop, slowly at first, and then in a rush. Steve was at her side in an instant with his arm around her shoulder.

'What's wrong? What's happened?'

Jessica looked up at Steve. 'She's dead,' she said.

He went pale. 'Who's dead? Not Tiffany? What's happened?'

Jessica shook her head. 'Mrs Rowntree.'

'Who?' Then, as the name filtered through his memory, he said, 'Oh. That's sad.' Confusion clouded his features as questions began to gather in his mind. 'But why are you …?'

'I wanted to tell her about how wonderful Faith is, how much we love her,' Jessica blurted. 'I thought it would be a comfort.' An even stronger wave of emotion hit Jessica and she buried her head in Steve's shoulder and wept.

'I'm sure she knew,' he said, stroking her hair.

Jessica gathered herself, willing the tears to subside. But she couldn't totally shake the sadness, and still hadn't when the phone in front of her began to ring. Steve answered it and she listened to the one-sided conversation:

'Hello, Steve speaking ... Oh, hi, Tiff. How's things? ... Oh shit, that's not good. Of course you can. Do you need me to come and get you or anything? ... No, thanks, but it's all sorted – apricot chicken. There's plenty to go around ... Hey, before you go, are you still in town at work? ... Could you do me, us, a favour? ... We're in need of comfort food, of the ice-cream, chocolate block, and chips variety ... We'll tell you everything when you get here. No, she's fine ... See you soon. Drive safely,' he said and hung up.

'That was Tiffany. Apparently the part of the Nairn road near her place is cut, so she can't go home. I hope it's okay that I said she could stay.'

Jessica nodded. 'I'll start dinner,' she announced, getting up. She was afraid of saying more. She could feel the emotion lurking, and didn't want a fresh round of tears.

'I'm happy to do it if you'd rather rest.'

'Thanks, but I'm fine.' She told herself there was no point dwelling on Mrs Rowntree. And as she went into the kitchen, she was surprised to find the sadness drain away as if she'd just risen up out of it.

Jessica was further surprised to find she felt quite cheery, even to the point of humming while she trimmed the chicken pieces, rolled them in flour, and then stirred the sauce. She noticed Steve looking at her with a slightly perplexed expression a few times. *Woman's prerogative to change her mood*, she thought, altering the saying to suit her circumstances. Not that she'd deliberately changed anything, it had just happened. Weird.

With dinner in the oven, Jessica went to check Faith for the last time that evening. Now the storm had passed and the weather looked clear, she could take her back to the paddock, but she decided to keep her in until the morning, just to be sure.

She was pleased to see the horse looked none the worse for their adventure. She'd checked her all over for any cuts and scrapes earlier. She glanced down her legs again in case some swelling had come up in the meantime. Thankfully she was unscathed. But Jessica cringed, as she always did, at seeing the old scars. A new wave of tears startled her. She told herself she was being stupid, brushed them away and swallowed the lump in her throat.

'Good girl, you sleep tight,' she said, giving the horse a final pat as she left.

Back in the house, she set up the spare room for her friend, putting fresh sheets on the bed and making sure to lay some clean clothes and a towel out.

Jessica went to the door as she heard Tiffany's car pull up. She recognised that as much as she was looking forward to seeing her best friend and sharing her adventures with her, she was actually almost more looking forward to seeing what comfort food she had brought with her. She wasn't really hungry, but was suddenly having a ferocious craving for chocolate and chips – together. She wouldn't have believed it if she wasn't feeling it, but she was actually salivating. She wiped away the moisture she felt creeping out of the corners of her mouth.

God, she hoped Tiffany had salt and vinegar chips. They weren't her favourite flavour – barbecue was – in fact she didn't really like the sharpness of salt and vinegar, but right now she really fancied some. What a day – it had even, apparently, upset her taste buds.

She opened the door wide as Tiffany got to it, laden with handbag and grocery bags.

'Hey there,' Tiffany said.

'Hey. Great to see you.' Jessica hugged her friend tightly. 'Ooh, goody, chips,' she said, pulling away.

'Yes, I come bearing plenty of comfort food, as requested,' Tiffany said with a laugh as she entered the lounge room. 'Thanks so much for having me in my hour of need. Bloody weather.' She sat down on the nearest lounge.

'You're welcome,' Steve said. 'But will your horses be okay?'

'Yeah, they've got plenty to eat and they can go into the shelter. Right, I have chips – salt and vinegar, barbecue and corn,' she said, pulling out the bags and putting them on the coffee table. 'Chocolate – dark, milk and white. And a couple of Cherry Ripe bars. I wasn't sure what level of crisis we're facing here. And finally, the ice-cream – honeycomb, chocolate and strawberry.' She extracted three small tubs. 'So, what's the emergency?'

Jessica wondered briefly if Tiffany realised she'd brought everything in lots of threes – well, except for the Cherry Ripe bars. If she wasn't so intent on staring at the food and stopping herself drooling, she might have pointed it out.

'Wow, you've thought of everything. Thanks so much. I'll put the ice-cream in the freezer for later,' Steve said, gathering the pots up.

'Can you bring back four bowls, darling?'

'You know dinner's almost ready?' Steve said, handing over the bowls.

'Yeah, I know. But I'm starving,' she said. She wasn't hungry at all – that was a lie. This yearning was coming from her mouth – her tastebuds – rather than down in her stomach. She tore open the bag of salt and vinegar chips and tipped some into one of the bowls. She rather fancied diving head first into the bag, but restrained herself. She then broke up some squares of each variety of chocolate and piled them into a bowl, watched on by Steve and Tiffany, who didn't seem interested in the food at all. Their loss. She noticed they were exchanging shrugs and raised eyebrows. But she didn't care, she couldn't stop herself if she wanted to. Some strong, unknown force had taken over.

Unable to decide between white chocolate – weird when she actually preferred dark – and the chips, she made a sandwich out of both, and shoved it in her mouth.

'Oh my God, it's heavenly,' she tried to say through her full mouth, but suspected it just sounded like a rumble. Orgasmic was the word. Jesus, it was good. Who would have thought?

'Are you okay?' Tiffany asked. 'Steve said on the phone something had happened. What's going on?'

Jessica told her cattle-moving story to Tiffany, who gradually became more and more bug-eyed. A few times the emotion threatened to engulf her, but she distracted herself from it with more chip and chocolate sandwiches.

'Try it, it's *so* good,' she urged. But Steve and Tiffany just watched her as if she had suddenly grown an extra head. She shrugged at their disinterest.

Finally Jessica told Tiffany about phoning the retirement village and why, and learning of Mrs Rowntree's demise. And then the tears started. But this time they were short-lived – like a wave sweeping through.

'It's okay,' she said, flapping her arm. 'I guess it just wasn't meant to be.'

'I'm sure she's up there somewhere and knows anyway,' Tiffany said kindly.

'Maybe.'

Jessica's junk food binge was interrupted by the ding of the oven timer signalling their dinner was ready.

Looking down at her meal, she felt a little queasy. She really shouldn't have eaten all that crap. She found it hard to believe she actually had. It was so out of character. Oh, well, too late now. Unless she threw up, an event that was appearing more and more likely. She forced the thought aside and concentrated on cutting her chicken up and moving it and the rice around her plate to try to disguise her reluctance to eat it.

'Someone's ruined their dinner,' Tiffany chided.

'Hmm.' Jessica couldn't understand it; apricot chicken was one of her all-time favourites, but she could barely look at it. And the smell really was making her feel ill.

'Are you okay?' Tiffany and Steve said, in unison.

'Yeah, I'm fine,' she said. Though that was a lie too. She felt all out of kilter. And something told her it wasn't from the chips and chocolate. She hadn't had that much, when she thought about it. She noticed Tiffany and Steve were staring at her with thoughtful, knowing expressions.

'What?' she demanded. 'Have I got chocolate on my face, or something?' She rubbed her cheeks vigorously.

'Um, you're not pregnant are you?' Tiffany said.

'Don't be silly,' she said quickly. 'Why would you …?' Slowly the pennies began to drop – the mood swings, the tears, the cravings. She wasn't sure about the queasiness – didn't you actually throw up with morning sickness?

Oh, wow, could I be? Really?

'Cravings, mood swings,' Steve said, thoughtfully.

'Weird combinations of food, floods of tears,' Tiffany added.

Jessica stared back at them. She couldn't make herself get up to check one of the remaining pregnancy test kits she had stashed in the bathroom cabinet – she didn't want the disappointment. While it was possible they might be right, she couldn't think of her dream coming true. She watched Tiffany get up and walk away from the table.

Jessica stared down at the box that had appeared in front of her.

'Please put us all out of our misery,' Tiffany said, sitting down.

Jessica looked up at Steve, who seemed to have gone a bit ashen, though she was relieved to note his eyes shone with excitement. In her dazed state, she picked up the box and left the table.

She peed on the stick and waited. All those weeks ago, she'd bought the super-sensitive version that could be done any time of the day so she didn't have to wait until the morning. God, five minutes takes forever when you're waiting for news that could change your whole life.

Apprehension flooded her. What if she wasn't a good mother? What if the kid grew up to hate her? She calmed herself down. One bridge at a time.

Steve appeared just before the time was up – he must have been watching the clock. They stood together, arms around each other, at the bathroom sink. Jessica had placed the stick upside down beside the taps so she couldn't cheat.

'According to my watch, that's five minutes,' Steve said. 'Shall I?' He pointed at the stick.

Jessica nodded. She crossed her fingers behind her back. She felt sick, but most likely it was tension, apprehension and anticipation causing the churning.

Steve picked up the white plastic stick. Jessica stared at his shaking fingers.

'Two stripes or one?' he asked, frowning at the object.

She'd thought she'd committed what they were looking for to memory, but her mind was blank. She picked up the box.

'Two.'

'We're pregnant, then,' Steve said a little matter-of-factly. 'Well, you are. Oh, my God, we're going to have a baby.'

Jessica brought her hands up to her face. Tears filled her eyes. 'Really? Oh. My. God. Really?'

'See for yourself,' he said, turning the stick to her.

She could barely make the little window out, it was swimming beyond her veil of tears. But after a few blinks, things gradually became clear. And there they were, two little grey lines.

'Um, guys?' Tiffany called. 'The suspense is killing me.'

They walked out and over to the table, still entwined.

'We're pregnant,' Steve said, looking at Jessica warmly. Jessica stared into Steve's eyes, thinking she'd never been so in love with him as she was right then. She looked at Tiffany and nodded, her eyes brimming with tears again.

'Oh my God, oh my God, *oh my God*!' Tiffany cried, leaping up and jumping around. She hugged them both and soon they were dancing around in a circle holding hands.

'I knew it,' she said, when they finally broke away and sat down.

'I guess we'd better not tell anyone for a while. What is it – twelve weeks when it's considered safe?' Jessica said.

'Probably best. My lips are sealed,' Tiffany said. 'Ooh, I'm going to be an auntie – well, sort of.' She clapped her hands. 'Well, this calls for honeycomb ice-cream.'

'Oh, I'm not sure I can face it,' Jessica said, cringing.

'But, it's your favourite,' Steve and Tiffany said in unison, aghast.

'What about chocolate or strawberry?' Tiffany said.

'No, thanks. But, actually, I would love a few sweet pickled gherkins,' she said.

'Of course you would,' Tiffany said, laughing.

Steve rolled his eyes. 'Well, thank God there's a jar already in the fridge. What am I in for?' But he was grinning.

Steve put the tub of honeycomb ice-cream on the table and the jar of gherkins in front of Jessica, smirking. Tiffany put a fork in front of her friend, also smirking.

'Thank you,' Jessica said primly, took the lid off the jar, speared a short, fat, green gherkin and bit into it. 'Yum. God, that's good,' she said, as she savoured the crisp texture and explosion of sweetness and tang in her mouth. 'I reckon barbecue chips would go well with these,' she mumbled through her half-full mouth.

Epilogue

Around a year later

'Say good luck, Mummy and Auntie Tiff, and wave bye-bye, Talia,' Steve said, lifting the three-month-old baby's arm and simulating a wave.

'See you soon,' Jessica said, blowing a kiss from atop Faith. She was grinning from ear to ear. Life was pretty darned near perfect. She'd just done a half-decent dressage test – even a little better than last week's – and was about to embark on the cross-country phase. Thanks to Faith's love of water – and jumping generally – she didn't have any fears or concerns. Anyway, she was in the lower grades. At this level it was all about fun – there wasn't much that could go wrong. The thought of the things that could go wrong crossed her mind now and then, but she'd since accepted – thanks to much encouragement from Steve and badgering from Tiffany – that what would be, would be.

She turned Faith away and went over to where Tiffany was warming up, ready to head out on her round before Jessica.

Halfway through Jessica's pregnancy, they'd made a pact: If Jessica taught Tiffany how to jump and started back in the lower levels, Jessica would come and do one-day events with her. It made the events so much more fun and, while they were essentially competing against each other, they were there purely for enjoyment.

As it turned out, Tiffany hadn't needed a lot of tuition from Jessica, which was lucky, because Jessica had found baby Talia Faith Harrington took up a lot more time and energy than she ever would have thought possible. Though Jessica suspected she gave her daughter more time than she really needed.

Far too often, Jessica whiled away hours sitting in the rocking chair, holding Talia or just watching her while she slept, thinking she was the luckiest woman in the world. The baby really was the sweetest little thing – slept really well, barely cried, and was so far meeting all her target weights and measurements.

And Steve doted on her. And on Jessica. He always had, but something had shifted and he was now extra devoted to 'his girls', as he referred to them. To the extent that he'd given up his Saturdays of tennis to come along to horse events and take care of Talia while Jessica rode. She and Tiffany regularly teased him that it was a good excuse – he'd been complaining on and off about knee and shoulder pain for the past few seasons.

Jessica loved that they now made these outings together as a family, and was careful to tell him so frequently. So close-knit were they these days that she regularly pushed the pram while Steve hacked his way around the golf course on a Sunday – his term, not hers.

One of the members of the local hunt club, Aaron Stanley, was the reason Tiffany hadn't needed too many jumping lessons from her best friend. Tiffany was smitten and Aaron seemed a really good guy. It had been love at first sight when Tiffany and Jessica had taken bottles of cold cordial down to the guys fixing the capped fences on Steve and Jessica's property and adding some extra logs to that part of the course along the creek after the storm.

It had been a hot day, and they'd watched them toiling from Jessica's lounge-room window and become intrigued when a few shirts had come off in the heat. Jessica maintained that she'd been providing moral support to Tiffany – she was a married woman, and heavily pregnant at the time. So she'd waddled the few hundred metres down to the workers, accompanying her friend. It had been a struggle, but if Tiffany was finally showing some interest in meeting a man again, which she clearly was, then who was Jessica to stand in her way?

Tiffany's eyes had locked with Aaron's over the top of the insulated water bottle and their fingers had touched as she'd handed it over. And the rest, as they say, was history – well, history in the making. If Jessica hadn't seen it for herself, she would never have believed it.

Six months on and Aaron had secretly consulted Jessica on ring styles and ideas for popping the question. She hadn't liked the pressure this put her under, but how could she not help? She hoped she could put on an Oscar-winning performance when Tiffany announced her news. Of course she'd come clean later, and she could imagine them dining on the story for years, but for now it was all about Tiffany and Aaron.

The best thing about it was that the four of them – five, with baby Talia Faith – got on so well. Quite often it seemed as if they spent more time together as a fivesome than as separate couples. Aaron didn't do eventing because he hated dressage with a passion, but he was here today strapping for both of them.

'Good luck, safe travels,' Jessica called out to Tiffany, who had just been given her two-minute call.

'You too,' Tiffany said, breathlessly. Tiffany suffered a little from nerves – understandable given she had come so late to the sport. But she said they disappeared after the first jump, and so far they hadn't paralysed her. And, like Jessica, she had a lovely, willing horse who was happy out on course.

A few butterflies fluttered deep in Jessica's stomach. She was up next. But these were of the friendly variety of butterfly – butterflies of excitement, of enjoyment – nothing like the birds of nervousness she used to fight against for focus. She'd come to realise that she'd been pushed far too hard by her father and that his aspirations for her had far outweighed her own. She'd just been on a merry-go-round that was going too fast to get off. She could find no other explanation for having been able to give up serious competition so easily. And there was no question that she'd have given it up for Talia – she'd do anything for her. She didn't even have any lingering feeling about giving up her place in the state team, which she'd officially done the day after the storm. Even the mutters of disappointment and few negative comments from people, which she faced quite regularly thanks to being back in the saddle in public again, didn't bother her these days. It was now all about having fun – both her and Faith.

The only problem facing her these days was winning too many events and being forced up into the higher grades. Jessica and Tiffany had come first and second in their first events last week. Too many points and they'd be out. They'd discussed staying in the lower levels and entering as non-competitors. They had no ambition beyond keeping safe and enjoying themselves.

Jessica wished they hadn't been put so close together in the draw; they would have liked to watch each other go around. But

Aaron was a keen photographer and would already be somewhere on the course staking out a good position from which to snap away as they went past.

'And go!' said the starter. Jessica watched as Tiffany and Brandy bounded out towards the first fence – a nice, inviting log. The first fence was usually a good indication of how the round would go, in Jessica's experience. If the horse was spooky, hesitant, not going forwards easily, then there was every chance the round would be a tough ride. The only fault Tiffany's Brandy had was that he tended to get a little distracted by spectators and anything else he could find along the way to look at. Today he had his ears pricked and was keen to get to the first obstacle.

Jessica only realised she was holding her breath when Tiffany sailed over and she let out a sigh of relief. She felt responsible for Tiffany and regularly worried about her safety – she was the one who'd got her involved in this sport where, really, anything could go wrong and there were so many things beyond their control.

Jessica thought back over the past year and a half and saw that everything had had to happen to bring her to this spot and set of circumstances. Yes, some things she would have liked to have been spared – the loss of her father, her cross-country accident – but she wouldn't have wanted to miss this outcome for anything.

'Rider twenty-one, two minutes,' the starter called.

She gave a final wave to Steve and Talia, who both waved back – Talia obviously with the help of Dad – before gathering Faith up a little more and getting totally focussed on the task at hand.

'And go!'

Faith leapt over the start line beautifully. She was concentrating and felt strong, calm and balanced beneath her.

'Good girl,' Jessica told Faith, and rubbed her neck as they landed after the first jump. What a great team they made.